The Secrets of Rhydian Hill

What Reviewers Say About Ronica Black's Work

The Breakdown

"The author puts everyone in desperate situations and then piles onto those problems, making a thriller that grips more tightly by the page. The romance is well paced and believably slow for two women who have every reason to shy from love but can't help their feelings. …Every character, no matter how small, is beautifully drawn."—*Lesbian Review*

A Love that Leads to Home

"If you love a slow-burn romance where the characters are carefully dancing around each other while being incredibly adorable, this story is for you. It was an emotional read for me, and if you want a good heart-wrenching story, read it."—*Hsinju's Lit Log*

Freedom to Love

"This is a great book. The police drama keeps you enthralled throughout but what I found captivating was the growing affection between the two main characters. Although they are both very different women, you find yourself holding your breath, hoping that they will find a way to be together."—*Lesbian Reading Room*

The Practitioner

"*The Practitioner* by Ronica Black is the angsty sort of romance that I can easily get lost in. I wanted to fill a tub and bathe in all the feelings. Hell, if I had one of those fancy, waterproof Kindles, I just might have."—*Lesbian Review*

"The beginning of this novel captured my attention from the rather luscious description of a pint of Guinness. I cannot tell a lie, I almost immediately wanted to be drinking it. …The first scene with the practitioner also pulled me in, making me sit up and pay attention to what was happening on the digital page. The relationship was like a low simmering fire, frequently doused by either Johnnie's personal angst, or Elaine's. This book was an overall enjoyable read and one which I would recommend to people wanting characters who practically breathe off the page."—*Library Thing*

The Midnight Room

"This book was immensely intriguing, delightfully educational for me, and deliciously intense and romantic. This grabbed me right from the beginning and held my attention all the way through. I most certainly recommend this book to new or returning fans of Ronica Black. Fantastic!"—*Rainbow Book Reviews*

Snow Angel

"A beautifully written, passionate and romantic novella." —*SunsetXCocktail*

"*Snow Angel* is a novella, and it flies by. It draws characters and scenes in large strokes, and it's good fun if you'd like a quick read that's particularly escapist."—*The Lesbrary*

Under Her Wing

"From the start Ronica Black had me. I loved everything about this story, from the emotional intensity to the amazingly hot sex scenes. The emotion between them is so real and tear jerking at times. And the love scenes are phenomenal. I feel I'm raving—but I enjoyed it that much. Highly recommended."—*Kitty Kat's Book Review Blog*

***"Emily" in* Women of the Dark Streets**

"A darkly disturbing brush with questionable magic that leads to an astounding one-eighty-degree turnaround after an apparent attempt at suicide. Mindboggling!"—*Rainbow Book Reviews*

The Seeker

"Stalkers, child kidnappers and murderers all collide in this fast-paced, dual-plotted novel. This is not Black's first novel, and readers can only hope it will not be her last."—*Lambda Literary Review*

"Ronica Black's books just keep getting stronger and stronger. …This is such a tightly written plot-driven novel that readers will find themselves glued to the pages and ignoring phone calls. *The Seeker* is a great read, with an exciting plot, great characters, and great sex."—*Just About Write*

Flesh and Bone—*Lambda Literary Award Finalist*

"Ronica Black handles a traditional range of lesbian fantasies with gusto and sincerity. The reader wants to know these women as well as they come to know each other. When Black's characters ignore their realistic fears to follow their passion, this reader admires their chutzpah and cheers them on. …These stories make good bedtime reading, and could lead to sweet dreams. Read them and see." —*Erotica Revealed*

Chasing Love

"Ronica Black's writing is fluid, and lots of dialogue makes this a fast read. If you like steamy erotica with intense sexual situations, you'll like *Chasing Love*."—*Queer Magazine Online*

Hearts Aflame

"Sleek storytelling and terrific characters are the backbone of Ronica Black's third and best novel, *Hearts Aflame*. Prepare to hop on for an emotional ride with this thrilling story of love in the outback. …Along with the romance of Krista and Rae, the secondary storylines such as Krista's fear of horses and an uncle suffering from Alzheimer's are told with depth and warmth. Black also draws in the reader by utilizing the weather as a metaphor for the sexual and emotional tension in all the storylines. Wonderful storytelling and rich characterization make this a high recommendation."—*Lambda Literary Review*

"*Hearts Aflame* takes the reader on the rough and tumble ride of the cattle drive. Heat, flood, and a sexual pervert are all part of the adventure. Heat also appears between Krista and Rae. The twists and turns of the plot engage the reader all the way to the satisfying conclusion."—*Just About Write*

"I like the author's writing style and she tells a good story. I was drawn in quickly and didn't lose interest at all. Black paints a great picture with her words and I was able to feel like I was sitting around the camp fire with the characters."—*C-Spot Reviews*

Wild Abandon—*Lambda Literary Award Finalist*

"Black is a master at teasing the reader with her use of domination and desire. Black's first novel, *In Too Deep*, was a finalist for a 2005 Lammy. …With *Wild Abandon*, the author continues her winning ways, writing like a seasoned pro. This is one romance I will not soon forget."—*Books to Watch Out For*

"This sequel to Ronica Black's debut novel, *In Too Deep*, is an electrifying thriller. The author's development as a fine storyteller shines with this tightly written story. …[The mystery] keeps the story charged—never unraveling or leading us to a predictable conclusion. More than once I gasped in surprise at the dark and twisted paths this book took."—*Curve*

"Black has managed to create two very sensual and compelling women. The backstory is intriguing, original, and quite well-developed. Yet, it doesn't detract from the primary premise of the novel—it is a sexually-charged romance about two very different and guarded women. Black carries the reader along at such a rapid pace that the rise and fall of each climactic moment successfully creates that suspension of disbelief which the reader seeks." —*Midwest Book Review*

In Too Deep—*Lambda Literary Award Finalist*

"Ronica Black's debut novel *In Too Deep* has everything from nonstop action and intriguing well developed characters to steamy erotic love scenes. From the opening scenes where Black plunges the reader headfirst into the story to the explosive unexpected ending, *In Too Deep* has what it takes to rise to the top. Black has a winner with *In Too Deep*, one that will keep the reader turning the pages until the very last one."—*Independent Gay Writer*

"…an exciting, page turning read, full of mystery, sex, and suspense."—*MegaScene*

"…a challenging murder mystery—sections of this mixed-genre novel are hot, hot, hot. Black juggles the assorted elements of her first book with assured pacing and estimable panache." —*Q Syndicate*

"Black's characterization is skillful, and the sexual chemistry surrounding the three major characters is palpable and definitely hot-hot-hot…if you're looking for a solid read with ample amounts of eroticism and a red herring or two you're sure to find *In Too Deep* a satisfying read."—*L Word Literature*

By the Author

In Too Deep

Deeper

Wild Abandon

Hearts Aflame

Flesh and Bone

The Seeker

Chasing Love

Conquest

Wholehearted

The Midnight Room

Snow Angel

The Practitioner

Freedom to Love

Under Her Wing

Private Passion

Dark Euphoria

The Last Seduction

Olivia's Awakening

A Love That Leads to Home

Passion's Sweet Surrender

A Turn of Fate

Watching Over Her

The Business of Pleasure

Something to Talk About

Decadence "Passionate Pursuance"

The Murders at Sugar Mill Farm

The Curse writing as Alexandra Riley

The Breakdown

Stranded

Behold My Heart

The Fame Game

The Secrets of Rhydian Hill

Co-Authored with Radclyffe

When Love Comes Around

The Secrets of Rhydian Hill

by

Ronica Black

2025

THE SECRETS OF RHYDIAN HILL

ISBN 13: 978-1-63679-880-6

This Trade Paperback Original Is Published By
Bold Strokes Books, Inc.
P.O. Box 249
Valley Falls, NY 12185

First Edition: November 2025

Credits
Editor: Cindy Cresap
Production Design: Susan Ramundo
Cover Design By Tammy Seidick

Acknowledgments

Thank you to my publisher, Bold Strokes Books. You guys really are the best.

A big thanks to my editor, Cindy Cresap, for her never-ending guidance and support.

Many thanks to all my family and friends who encourage me and keep me going.

And of course, a huge shout out to the readers… THANK YOU!

Prologue

Jenny awoke to a soft banging, echoing throughout the dimly lit bedroom. Confused, she turned over and skimmed the bed for Ken, but she found only cold sheets. She sat up and glanced around as the banging continued, rhythmic-like, like the polite knock of someone at the window. She swung her legs to the floor and padded across the cool pine to the window where she pulled back the sheer curtain to peer out into the moonlit night. Rain flecked the pane and she saw that one of the decorative shutters was loose and clamoring in the wind. She breathed a sigh of relief at having found the source of the noise, but then grew anxious again, wondering where Ken was.

She slipped into her robe and headed down the creaking staircase and searched, first the living room, then the kitchen, but Ken was nowhere to be found. She stood in the dark in the kitchen as distant voices came to her from outside. She looked through the window above the sink and saw movement out at the dock. The waves were thick and lugubrious in the blowing storm, rocking Ken's boat back and forth. Two forms stood on the bow, struggling to balance themselves.

"What the hell?" she whispered.

It was after midnight. What was Ken doing out on the boat, and more importantly, who was he with? She tugged her robe tightly around her and stepped out the front door. The wind whipped sharp rain against her face as she descended the porch steps. The voices grew louder and sounded stressed, angry, but she could make out nothing more. She trotted through the wet grass to a nearby elm where she hid. Whatever was going on, it was obvious that Ken didn't want her to know about it, so she was careful to remain unseen.

That's when Ken shouted. Startled, Jenny peeked around the tree and watched as he threw his hands in the air. He appeared frustrated and at a loss, like he'd given up trying to reason with his counterpart. The other man didn't seem to appreciate the gesture. He stepped closer to Ken and raised his arm, aiming something directly at him. Ken said something, something rushed and panicked, but it was cut off quickly by the sharp crack and quick spark of gunfire. She jerked and covered her mouth to keep from screaming as she watched Ken stumble backward and fall overboard into the churning water.

The other man hurried to the edge of the bow to look down into the sea. He fired two more shots and then hopped off the boat and ran down the dock in the blowing wind and rain. She knelt, body pressed tightly to the tree, trying not to weep, and caught sight of his face as he ran past her.

No. It couldn't be. Couldn't possibly.

She almost called out to him, to rage at him for shooting Ken, but she refrained and waited until she heard him peel out of the gravel driveway before she stood and rushed to the sea where she tore off her robe and waded out into the cold water. She yelled for Ken as she swam, searching madly as she bobbed in the wake. Then she saw him. Floating near the dock. She called his name again and then lowered her head to swim as quickly as she could. When she reached him, she turned him over, saw he was unresponsive, and pulled him back to shore, just as she'd practiced all those years ago as a lifeguard. She prayed as she swam, hoping she could save him. Her heart pounded and she swallowed water twice before her feet touched ground. With all her strength, she dragged him onto shore and collapsed next to him.

"Please," she said, breathless. She checked for a pulse, checked for signs of breathing. Nothing. She began CPR, doing her best not to pass out with fatigue. In the distance, she heard someone. Then another. She saw the swinging beams of flashlights coming from her neighbor's house. She called out so they could find her and continued breathing into Ken's mouth. But she knew it was hopeless. Ken was limp, lifeless, and losing far too much blood into the foamy water rushing around them. She rested her head on his chest and cried as she cradled him in her arms.

Ken was gone.

She'd seen who'd done it and couldn't believe it.

What was she going to do?

CHAPTER ONE

"Dr. Walford?"

Gianna Walford stopped in her tracks in the middle of the bustling emergency department and turned to face the new young nurse who stood looking pensive and intimidated. "Yes?"

"Your patient is asking for you. The one in room four."

"Right. What's your name again?"

"Heidi." She pivoted to walk away.

"Wait. You said room four?"

Heidi nodded.

"The one with the perforated bowel?"

"Yes, ma'am."

"I sent her up to surgery a half an hour ago."

Heidi appeared confused. "She was brought back down. She's being transferred to—"

Gianna didn't allow Heidi to finish. "She was brought back down?"

"Yes, ma'am. She's being transferred to…" She studied her tablet, swiping her finger across the screen quickly. Gianna stepped up and took the tablet from her. She stared at the screen in anger and returned the device.

"Dr. Malloy ordered this?"

"Yes, ma'am."

Self-righteous bastard. It was no wonder. She'd had nothing but problems with the surgeon from day one and it seemed nothing had changed.

Gianna called out to the charge nurse, Elaine. "Page Dr. Malloy for me."

Elaine glanced up from her computer screen nestled in the circular nurses' station. "He just went into surgery."

"What? Why in the hell is he not operating on my patient in four?"

Gianna marched up to her and waited while Elaine searched through the information on the computer. After a few long seconds, Elaine had an answer. "Says here he wants her transferred back to the hospital that performed the original bowel surgery on her."

"That's crazy," Gianna breathed. "She's got a perforated bowel and it can and needs to be fixed here."

"He examined her, said she's stable enough for the transfer."

Gianna sighed, ran her hand through her hair, and walked away cursing beneath her breath. This was just like Malloy. Pushing certain patients onto others so he could do the surgeries he preferred. It wasn't supposed to happen. There were regulations in place so it wouldn't. Yet Malloy often found ways around them.

She dodged an incoming gurney escorted by paramedics barking out vitals and approached treatment room four to pull back the curtain. Her patient, Donna Perry, was lying on her own hospital gurney, angled slightly to one side with her hand on her abdomen. Her face was ashen despite her fever. It was obvious she was still in pain.

"Ms. Perry, what can I do for you?" Gianna stood at her bedside and quickly gave the machines monitoring her vitals a quick look-see. So far, all continued to be well, minus the elevated pulse.

"How long will I have to wait for the transfer?"

"They should be here soon."

"I'm in a lot of pain."

Sweat beaded near her hairline and she winced as another stab of pain caused her heart rate to spike yet again.

"We can help ease that for you."

Gianna walked back to the curtain, tugged it aside, and asked Heidi to join her in the room. Heidi, who still seemed intimidated, hurried in and reported on the last dose of pain medicine given as she swiped at her tablet. Gianna ordered a small dose of morphine and returned to Donna's bedside.

"Thank you," Donna said, watching as Heidi injected the medication into her IV and left.

"Thank you for your patience," Gianna said.

Her brow crinkled. "Doctor? Am I being transferred because I'm on Medicaid?"

Gianna inhaled quickly but smiled, hoping to hide it. She cleared her throat and spoke. "No, of course not. That's against the law."

"I just don't understand then. You said I needed the surgery and that you could do it here, yet Dr. Malloy says different."

Gianna kept her face expressionless. Malloy didn't want to do the surgery, why, because he obviously had a more lucrative or interesting one lined up. But she knew what he was no doubt telling everyone, so she went with that, wanting to comfort her patient.

"He believes that the surgeon who just operated on you would be the one best to operate on you again."

"But why? When he could just do it here?"

"Probably because your previous surgeon is more familiar with you and your case."

Donna's gaze dropped from Gianna's and drifted to the right. She appeared hopeless and solemn. Gianna reached for her hand.

"Try not to think about all that now. Just try to rest. Your ride should be here soon, okay?"

She nodded.

Gianna gave her hand a gentle pat, offered her another smile, and left the room. She crossed quietly back to the nurses' station when what she really wanted to do was to storm up to surgery and burst through the operating room doors, demanding to know just what the hell Dr. Malloy was thinking. But she couldn't do that. He was in the middle of surgery. And besides, he'd just gaslight her like he did everyone. So she did what she could. She asked Elaine to call Regina down.

If she couldn't talk to Malloy, she'd go above him to the hospital administrator.

She checked in on another patient as she waited, inspecting the stitches her medical student had given, and when she emerged from behind the curtain a few minutes later, Regina was there and she didn't look too pleased.

"Dr. Walford, you rang?"

Gianna led the way into a private glassed-off room and closed the door behind them. "Do you know about my patient, Ms. Perry? The bowel perforation? The one Dr. Malloy refused surgery on?"

"I do."

"And you're okay with that?"

"She'll be better off at County. Under the care of her original surgeon."

"Better off? She has a perforation, Regina. Obviously, her previous surgeon didn't do something right. And we both know Malloy can fix it. Right here, right now."

"Dr. Malloy has made his decision."

Gianna laughed and crossed her arms over her chest. "And his decision stands? Regardless of what your attending thinks? Regina, she's in a great deal of pain and who knows how long she'll have to sit here and wait for that transfer to County? Not to mention how long she'll have to wait at County before they take her into surgery."

"That's up to County and it's not our concern."

"No, our concern is to provide the best treatment possible for our patients right here, right now. Well, she's still here. And she needs surgery, ASAP. For Christ's sake, she could go into sepsis while she waits."

"You're getting carried away, Doctor."

"Am I? Well, forgive me if I am, but I'm getting sick and tired of all this bullshit."

"Now you're out of line."

"Why? Because I'm upset over the treatment, or lack thereof, of my patient?"

"You always seem to be upset over something as of late, Doctor."

"Well, that should tell you something."

"Oh, it does." Regina looked at her watch. "How much longer are you on shift?"

"Two hours. Why?"

"Why don't you go home, Dr. Walford? Cool down and relax. I believe Dr. Melrose has the day off. Go do something with her. Get away from the ED for a while."

"You want me to go be with my girlfriend? That's your solution to all this?"

"Your patient has been examined and is stable, Dr. Walford. She's awaiting transfer per Dr. Malloy's assessment. There's nothing left for you to concern yourself with. So, yes, I'm telling you to go on home for the day."

Gianna blinked at her in disbelief. "So this is where I stand?"

"You're overworked and overstressed. You need some time away. Why don't you take some vacation time while you're at it?"

"Are you kidding me?"

"No, Dr. Walford, I'm afraid I'm not. You've done nothing but complain as of late, about the way this hospital is run, and I don't appreciate it. Because that's my job, not yours."

"Yet, you're telling me how to do *my* job. You're telling me to ignore my patient in need and pass her off to another hospital. Please tell me it has nothing to do with her being on Medicaid."

"I'm not even going to respond to that." She checked her watch again. "If that's all, Dr. Walford, I have an appointment to get to."

Gianna inhaled sharply again and tried to control her rising temper. Regina took that as her cue to leave.

"Go on home, Doctor." She walked out the door, leaving Gianna alone and fuming.

❖

The few tears Gianna shed over the situation at the hospital were frozen on her cheeks before she even arrived at her building. She didn't bother wiping them away, nor did she bother slathering on another coat of Chapstick to her windblown lips. No, she wore the tears and her dry, cracking lips like a badge of honor. She'd lost this battle, and the handful before, but damn it, she would win the next. She was determined.

She nodded to the doorman as she entered the warm building and headed for the elevator. She still had Tiffany, and Tiffany would understand. She was a surgical fellow and she loathed Malloy just as much as she did. Maybe even more. She couldn't wait to tell her about this latest fiasco.

She exited the elevator on the seventh floor and walked quietly down the hall to the high-rise apartment she shared with Tiffany. It had a beautiful view of the Chicago skyline and she and Tiffany had decorated it together and really made it a welcoming home. God, she hoped the fireplace was going. She needed a glass of good wine to sip on as she sank into her favorite chair by the glowing fire.

She unlocked the door and walked inside to toss her keys onto the counter. To her delight, the fireplace was lit, along with several accent lamps, giving the place a warm, cozy feel. She hummed along with the smooth jazz that was playing over the sound system as she crossed to an open bottle of wine near the sink. She gratefully poured herself a nice, full glass and kicked off her shoes to head down the hall to find Tiffany.

She didn't bother calling out, knowing the music would drown her voice. Tiffany was probably in her office, going over patient files or studying some new and advanced surgical technique. The hospital they worked at was the most innovative in Chicago, and

Tiffany? She was one of the top surgeons and Gianna was damn proud of her.

Gianna stopped at the office and peeked inside. It was empty, Tiffany's two oversized computer monitors in sleep mode. Perplexed, she continued down the hall and froze when she heard laughter. It was coming from the bedroom and it sounded like *two* women rather than one. She forced a swallow and took the last step to stand before the open double doors.

The full wine glass fell from her hand and shattered on the floor as she focused on the two bodies locked in an erotic embrace amongst the tangled sheets on the bed.

They turned at the noise of the glass breaking and a look of sheer horror contorted their faces. Tiffany immediately called out to Gianna and struggled to free herself from the bed.

But Gianna simply lowered her head and walked away, knowing that her life, as she knew it, was over.

Chicago, it seemed, had nothing more to offer her.

It was time to move on.

Chapter Two

I don't understand," Jenny said. "I've told you all I know. Why aren't you going after him? I saw him do it. He was there. He shot Ken."

"If you're referring to Gary, we've spoken to him. He has an alibi," Detective Ridley said.

"So, what, you're just going to believe him and pin this on me?" She was angry and terrified. She'd seen Gary, Ken's brother, with her own eyes. He'd shot and killed Ken. How could he have an alibi? Her hands shook on the shining metal table nestled in the back corner of the interrogation room. She quickly moved her hands to her lap.

"You were found with the deceased, covered in his blood. By your own admission, you'd had an argument with him that evening, and you were the one with the motive. You wanted that house and his fishing business." He studied her closely and she could tell he was waiting to see her reaction to what he'd just said.

Flustered, but too damn angry to be very concerned about it or what he thought, she let loose. "Are you serious? I love—loved Ken. Sure, we had our disagreements, but I would never—"

"Disagreements over the business."

She blinked, caught off guard. "Yes, sometimes. He wasn't very good with numbers, or money for that matter."

"That's motive," Detective Ridley said as he pointed a thick finger at her.

"I was trying to help him, not harm him. Jesus."

Ridley leaned back in his chair and continued to study her with his dark, beady eyes. This was the third time they'd called her down to the station to question her and she now knew for certain that they considered her a serious suspect. The realization chilled her to her bones and her entire body began to shiver just like it had that night she'd pulled Ken from the water. She clenched her eyes as the memory washed through her, swashing her constitution like the sway of a storm-laden ship. It made her sick and she reached out to brace herself against the table.

"You okay?" Ridley asked.

"No. I'm not okay. You're accusing me of murder."

He sighed. "I can't yet prove it, but you should stick around town for now."

She bored a stare into him, ignoring his pockmarked cheeks and ruddy nose. "I can go then?"

"For now."

She stood, slung her purse over her shoulder, and hardened her jaw as Ridley spoke again. "Like I said, don't go far."

"Just do your damn job and look into Gary's alibi again. Because it's bullshit." She turned on her heel and stormed out of the suffocating interrogation room. A few other detectives watched her as she hurried down the hall and out of the sterile building. She blinked in the harsh, winter sunlight and made her way across the parking lot to her car. She sat in her older model Honda Civic for a moment, trying to recuperate from the interview before she started the engine to head home.

She couldn't believe what was happening. First Ken had been killed and now the police actually thought she was responsible. How could that be? She'd never harm a fly, much less a human being. Ridley knew that. He'd questioned the people in town. They'd no doubt told him. She'd grown up in Sunset Cove, just off the coast of North Carolina, and everyone knew her, knew her late family. This was nuts.

She wiped at a tear as she started the vehicle and drove from the parking lot to head home. She kept the volume to the radio turned all the way down, preferring the silence to noise. She had a lot to mull over and noise of any kind would only disrupt that.

Two cars whizzed by as they swerved around her to pass. She let them go, keeping her speed at the proper limit, lost in her thoughts. It was raining again, speckling her windshield just enough for her to need the wipers. The sky was overcast and dreary, just like her mood.

She had to continue to pack once she arrived back at the house. Ken's family had requested she leave the property pending the handling of his affairs. It was rude, insensitive, and unnecessary, but then again, his family had never been very kind to her. Nor did they believe her. They, like Detective Ridley, didn't seem to believe in her innocence. And who knew what Gary had been telling them.

The whole family was in chaos over Ken's death. They were already fighting amongst themselves over the house and boat and Ken hadn't even been dead a week. It was sad. It was repulsive. And she wanted nothing to do with any of it. So how could Ridley possibly think she had a motive? She didn't want that house. It was old, built in the 1930s and it needed major renovations. The only reason she'd agreed to stay there was because Ken loved it and wanted to do the work himself. He'd loved her and wanted her with him, so she'd moved in with the hopes of helping him. She was good with her hands and always had been and Ken appreciated that. He also loved how she was just as good, if not better, at shrimping than he was. She'd often go out on the boat with him to fish and haul in a good catch to go sell. She'd been doing that since she was a kid, alongside her father, who had also been a shrimp boat captain. The sea was like a second home to her.

She let out a sigh as she once again thought of Ken. He'd only been gone a short while, but it felt like an eternity. The deep ache in her chest only seemed to be getting worse rather than better. Whoever said time healed all wounds evidently hadn't lost someone to senseless murder. She wiped at a tear and sniffled, trying to control the sobs that threatened. She couldn't believe she even had any more tears left to cry after all the sobbing she'd done. But here she was, crying all the same. Missing her boyfriend of five years. Five good years. Five years full of love and happiness. And all of it had been taken in a matter of seconds. By someone Ken had trusted, loved. His own brother. Gary.

How could this be? It was a nightmare and she couldn't seem to wake up.

The whining wipers brought her back from her trance. The remaining traffic fell away around her, leaving her alone on the desolate country road leading back to the seaside house. The rainfall increased and she leaned forward to focus better. The road curved sharply again, and she braked to slow. She knew the old road like the back of her hand, which was why she drove so carefully on it. Many an accident had occurred there, taking lives and seriously injuring others.

She gently pumped her brakes again, and she was just about to go into the thick of the curve when a truck came up out of nowhere and rammed her side, pushing her off the road. She shrieked and slammed on her brakes and tried to control the vehicle, but it was no use. The car skidded off the pavement and careened quickly through a grassy knoll, bumping and bouncing along the way. She shrieked again as a large tree loomed in front of her. She yanked the wheel at the last second, sending her and the car crashing into the tree at an angle. The impact was powerful and jolting. She was thrown against her seat belt as the door caved in on her. Her teeth gnashed and her eyes felt as though they'd rattled in her head. Then all movement ceased and the car hissed and clicked, sounds she could hardly discern from the buzzing in her ears. She opened her clenched eyes and saw smoke rising from the hood. She could smell the spilled and burning oil, the gasoline and the wet grass. She tried to call for help but her voice was weak. She turned to glance back at the road. The truck, the one that had rammed her, was idling. The driver watching.

She recognized the vehicle. Even in her injured state. It was Gary's. And he was sitting behind the wheel, staring her down.

A wave of pain overcame her and she winced and lowered her head to close her eyes once again. She heard the sound of a revving engine and squealing tires and when she turned to look again, the truck was gone.

He tried to kill me.

Gary tried to kill me.

Panicked, in pain, and worried about the scent of gasoline, she unbuckled her seat belt and forced herself to crawl into the passenger seat. She cried out as she did so, a stabbing pain coming from her left knee. But fear kept her moving and she pushed out the passenger door and fell onto the wet grass.

She stared at the green blades topped with beads of rain for a long moment before she had the strength to shove herself to an awkward stand. Then, she limped to the road and waved down the next car to come along, knowing she had no choice now. She had to get the hell out of Sunset Cove.

CHAPTER THREE

There, that ought to do it.

Gary sped away and made a turn toward his home, thankful there still weren't any cars around to see him.

Serves that bitch right. Telling everyone who would listen that he killed Ken. Ha. Who was she kidding? No one would believe that. He and Ken, they were brothers, nearly attached at the hip. It sounded like the bullshit that it was.

Still…he'd had to do something to shut her up. He couldn't risk her continuing to run her damn mouth. People might get suspicious, she might wear them down. They might take a harder look at him and he couldn't have that. No, he needed the police and everyone else to continue to see him as the grieving brother, someone to feel badly for, not someone who could possibly cause harm to another.

You better go back and check on her. Be sure she's really dead.

He rubbed his stubbled jaw and answered the voice in his head. "Nah, she'll die. All alone on that road and the way her engine was smoking with all that spilled gasoline. They'll be lucky if they can even identify her remains."

He fumbled for a cigarette in his console and lit it to take a deep draw.

He checked his rearview mirror for signs of a fire. He saw nothing but gloomy skies.

Go back.

"It's too late now. Someone might see."

She's not dead. You saw her moving.

"She was trapped in that car. She's not going anywhere."

She'll tell them it was you who ran her off the road.

"So what? Who's going to believe her? No one. That's who. They haven't believed her so far, so what's changed?"

He sucked harder on his cigarette. None of this would even be happening if Ken had just loaned him that money. Goddamned Kenny. So selfish. Even to his dying breath. Never willing to lift a finger to help him. No siree, Bob. Not a finger.

And why? Ken had everything. He had the house. The one that had been in the family for generations. He had his shrimping business. And he had Jenny.

Jenny.

The goddamned woman of Gary's dreams. Who Ken just happened to get to first. Had Gary gotten to her, asked her out first, he'd be the one with her. Not Ken. Fucking Kenny. That little runt bastard of a brother. He had everything. Always had. He'd been favored by everyone from the word go. Kenny this and Kenny that. Oh, look at what Kenny can do. Isn't he something? Say, Gary, why can't you do that? Why can't you be more like Kenny? Be more like your brother? You know, they say that younger brothers are supposed to take after their older brothers, but in your case it's different. You should look up to Kenny, even if he is your younger brother.

"Fuck that."

He pulled the cigarette away and blew smoke out the side of his mouth. He took care of that problem once and for all. Now there'd be no more comparisons. No more should haves and could have beens. Ken was gone. And he was finally free.

If only he had Jenny. If only she hadn't seen what he'd did to Ken.

Damn it.

Now, she'd become a liability. One he couldn't let live.

It hurt him terribly to have to off her, but it was her or him and he chose himself. After all, she'd rejected him, time and time again. So it was her own fault really. She'd chosen Ken, even when Gary had made his true feelings known and offered to give her the world if she'd just run away with him. But she'd said no. That she'd loved Ken. And that he was an awful brother for even suggesting such a thing.

He smirked. Maybe so. But then again, Ken had everything and he had nothing. He was only looking out for himself. Trying to get just a little of what Ken had in life. One couldn't blame him for that.

He sped up despite the rainfall. He needed to get home quickly and finish establishing some sort of alibi. The groceries he'd purchased on the other side of town were next to him on the floorboard and he'd made sure the cashier had noticed him when he checked out. Now all he had to do was get home, unload, and start cooking dinner. The cops would stop by, no doubt. Just as soon as the accident was reported. But he'd be well settled by then. The house would smell like a freshly made meal and the game would be on and he'd be casually enjoying a beer as he took it in. And they'd hopefully buy this alibi just like they'd done the last. Easy peasy.

He wondered as he eventually slowed to turn into his drive, how long it would take before someone came across the accident. Would Jenny be dead by then? Or would she hang on, barely conscious? Would she tell them it had been him? Or had she even seen him at all? If she had, would she even remember?

Either way, he should be in the clear. And if she wasn't dead, if she somehow survived, she'd better take it as a warning to keep her mouth shut.

"Otherwise, I'll have to try again. And this time, I'll make sure she dies."

Chapter Four

"Welcome home!" Lauren said as she tugged Gianna inside to envelop her in a tight hug. Gianna, completely helpless to escape, merely smiled and enjoyed the embrace as Lauren's kids joined in with their loud but warm welcomes. The youngest, Haley, was even holding a homemade sign that said "Welcome Home, Auntie GiGi."

"Thanks, guys," Gianna said as she drew away from the hug. "This is all so unexpected."

"We wanted to surprise you," the oldest, Avery, said.

"And we made you a poster," Haley added.

"Yeah, and we hung balloons," Jaden, the middle child, said. He brought her a bright blue one and smiled proudly.

"Gosh, thanks, bud. Thank you all. I've never felt so welcome." Not since her last visit anyway. Lauren and the kids always made her visits a big deal, but she pretended to be surprised each and every time. It tickled the kids to no end.

Lauren pulled her farther inside. "Come in, come in. Doug's still at work, but we've already got dinner ready for you."

Gianna stumbled along after her as Jaden and Avery dragged her luggage across the living room and down the long hallway.

"They don't have to do that," Gianna said, staring after them. They'd never taken her luggage for her before. They'd been too small last time she was there to even try.

"It's okay," Haley said. "Mama says it's called manners."

Gianna laughed and looked to Lauren. "You've done well."

"I try."

Lauren insisted she sit at the table as they entered the kitchen and she called for Avery and Jaden. The duo returned from the hallway and began helping her set the table, while Haley put down her sign and climbed up into her booster seat to grab a sippy cup full of what appeared to be juice. She gulped loudly and then let out a satisfied sigh along with a grin.

She was adorable.

They all were.

Such a wonderful family. And it was so good to see them. It had been two years now. Two years too long since she'd been home.

"We made chicken," Jaden said as he carried a serving dish over to the table. "Mom said you like it."

"I do. And I especially like your mom's chicken."

"Yeah, she makes the best," Avery said.

"I like steak!" Haley announced.

"Me too," Gianna said with a wink. "We'll have to have that another night."

Haley nodded and drank more juice.

Lauren carried over the last two dishes of food and settled down next to the kids. "So, how does it feel to be back in Flagstaff?"

"Good. Really good."

"You don't like Chicago anymore?" Avery asked.

"I do. It's just time for a change."

"Does this mean your going to stay in Flag?" Jaden asked, a hopeful look on his young face.

"'Fraid not, Jay."

"Where will you go?" Haley asked.

"I'm going to Oregon. To a small coastal town called Cliffside. I'm going to be the doctor there."

"Neat!" Jaden said. "You'll be next to the ocean."

"Sure will."

"Can I come visit? And learn to surf?" he asked.

"I'm not sure you can surf where I'll be, bud. The shore is rather rocky and it's cold and foggy a lot of the time."

"Oh."

"But you can absolutely come to see me. Anytime."

He perked up and looked to Lauren. "Can we, Mom? Please?"

"Let's give Aunt GiGi time to get settled first and then we'll see. Okay?"

He nodded and dug into his chicken and noodles.

"Why don't you want to stay here, with us?" Haley asked, pushing out her lower lip as tears filled her eyes.

Gianna's heart lurched. "Oh, sweetie."

"Aunt GiGi wants to see a new place where she can explore and see new things," Lauren said.

"But she'll be lonesome," Haley said.

Lauren looked to Gianna. Gianna lightly gripped Haley's tiny hand. "I will never be lonesome, sweetie. Know why? Because I have you all and you're just a phone call away."

"We can FaceTime?" she asked.

"Sure can."

"All the time?"

"When Aunt GiGi's not working we can," Lauren said.

"Yay!" Haley raised her fork in the air.

Lauren pointed at her chicken, which she'd cut up for her. "Eat your dinner, Hales. Before it gets cold."

Gianna took a bite of her own food and complimented the chef. But Lauren insisted that the kids had helped, and Avery and Jaden nodded in agreement. Gianna was impressed and offered to cook dinner for them the following night.

"Can we have steak?" Haley asked after slurping up a noodle.

"Yes," Gianna said with a laugh.

"Right on," Jaden said as he forked a bite.

"I thought we'd go up to Snow Bowl tomorrow," Lauren said after swallowing a bite to sip her soda. "Let the kids ride the inner tubes."

"I want to try out my new snowboard," Avery said.

"Me too," Jaden added.

"They got snowboards last Christmas and they didn't quite get the hang of riding them last season," Lauren said.

"We did alright," Jaden countered.

"You did. But you need more practice."

"So, let us ride tomorrow."

Lauren sighed. "What about Haley? And Aunt Gigi? She's our guest. We want her to have fun too. And if we're all split up, it won't be as much fun."

Gianna saw the look of disappointment on the kids' faces. "Let 'em snowboard. You and I can stay with Haley. Besides, I'd love to see the kids try out their boards."

"Please, Mom?" Avery said.

Lauren set down her fork. "Oh, alright."

"Yes!" Jaden said.

"But only for a couple of hours. Then we inner tube with Haley."

They nodded, pleased they'd succeeded in winning her over.

Gianna glanced around the table as they all quieted down to eat. The kids were thriving, Lauren seemed healthy and happy, and the house was warm and cozy. She couldn't be happier herself and she was glad she'd come home for a visit before heading off to the coast. She'd had the option of moving on to Cliffside early, to rent another place until her home was ready, but she'd wanted to see everyone here and she'd needed some feelings of nostalgia after the mess she'd left behind in Chicago.

Tiffany was still calling her and sending her long texts, begging her to come back, apologizing, saying the affair was nothing, blaming their busy schedules and the fact that they didn't have enough time together. It was all excuses and she wasn't buying it. She'd known the woman she'd caught Tiffany with. Her name was Katherine, and she was one of the hospital's major donors and someone she'd considered to be a friend. The betrayal had been nearly catastrophic, and she couldn't have escaped quickly enough. So coming back home had been an easy decision. It was safe, familiar, a place where she could quietly lick her wounds until it was time to move on to Oregon. Not to mention the fact that she would be surrounded by loved ones.

Yes, she'd made the right decision. She was back with her people, where she was wanted and loved. That included her folks, whom she also planned on visiting, as well as her other best friend, Jake.

"Hey, why don't we invite Jake up to the slopes tomorrow too?" Gianna asked.

The kids glanced over at Lauren, appearing alarmed.

"What?" Gianna asked.

"Well, it was supposed to be a surprise. But I might as well tell you. Jake's working for the ski patrol up at Snow Bowl now. So, he'll be there."

"That's great."

"Tell her the best part, Mom," Jaden said.

"He's actually the head of ski patrol. In charge of it all."

"Really? Good for him."

"He's still doing his paramedic work at the fire department too, in his off time and during offseason. But for now, he's commanding the ski patrol."

Gianna sipped her soda. "I'm so happy for him." Growing up, she and Lauren and Jake had been avid skiers and Jake had always talked of working for the ski patrol. He'd just never gotten around to it once he was hired on at the fire department. She was glad that he'd finally taken the time to do what he needed to make his dream a reality.

"I can't wait to see him," Gianna said. "It's been too long."

They finished dinner over more conversation about going up to Snow Bowl. Haley was excited to try out her new inner tube and she was more than eager to ride down the hill by herself for the first time. Lauren, of course, told her she would also have to wear her new helmet, which Haley pouted about until Lauren told her she'd bought her a pink one. That seemed to seal the deal.

After dinner, Gianna insisted the kids go play while she helped Lauren clean up. Lauren seemed glad to have some quiet time with her, but it was Gianna who spoke first as she dried a plate and put it away.

"You're looking really good," she said. "I'm assuming things are going well?"

Lauren smiled wistfully but kept washing the dishes. "Mm-hm."

"Wait. What does that mean?"

"Nothing."

"Lauren, I've known you almost my entire life. I know when something's off."

"Nothing's off." But then she sighed and slumped her shoulders. When she turned to look at Gianna, her face was one of deep concern. "GiGi, I'm pregnant."

Gianna almost dropped the wet bowl in her hand. "What?"

"I found out day before yesterday."

"You're—sure?"

She nodded. "Went to the doctor and everything."

Gianna studied her. "Congratulations?"

Lauren snorted. "Thanks."

"So…this is bad news, then?"

"It's just not a good time. It's—unexpected and well, we're barely making it as it is. I was even planning on going back to work."

"What does Doug say?"

"I haven't told him yet."

Gianna set the now dry bowl aside. "Come here." She hugged her for a long moment and kissed her cheek as she drew away. "It's going to be okay. You hear?"

But Lauren only wiped away tears, obviously unconvinced.

Gianna took her damp hands in her own. "You know I'm here for you, right?"

"Yes."

"That means you can ask me for help, Lauren. Especially if you're struggling financially."

"I can't do that."

"Why not?"

"It doesn't feel right."

"Lauren, how many times have you helped me with things over the years? Including now. Giving me a safe place to land after my breakup. I owe you, girl. So, please, let me help."

"I don't think Doug will allow it."

"Let me talk to him."

"He'll only be embarrassed." She shook her head. "Let me do it. I need to give him the news about the baby anyway."

"You sure?"

"Yes."

Gianna embraced her again. "It really is going to be okay."

"I hope so."

"It will."

Gianna closed her eyes as she held her. She felt the gentle shake of her body as the tears overwhelmed her, and she hoped that she was right and that things would be okay. But deep down she wondered, how could she promise something she couldn't even reassure herself of?

There was only one thing that was certain for the both of them. Time would do the telling.

Chapter Five

Ma'am, are you sure you don't want me to take you to the hospital?" the kind driver asked from behind the wheel. She was young, maybe all of seventeen, and she'd picked Jenny up from the side of the road. But she'd asked nonstop questions since.

Jenny trembled in both fear and pain. She looked over her shoulder to make sure Gary wasn't behind them, following them in the rain. She brushed her wet bangs away from her forehead and examined the blood on her fingertips.

"No, no hospital," she finally managed to say.

"But you're hurt. Like really hurt bad."

"I'll be okay."

The girl sighed and kept driving. Jenny checked behind them once again. "Can you drive a little faster? I'm in a bit of a hurry."

"It's raining and rain makes me nervous. I don't want to get in an accident like you did."

"Someone ran me off the road," Jenny said.

The girl lifted her eyebrows in the reflection of the rearview mirror. "Seriously? Oh, my God. I should take you to the police then."

"No. Please. I just need to get home." She prayed Gary wouldn't be there waiting for her, but she reassured herself that he wouldn't be. Not if he was smart. He would know that if she had survived the accident, she'd most likely inform the police and they'd be looking for him. Ken's house would be the first place they'd look, next to his own home.

"You have someone there to take care of you?"

"Yes," she fibbed.

"Okay." That seemed to settle the young woman's nerves, and she remained silent the rest of the ride. Jenny, who was fighting off shock, stared at the silver cross hanging from the rearview mirror, watching it dance with the movement of the vehicle. The rain continued to fall, heavier now, and a light fog had settled over the surrounding forest, trying to lull her to sleep. But she battled the weighing fatigue and forced her eyes open until at last they pulled into the drive.

"Do you need help getting out?" the girl asked.

"I'm fine, thanks."

Jenny shoved open the door and winced in pain as she climbed from the vehicle. She turned and gave the young woman a polite wave before she closed the door. "Thanks again."

"Sure thing." But she didn't seem okay with leaving Jenny on her own. She appeared apprehensive and unsure, like maybe she was about to crawl from the car to assist her to the front door.

Jenny leaned down to knock on the driver's side window. The young woman lowered it.

"I'm really okay. My boyfriend is just inside. He'll help me."

The girl nodded.

Jenny waved again and hobbled up to the front porch. The young woman waited until she was inside before she drove away. Jenny locked the door and eased onto the bench in the foyer. She was drenched and in awful pain, her body bruised and scraped and her knee dislocated or something. It hurt like hell to walk. She took several deep breaths, ran her cold hands through her wet hair and began stripping out of her clothes. She started with her shoes, which she kicked off and then lowered her pants and pulled off her sweater and shirt. She walked through the house slowly, limping along the way, and opened the fridge for some orange juice. She drank straight from the container and downed nearly half of it, dripping some of it on her chin which she swiped away with the back of her hand. She had no appetite, despite it being around dinner time, so she returned the juice to the fridge and crawled her way up the stairs. It was slow going and very painful, so it took her a while. But she finally made it, and she sat on the edge of the bed in her panties and bra and gathered her breath. When she had recovered a bit, she stood and switched on the television and changed it to the local news. She was curious to see if her accident had been reported, but what she saw instead made her blood run cold. They were reporting on Ken's death and her driver's license picture came up on the screen. The police had declared her a major person of interest in Ken's death, and they were now officially releasing to the public that it was a homicide. They were asking for anyone who had any information to call the police tip line. She threw the remote across the room and cursed.

How could they? And how could they not even mention Gary?

She stumbled over to the closet and pulled out her rolling suitcase. She unzipped it and began packing it full of clothes and necessities. She included the wad of cash that she and Ken kept hidden in the sock drawer for emergencies. If this wasn't one, she wasn't sure what would be.

She then slid into some waterproof athletic pants and a long-sleeved shirt and covered that with a windbreaker she often wore on the boat. Next, came some socks and all-terrain type shoes and she was ready to go.

Her heart raced as she slid her way back down the stairs, in pain and in fear of Gary or the police showing up to stop her.

When she made it back to the bench, she sat again and reached for the telephone on the nearby accent table. It was a land line, one they'd hardly ever used, but Ken had insisted on keeping it. She dialed the local cab company, whose number she found in the old address book in the drawer of the table, and requested a cab immediately.

As she sat and waited, with her nerves on edge, she glanced around at the house and wondered if she'd ever see it again. A profound sadness overcame her, as memories of Ken and her working on the interior of the house flooded her mind. They'd started the renovation just over a year ago and had taken things one small project at a time, beginning with the downstairs. She recalled the way they'd worked together, stripping old wallpaper off the walls while listening to classic rock, both of them singing off key. They'd had fun despite the hard work and she knew it was because they'd done it together. They'd enjoyed each other. Always had. She wiped away her tears and tried to shove down her emotions. She couldn't afford to cry right now. If she did, she was afraid she'd never stop.

The cab pulled up out front and she wiped her wet cheeks again and rolled her suitcase out the front door.

The driver met her at the steps to take her luggage for her. She thanked him and climbed into the car, trying to ignore his concerned stare. She knew she looked a wreck, but there wasn't anything she could do about it now except to try to behave as calmly and casually as she could. So she gave him a polite smile and tried for small talk about the weather, which was starting to clear up a little.

He seemed happy to chat and when he crawled behind the wheel, she offered him the cash she had up front and asked him to take her to the nearby truck stop.

He readily agreed and they made more mindless small talk along the way, which she was grateful for. Anything to keep her mind off of the crash and Ken and Gary.

Amidst their easy conversation, she stared longingly out the window at the retreating sea, along with the surrounding dunes and then eventually the woods where she'd grown up playing. She quietly said goodbye to the life she knew and hoped with all she had that better things lay ahead.

❖

After she bid farewell to the cab driver, Jenny stepped into the nearby truck stop café and was hit with the overpowering smell of fresh coffee. Suddenly, she craved a hot cup like she never had before. Still limping and trying to ignore the blatant stares, she walked over to a table and sat. She kept her head low and tried to hide her trembling hands. A bubbly middle-aged waitress was at her side in a nanosecond, smiling a toothy smile that quickly faltered as she got a good look at Jenny.

"Say, darlin', you sure do look a sight. You okay?"

"Fine, thanks. Can I just get a cup of coffee, please?"

"That all you want? I got my best guy behind the grill, he can cook you up anything you like. You look like you need a good meal to me."

"Just the coffee, please."

"Suit yourself." She tore off the ticket and left it with Jenny and then returned a second later with a pot of coffee. She filled her cup and left her in peace.

Jenny gripped the mug with two hands and brought it up to her dry and cracking lips. She sipped the piping hot liquid and nearly groaned as it filled her mouth and spilled down her throat, instantly warming her. She breathed deep and tried to relax while keeping her eyes peeled on the vast parking lot. Semi-trucks were lined up like long soldiers in the parking area, while others were pulling in for fuel or a nice wash after all the mud and rain. Truckers wandered in and out of the café, stiff from their extended hauls, talking and musing, paying her little mind. Forks scraped plates and eager lips slurped coffee, and soon she was fighting sleep, lulled by all the constant but steady commotion.

Her waitress returned and slid a plate of apple pie in front of her. "It's on the house."

Jenny blinked up at her.

"Like I said. You look like you could use it."

"Thank you."

"Don't mention it."

She refilled her coffee and started to walk away, but Jenny stopped her.

"Excuse me?" Jenny glanced around nervously. The waitress raised an eyebrow. "Do you know of any drivers that might be willing to give me a ride?"

The waitress scrunched up her face. "Listen, sweetie. I ain't your pimp. You run your business out in the parking lot just like everyone else."

"No, I don't mean—I'm just looking for a ride out west. Nothing else, honest."

"No fooling?"

"I was hoping you knew of someone trustworthy. Someone safe."

The waitress glanced back at the counter where men were sitting on stools, eating and chatting. They were all dressed similarly to each other in dirty denim, flannel shirts, and worn ball caps. She'd be hard-pressed to choose one on her own, based on appearances alone.

"West, you say?"

"Yes. I need to get to Oregon. But I'll settle for as far as they can take me."

She looked back to Jenny. "You ain't in any trouble, are you?"

"No," she swallowed. "I just need to leave. I have—my boyfriend—isn't very nice."

"Say no more." She left her and walked up to the counter to speak with an older gentleman sitting at the end. She pointed back to Jenny and then led the man over to her.

"This here's Floyd. He'll take you all the way to California if you're wanting to go."

"Yes, that would be great." She held out her hand and prayed it wouldn't tremble. "I'm Jenny."

"Floyd," he said gruffly but with a gentle smile. "You okay enough to travel? You look like you're hurt pretty bad."

"I'm okay. I just really need to get going."

He tugged on his cap. "Well, I just need to refuel and then we can set out on the road."

The waitress took the ticket for the coffee and crumpled it up. "Coffee's on the house too, darlin'. You just stay safe."

Jenny smiled. "Thank you."

"You ready?" Floyd asked, offering her his hand. She took his rough palm and pulled herself up. Floyd eyed her with obvious concern as she tugged on her suitcase and limped toward the door. "Here, let me." He took the luggage, and they headed out into the waning sun and walked slowly to his truck on the slick pavement. He opened the door and helped her inside, which was quite difficult with her sore knee, but she finally managed. She settled into the comfortable seat and waited while he opened his door to place her suitcase in the back in the sleeper.

"Feel free to lie down back there whenever you need to," he said.

She nodded.

Floyd then started up the rumbling engine and pulled them around to refuel the truck.

She checked out the interior of the cab while she waited, searching for anything suspect. She'd never hitched a ride with a stranger before, but her father often had when he'd been younger, and he'd told her the truckers were the nicest. Of course, that was fifty years ago, but she hoped it was still true. Floyd seemed like a nice enough man, but she was still anxious about sharing such close quarters with him. Anything, however, was better than staying in town and leaving her fate up to the police. Gary would kill her for sure before they got their heads out of their asses.

Floyd climbed back inside, buckled his seat belt, and stared into her.

"I want you to do something for me before we go."

She rested her hand on the door handle, ready for a quick escape.

He reached around his back, going for his pocket. "I want you to talk to my wife." He pulled out his phone.

"Sorry?"

"I don't give rides to no one she don't see and talk to first."

He dialed and held up the phone to FaceTime. She answered right away.

"Yes, my love?"

"Hi, sweetheart. I have a new companion. Another one needing help."

"That so?"

"Her name is Jenny and she's going all the way to California. Got troubles with her old man." He turned the phone toward Jenny. The older woman had a stern look at first as she gave Jenny the once-over, but then her face cracked with a kind smile.

"You're just an itty-bitty thing, aren't you?"

"I'm not. Not really."

"Well, compared to me you are, honey." She let out a throaty laugh, one that seemed to last an entire minute, before she grew serious again. "You want to ride with Floyd, do ya?"

"Yes, ma'am."

"Got man trouble?"

"Yes, ma'am."

"Hell, I've been there. In my younger days." She pushed out a breath. "Floyd's a good man. You can trust him. He'll take you to California, rest assured. But your man, he ain't gonna come after you, is he? I don't want my Floyd getting hurt."

"No, he doesn't even know I'm gone." She hoped that was true.

"Well, you all better get going then. Floyd?"

He turned the phone back to him.

"You take care now. And call me later."

"I will, sweetheart."

They said their goodbyes, and Floyd ended the call. Then he started the engine back up and they headed out.

"You a talker?" he asked as they entered the highway.

"Not really."

"Well, I am. I hope you don't mind."

"Not at all."

"Your man, he did a number on you, didn't he?"

She shifted in her seat.

"You ain't got to say nothing. I can see it on you." He shook his head. "I'm real sorry that happened to you."

She didn't respond, just wiped at a tear.

He reached over and handed her a tissue. "You're safe now, honey. Ain't no way he'll find you in here or where we're headed."

"Thank you," she said as she wiped her eyes.

"No need to thank me. I like having the company."

"You're very kind."

"I am, yes. But some aren't. You know that, right? What you're doing, it's dangerous."

Again, she said nothing.

"But I suppose you staying is even more dangerous. Hell, that's a shame. That's a downright shame."

He adjusted the radio, found a mellow country station, and eased back in his seat. "You go on and rest now. I've got the road."

She nodded and slumped down in her seat, her eyes already falling shut. As she drifted off to sleep Floyd's words kept replaying in her mind.

You're safe now, honey. Ain't no way he'll find you in here or where we're headed.

CHAPTER SIX

Gianna followed Lauren inside Josephine's Modern American Bistro near downtown Flag and settled in at a table near one of the two burning fireplaces. She slung her purse over the back of her chair and folded her chilled hands on the table to smile at an exhausted-looking Lauren.

"You okay?" Gianna asked softly, knowing they'd had a very long day on the slopes with the kids, who'd had a blast but were currently at home with Doug.

"Just tired," she said, avoiding her gaze to glance over the menu.

"You got some sun," Gianna said.

Lauren touched her pink cheeks but didn't look up. "So did you."

"Guess we should've been more generous with the sunscreen."

"Guess so."

The waitress appeared and Gianna ordered some wine and told her they'd wait on a starter until Jake arrived. The woman walked away and Gianna reached for Lauren's hand. "Hey, what's going on? You've been down all day, though you really tried to hide it with the kids. I've got to give you credit for that."

"Nothing." She continued to look at the menu and carefully removed her hand from beneath Gianna's.

"Is it Doug? I heard the two of you arguing last night—"

She shot her a hard look. "You were listening?"

"No, of course not, Lauren. But I couldn't help but overhear. You were having a disagreement."

Lauren released a breath and focused somewhere out the window. "He's upset about the pregnancy. Says we can't afford it."

"I can help," Gianna said.

"He said that would make him uncomfortable."

"Well, he needs to get over that."

"Don't," she said, holding her gaze once again. "I can't handle you being that way right now. He's my husband and I have to respect his feelings too."

Gianna eased back against her chair. "Okay."

"So, please don't bring it up around him."

"What, the baby or the money?"

"Either."

Gianna sighed and thanked the waitress for her wine before taking a nice, long sip. It was chilled to perfection and just what she needed after a long day on the slopes, watching the kids snowboard and inner tube. She'd ordered a glass for Jake, but the waitress had set it in front of Lauren who let it remain.

"There's Jake," Lauren said, suddenly brightening. "Please don't mention the pregnancy to him either. I don't feel like discussing it anymore tonight."

"Lauren, he's going to be hurt that he's the last to know."

"I know, but please, don't."

Gianna nodded and stood to hug Jake as he walked up to the table, all smiles.

"It's good to see you, GiGi," he said, holding her at arm's length to take her in. "It's been too damn long."

"It has."

He then embraced Lauren, who beamed at him like nothing in the world was wrong. But Jake had always seemed to have that effect on her, and for a long while Gianna thought for sure the two of them would get together and eventually marry. But Jake went off to the military after college and Lauren had met Doug. The rest, as they say, was history.

"What are we having?" Jake asked as he sat and rubbed his hands together. He, too, had the raccoon look from the sun on his face and he quickly pulled out some Chapstick to glide over his pink lips. "That wine any good?"

"It's wonderful," Gianna said, sliding it toward him so he could try it.

He took a hefty sip and waved the waitress over to order a bottle. Then he asked Lauren and Gianna about a starter. He was just coming in from work and he was starved. Gianna didn't argue, feeling rather hungry herself.

They ordered the southwestern crab cakes and Jake filled them in on his new position as director of the ski patrol. They hadn't seen him on the slopes earlier; he'd been too busy working to try to find them. Gianna said she understood and asked him how he was liking it. He said he'd never been happier. His smile lit up his striking blue eyes and it appeared as though he was right, and Gianna couldn't be happier for him.

"So what's up with you two?" he asked after they'd ordered their entrees and were digging into their newly arrived crab cakes. "You still moving to Oregon?" He aimed the question at Gianna.

"In a week or so."

"What's the holdup?"

"I'm waiting for the previous doctor to move out of the house."

"Oh?"

"He's retiring and I'm taking his place. So I'm moving into the house where I'll be living upstairs and seeing patients downstairs."

"No kidding? Like an old-fashioned town doctor."

"Exactly."

"It sounds so quaint, doesn't it?" Lauren said, careful to avoid drinking her wine. She sipped on her lemon water and Gianna had noticed but she wondered if Jake had. He was already refilling his own glass of chardonnay and trying to do the same for Gianna. She let him, but told him she needed to slow down some.

"Oh, come on, live a little. It's a beautiful evening and we're all together again."

"This is true," Gianna said, then took another sip.

Jake eyed Lauren. "What's with you? Why aren't you drinking?"

"I just don't feel like it tonight."

"She's rather dehydrated from all the sun exposure today," Gianna said. "So I encouraged her to drink her water instead."

Jake rubbed his scruffy jowl and snorted. "Oh. For a second there I thought you were going to tell me you were pregnant."

Lauren's face went ashen and her mouth fell open. She tried to recover but it was too late. Jake had seen it all.

"Laur?"

"I—"

"You're pregnant?" he whispered.

Her eyes widened and filled with tears. Jake reached for her hand. "Hey," he said. "It's okay. It's okay, Laur."

"No, it's not okay. We can't afford it, and Doug—he's upset—" She broke down.

Jake frowned. It was no secret that Jake didn't care much for Doug. He just didn't like the way he handled things and he definitely didn't like how he sometimes put his own wants and needs before his family's.

Lauren brushed away her tears and forced another smile. "But you're right. It's okay."

"Listen, if you need help, I'm here. I have some savings—"

She shook her head. "No. I can't."

"I've already tried," Gianna said. "She won't take money from me either."

Jake looked perplexed. "Well, why not, Laur? We're your friends. Your best friends. Let us help."

"Doug says no." She grabbed her glass of water and downed the rest of it. "And I can't talk about it. Don't want to talk about it."

Jake pressed his lips together and gave Gianna a look. "Okay. Whatever you want. Just know that the offer stands."

"Thank you," she breathed as the waitress refilled her glass of water.

They sat in silence and Lauren began to softly hiccup from crying. Gianna and Jake tried to soothe her and discuss other things, but she remained distant and melancholy the rest of the evening, though she did try to converse with them occasionally. When they left, she and Gianna both hugged Jake goodbye, with the promise of trying to get together again before Gianna left for Oregon.

Lauren drove them home, with Gianna a little too tipsy to drive after all the wine.

"It really is going to be okay, Lauren," Gianna said as they drove in the dark.

"I know. It just seems bad right now is all."

"You know you have options, right?" She hadn't wanted to bring it up earlier, but she felt it needed to be said.

Lauren shook her head. "No. I'm having it. Even if Doug doesn't want me to."

"He doesn't?"

"No."

"Oh, Lauren. I'm sorry. No wonder why you're so upset."

"I just feel so alone." A tear slipped down her cheek, reflected in the oncoming headlights.

Gianna squeezed her hand. "You're not, sweetie. You have Jake and me. And we're always here. Got it?"

"It would just be nice if I felt the same about my husband."

"I know. But he may come around. He did with Haley and she was a surprise."

"Yes, but he was adamant that Haley be the last. And somehow he's implying this is all my fault. As if I did this on my own."

"Jesus. He's that bad?"

She swallowed. "He is."

Gianna continued to hold her hand as they rode the rest of the way home in silence. She wasn't sure what to do for her friend, but she knew she needed to do something.

CHAPTER SEVEN

Gary eased his truck up the gravel drive and parked in front of the quiet house. He sat for a moment before he switched off his engine, just to make sure he was alone. When he was reasonably assured, he killed the engine and slid down from the truck to hurry up the porch steps. He glanced around before he gave the door a hard series of knocks. When he heard nothing in response but the distant barking of dogs, he tried the doorknob. It turned.

With one last cautious look over his shoulder, he pushed the door open and stepped into the house. The wind shoved at the door as he closed it and he stood in the foyer, taking in the sound of the wind whistling, still trying to get in.

"Hello?" he called out.

His voice echoed throughout the downstairs, but he heard nothing by way of a reply. "Guess I'm all alone." He walked slowly into the kitchen where he found a small stack of mail. He sorted through it quickly, finding nothing but bills and advertisements. He moved on to the fridge, tugged it open, found beer and orange juice but little else. The house was not only desolate and quiet, it appeared to be hardly lived in. He grabbed a beer, because, hey, why not, and trudged toward the stairs.

"Hello?" he called again. "Anyone here?" He sipped the beer as he reached the top step. "It's your old pal, Gary. Remember me? The guy you turned down again and again?" He stopped at the threshold to the bedroom and leaned against the doorframe. The bed was presentable, covered with a homemade quilt, one he recognized as one his late grandmother had stitched, and the rest of the room was nice and neat as well. It made him sick to be in there. To be where Ken and Jenny had shared a bed. Had made love. Had been happy.

He pushed off from the frame and ambled inside, downing more beer. "Where are you, Jenny? You home?"

He stood before one of the night tables, the one he assumed was Jenny's based on the scented hand lotion and small jewelry box resting on it. He pulled open the drawer and sifted through the contents. He found more lotions, small sample-sized bottles in varying scents. The rest was books, mostly paperbacks, and a lone tube of K-Y Jelly. His stomach clenched and he slammed the drawer closed.

Ken couldn't even get her properly excited enough without having to use lube. What kind of man was he? Gary scoffed. "Not much of a man at all." He crossed to the dresser, ignoring the banging from the shutter fighting the wind, and pulled open those drawers. The top two were empty. The rest had what appeared to be Ken's clothing inside, mostly socks and boxer shorts. He moved to the closet, saw the gap where clothes that should've been hanging weren't. He lowered his beer.

"Fuck. She took off."

He'd suspected as much after the police came calling, asking him about the accident and if he knew where she currently was. He'd been surprised to hear that she was missing. He'd thought for sure she'd be either dead or badly injured. But gone? No way. He hadn't seen that one coming. So he'd feigned his innocence, given them his alibi for the accident, which he'd been prepared to do, and then laid low for a few days. When he felt it was safe, he'd driven here, to Ken's, to see for himself. And now he knew. She was gone.

Great. What would the police think? She'd already accused him of murdering Ken and now she comes up missing? They'd hound him for sure. And if they happened to find her before he did, she'd tell them about the accident. About how he'd run her off the road. It wouldn't be good. Not good at all.

He hurried back down the stairs to the foyer where he took a seat on the bench to finish his beer. He then threw the bottle against the wall where it crashed and shattered. But he didn't care about the noise or the mess. Fuck this house. Fuck Ken. And fuck Jenny. All he'd wanted was a little loan to start up his own shrimping business. He just needed to repair his boat, get a little start-up cash. Why couldn't Ken have just done that for him? It would've saved them all so much trouble.

"Damn it, now I have to hunt her down and kill her all over again."

He yanked off his ball cap and ran his hand through his greasy-feeling hair. Then he looked over at the phone on the little table next to him. An address book sat next to it, open. He reached for it and read through the listed numbers. He smiled as he spotted one of particular interest, right there in the center of the page.

Maybe finding her wouldn't be so hard after all.

CHAPTER EIGHT

"You say you need to get to Oregon?" Floyd asked as he took a big bite of his bacon, lettuce, and tomato sandwich and chewed. They'd left North Carolina two days before, which had been their starting point, but Jenny still felt like they weren't far enough away to be safe from Gary.

Jenny nodded and lowered her spoon to sip her coffee. She'd finally been able to eat again, thanks to Floyd, who'd gently kept encouraging her, offering her coffee cakes and Danishes at each stop. Now she was up to eating oatmeal with brown sugar and dry toast, along with her black coffee, and thankfully, she was starting to feel a little better. She was still injured, no doubt about that, but her scrapes and bruises were healing, so she looked a little less alarming. She couldn't hide how thin she'd become since Ken's death or her prominent limp however, and people still stared.

"You might want to consider riding with a friend of mine," he added after wiping his liver-colored lips with a napkin.

She really didn't want to have to hitch another ride because Floyd was right, it was dangerous, and she'd been very lucky to find such a good person like him. Her chances of finding another? Probably not so great. That is, unless Floyd knew him personally. Still, she really didn't want to have to do it. But how else was she going to get to Oregon ?

Floyd slurped his Coke through the straw. "Name's Scottie. I'll give him a call on the radio when we get back in the truck and see if we can meet up with him, seeing as how we're almost to California."

They were currently in Arizona. Flagstaff to be exact, and there was snow on the ground. As beautiful as the mountain college town was, she'd done very little in the way of sightseeing since arriving. Or done any sightseeing at all on her journey thus far. She'd been in more of a daze as they traveled through state after state, too busy thinking about Ken, and going over and over the happenings of the past two weeks to pay anything out the window any mind. She still couldn't believe that any of it had actually happened and that this was her life now. Running from a killer, running from the law.

How the hell had this happened? And why the hell had Gary up and killed Ken?

"You alright, darlin'?" Floyd asked, pausing with his sandwich in midair.

"Hm? Yes, fine."

"You look like the weight of the world is on your shoulders."

"I feel like it is."

His kind eyes, which were nestled behind a web of wrinkles, scanned her face, appearing concerned. "You'll get yourself settled and you'll be okay. Mark my words. But I'd definitely get that knee of yours looked at. You don't want to wait too long on that."

He'd tried to take her to the hospital a few times, but she hadn't let him. She was afraid of the questions, and more afraid of the answers she'd have to give.

"I mean it now. You don't want to end up with a permanent injury."

She took another bite of her oatmeal and reassured him that she would.

"That's another thing," he said. "How are you for money?"

"I have some." She'd taken what savings she and Ken had out of the sock drawer back home when she'd packed. It wasn't much, but it was enough to get by for a while. And if things went as she hoped, she'd have a place to stay. She just prayed that nothing had changed. If it had, she'd be in a world of hurt.

Floyd reached in his back pocket and retrieved an envelope to slide across the table.

"What's this?"

"A little spending cash."

She pushed it back across the table. "Floyd, I can't."

He shoved it back to her. "Yes, you can. And you will. That's from me and the missus. She's insisting and you know how she is."

Jenny laughed softly, having overheard many of their conversations by now. "I do."

"Then you know she'd tan my hide if I let you refuse it."

Slowly, she lifted the envelope and tucked it into the pocket of her windbreaker.

"We should probably get you a heavier coat too while we're here. I know you can't be warm in that jacket."

"I can wait and get one later."

"No, it's best to get it now. I know you're cold. You were trembling on your way in here." He finished his sandwich and eyed her empty bowl of oatmeal. "You ready?"

"Sure."

He helped her up and they paid their tab and headed for the door. As they were walking out, a couple of women were on their way in, and one of them slipped on a patch of ice next to the doormat and bumped into Jenny, nearly causing her to fall.

"Oh, my God, I'm so sorry," she said, grabbing Jenny by the arm to steady her. "Are you okay?"

Jenny looked briefly into her eyes, saw the genuine concern and kindness, and then lowered her head to move on, afraid she might be recognized. "Yes, thank you."

Floyd was careful to lead her away as the woman called out. "You sure?"

Floyd turned and waved, trying to reassure her. Jenny didn't hear her call out after that, so she hoped that was the end of it.

"That could've been very bad," Floyd said. "Had you fallen and hurt that knee some more."

"I know." But she was more worried about the woman and her overly concerned look. She hoped she'd moved on by now and gone on into the restaurant to sit down and eat. But she could still feel her eyes on her, and when she crawled back up into the truck with Floyd's help, she snuck a peek back toward the diner, where she saw her, a slight but fit blond woman, staring at her through the large windows.

Jenny lowered her head again and felt great relief when Floyd finally drove them away.

"Do you think she recognized me?" she asked as they pulled into the parking lot of the nearby Walmart.

"Nah."

"The way she looked at me…"

"We've been checking. You're picture's not out nationally yet."

"No, but it is back in North Carolina."

"I think you're fine." He eased into the back of the lot and parked. "I'm going to run in here and get you a coat and a few other things. You need anything I don't know about?"

There was one thing. "A book."

"A book?"

"Any sort of paperback is fine."

"How about one with all those muscular men on the covers? The wife likes those."

"No, not one of those," she laughed. "But anything else will be fine."

"A mystery?"

"Sure." She enjoyed mysteries.

He nodded and climbed from the rig to cross the sludge-covered pavement. She closed her eyes and drifted off as she waited for him to return. Floyd was indeed a good man, and she'd already copied his address down from some of his mail she'd found strewn about the truck. She knew she couldn't repay him now for all his generosity and kindness, but hopefully someday she'd be able to.

She then wondered about his friend, Scottie. Was he just as good a man? Would he be safe to ride with? Would he even be willing to take her to Oregon?

She shifted in her seat and relaxed further as the heat from the vents soothed her tired and achy bones. A face flashed across her mind. It was the blond woman back at the diner. Her piercing green eyes seemed to penetrate her very soul with their strong concern and questioning. Who was she?

She knew she'd never know.

But in her heart of hearts, she wished she could.

❖

Floyd returned with a cart full of goods, which included instant oatmeal and protein bars for her, as well as some other food for her to munch on. He also had purchased her a new coat, which she really liked and tried on right away. It was bright blue and quilted and very warm. She sunk down into it and thanked him profusely. It seemed she was always cold, even inside the truck, so the coat was definitely appreciated.

Floyd blushed and waved her off as he settled back behind the wheel. He adjusted the heat, rubbed his hands together to warm them, and then got on the radio. He called out for his friend Scottie, whose call sign was Coyote. He didn't respond, but Floyd said that wasn't unusual. That Scottie was most likely stopped somewhere eating or refueling.

They left Flagstaff in the rearview with Jenny staring into the mirror mounted on her door, wondering once again about the mysterious woman who seemed to be disappearing along with the sleepy, snowy college town.

"Whatcha thinking about, kid?" Floyd eventually asked.

"Mm, not much." How could she tell him she was thinking about a stranger who'd pierced her soul with one look?

"Well, I got something that might cheer you up."

"Yeah?" She wasn't convinced, but she looked over at him anyway.

He reached into the Walmart bag and pulled out a big, hardcover book. She smiled as she took it from his meaty hand.

"You got me a book?"

"Of course. You thought I forgot, didn't you?"

She quickly scanned the ominous-looking mystery cover and flipped it open to read the synopsis on the lapel.

"Now, the lady in the store said it was good, and that it was popular. So, don't get upset with me if it stinks."

"Are you kidding? I'd never get upset with you." She smiled at him and hugged the book to her chest. "Thank you, Floyd. Really."

He smiled back. "You're welcome."

She relaxed back into her seat and stared longingly into the cover for a long while before she finally opened the book again to begin reading. She saw Floyd glance over at her from time to time, and she could see him smile, as if seeing her enjoy the book was pleasing to him. Eventually, he stopped and focused solely on the road as they drove on into the growing darkness. He tried Scottie again on the radio and to her surprise, Scottie came back, calling Floyd "Mayweather," which made her laugh. Floyd did kind of look like he could've been a boxer, back in his heyday.

The two men discussed meeting up, and Scottie reported that he wasn't far behind them. They decided to meet at the next truck stop just inside the California border, which meant she and Floyd would have a two-hour wait. She didn't mind however, she was ready for a good stretch and a decent meal, and she knew Floyd must be as well.

So when they finally pulled into the truck stop, she eagerly opened her door and tried to climb down without Floyd's help, which was a mistake. Her knee screamed and she nearly tumbled to the ground. Somehow, she managed to hang on and call for Floyd, who then eased her to the ground and chastised her for not waiting for him. He helped her inside and they settled into a quiet booth in the far corner near the back where they ordered dinner.

She heartily dug into her cheeseburger, happy to have something more substantial, but she couldn't eat very much. Her eyes were bigger than her stomach, so she gently pushed the plate aside after having a couple more fries and sipped her watered-down Coke. She focused on Floyd, who was finishing up his double cheeseburger and fries.

"So, this Scottie. He's a good guy?"

Floyd dipped a fry in ketchup. "Uh-huh."

"You know him well?"

He paused mid chew. "I've known him longer than I've known my wife."

"Oh?"

"Mm-hm. We served together in the Navy." He took another bite of his burger, shoved the wad of food into his cheek, and spoke again. "So, I know him real well. You can trust me on that."

"Yes, but can I trust him?"

He smiled and then finished chewing his food. "I'd bet my life on it."

She pushed back against her seat and breathed a sigh of relief.

Floyd sipped his drink. "Darlin', I wouldn't send you off with him if I didn't completely trust him."

"Okay."

He smiled again. "Just wait until you see him."

She had no idea what he meant by that, but the second Scottie walked through the door, some two hours later, she understood.

Scottie wasn't much bigger than her and he walked with the help of a colorfully plaid cane.

"Mayweather, you SOB, how the hell are you?" he called out as he headed toward their table.

Floyd stood and beamed at him. "I'm better now that you're here, you sorry excuse for a man."

Scottie belted out a roar of a laugh, along with Floyd, and Jenny couldn't help but be amused.

CHAPTER NINE

Gianna stood on the front porch of her parents' new manufactured home and took in the brilliant sunrise. The sun shone off the stark white snow almost to the point where it stung her eyes. She kept staring out across the land nonetheless, transfixed by a deer near the tree line. She dared not to even breathe, for fear of scaring it off. It raised its head, as if it could hear her thoughts, and then, after spotting her and staring at her for a moment, it leapt away, back into the brush, making her smile.

Her attention then went to the steam rising from her coffee mug and she tentatively took a sip and snuggled further into her faux down jacket, which she wore over a hooded sweatshirt and jeans. Her toes were getting cold, even through her boots, and she knew she wouldn't be able to stay out in the chilled morning air for much longer. So she took in her surroundings again, relishing in the vast countryside, appreciating the twenty acres of land on the outskirts of Flag that her parents had built on. And she once again thought over the offer they'd made her when she announced that she was leaving Chicago.

They'd said she could live with them while building her own place on the property. She'd seriously considered it for a while, but had ultimately made up her mind to live elsewhere. She needed a new start, a fresh beginning in some place she'd never been before. She needed to make her own way and build her life from scratch, and she couldn't do that here, regardless of how much she loved it.

She inhaled one last scent of the nearby ponderosas and walked back inside. The house was quiet and still smelled of new carpet and furniture. Her folks had also started anew, by replacing almost everything from her childhood home. And while she knew it had been time for them to do that, her heart still ached for the old house. She missed her childhood room and all the memories the house had held. It hadn't mattered to her that her mother had turned her old room into a craft den. It had still been hers. Same faded flowered wallpaper, same framed pictures on the wall. She'd just liked being able to go in there to sit on the purple fabric chair and inhale the familiar scent and bask in the sunlight streaming in through the sheer curtains. Sometimes she'd even rummaged through the closet and dug out her trophies and knickknacks from the past, which had always brought tears to her eyes and then a smile to her face.

She couldn't do that anymore. At least not here. All her belongings were packed up in the U-Haul, waiting for her to unload once she reached Oregon. She wondered if she'd feel the same when going through them there. She wondered how she'd feel about unpacking in general. Would she like Cliffside? Would Cliffside like her? From what she'd seen on her brief visit, she'd liked it very much. It was a small town, nestled by the sea, with beautiful looming cliffs overlooking the crashing waves. The people had been friendly enough and most, if not all, had welcomed her, seemingly excited to have a new doctor. A few had questions, wanting to know more about her and her personal life, but the rest had left her in peace, just content in having met her.

She refilled her mug and put on another pot of coffee. Her folks hadn't cared for the Keurig she'd bought them. So they'd packed that up for her to use in Oregon. She laughed as she sipped, forever amused by the way her folks always stuck to their guns and lived life as simply as they could.

"What's got you laughing this early?" her father said as he walked up next to her, already freshly showered and dressed in his typical jeans and college sweatshirt.

"You."

"Me?"

He stood waiting for the coffee to finish brewing and raised an eyebrow at her.

"The way you and Mom turned your nose up at the Keurig I bought you."

"Oh, that thing? No, thank you. I'll make my coffee the old-fashioned way."

She laughed.

"That funny?"

"Yes."

He'd always been a practical man. Working a blue-collar job as a pipe fitter, putting in extra hours to help pay for her activities outside of school. Often times traveling far and wide to work, never once complaining. She'd always been grateful, but as an adult, she'd finally fully realized all the sacrifices he'd made for her. Which was why she tried to spoil them with top-of-the-line gadgets and gifts now that she could afford it. But they seemed happy with what they had and rarely wanted for much. The one thing her father did accept from her, however, after many tears and long, warm hugs, was the new Dodge Ram truck she'd bought for him for Christmas the last time she'd been home. He'd desperately needed a new truck but had been reluctant to let the old one go, having grown attached to it. But as soon as he saw the new one, all shiny and red and sitting out in the snow with a big bright bow on it, he forgot all about his old truck and hopped right in to start up the new one.

He mumbled to himself at the counter as he filled his own cup with the freshly brewed batch. He blew on it and took a hearty sip. "Ah, that's the stuff."

She smiled wistfully, her heart already aching at having to tell him goodbye.

"So, you ready to hit the road?" he asked.

They settled at the kitchen table, both warming their hands on their mugs.

"Just as soon as I say goodbye to you and Mom."

"She's getting dressed and then she'll need to feed Lionel. You know how she is with him."

As if on cue, the large tuxedo cat walked into the room and yawned before sitting to lick his paw. He seemed to know better than to beg her father for his breakfast, preferring instead to wait to harass her mother. He was, after all, her baby. She'd found him as a kitten, crying in a bush along a popular hiking trail. She'd brought him home and nurtured him, bottle-feeding him until he could eat solid food. He'd remained by her side ever since and she'd named him Lionel because he had an affection for Lionel Richie songs, meowing like the dickens anytime one was played.

"Good morning, Lionel," Gianna said with a smirk. He gave her a look and then continued to lick his paw as if she didn't exist.

"Damn cat," her father said.

"You watch your mouth," her mother said as she breezed into the kitchen. "That's your son."

"Like hell."

She smacked him playfully on the back of the head and opened the fridge to retrieve Lionel's canned food, which she scooped out into his bowl. Lionel immediately meowed and came to weave between her legs.

"You all ready to go?" her mother asked her as she set the bowl on a place mat next to the fridge. She lowered her reading glasses, which were attached to a decorative chain she wore around her neck. With those glasses, her hand-knitted sweater, and her hair worn in a tight bun, she still had the look of a school librarian, which was what she'd been for forty years before recently retiring. Gianna could still remember going to the library after school to sit and read from any book she wanted while she waited for her mother to finish up with work.

"Mm-hm," Gianna said. "But I was hoping to talk to you both first."

"Oh?" She sat next to her father at the table and waited.

"I want you to promise me that you'll check in with Lauren every week."

"Well, of course. That's a given," her mother said. "Especially after what you've told us."

"I appreciate it."

"I hope she knows she can come here anytime, for any reason," her father said.

"She knows. I made sure."

He nodded.

Gianna continued. "I'm not sure what's going to happen there, with Doug. But I made her promise to keep me updated and I…left her with some money."

"How did you manage that?" her mother asked. "I thought she'd refused."

"I set up an account at the credit union. It's in my name but she has a debit card to use whenever she needs to."

Her father sighed. "I understand why you did it, but I hope it doesn't cause problems if he finds out."

"I told her to just blame me. To tell him I insisted that she have access to my account just in case I needed her to get things for you two."

They exchanged looks but then nodded their understanding.

"She also knows that she can come to Oregon anytime," Gianna said. "To visit, or to…whatever. I told her I'd pay to help her move if she ever wanted to do that."

"What did she say?" her mother asked.

"She just cried."

"Poor thing."

"I hate leaving her like this, but I've got to get to Cliffside. I have no choice."

Her father patted her hand. "You go. We'll keep an eye on Lauren for you."

"Thanks."

"You know we love her and those kids like they're our own."

"I do."

She stood. "I better get a move on."

They embraced and planted wet kisses on her cheeks. She'd only spent a few days with them, but it felt like forever, and she knew she was going to miss them all over again.

"You'll come and visit?" she asked.

"Promise," her father said, walking with her to the door. "You can count on it." They stepped with her onto the porch into the brisk winter air. "You sure you got everything?"

They'd loaded everything up the day before and the SUV and U-Haul trailer were ready to go.

"I've got everything, Dad. Double- and triple-checked, just like you taught me."

He hugged her again. "You drive safely. And call us."

"Every weekend." She gave them one last smile and walked down the steps to her vehicle, which she'd already started from inside with her remote. She climbed in, cranked the heat some more, and buckled her seat belt. Then, with one last wave, she set out for her brand-new life.

She set out for Oregon.

CHAPTER TEN

The local cab company wasn't that far from Ken's house. So after Gary had called and gotten confirmation that a cab had been to the house recently, he headed straight to their hub and breezed in through the jingling door. A woman behind the counter seemed surprised to see him, as if she rarely saw anyone come through the door that wasn't one of her drivers.

"Can I help you?"

Gary smiled his best smile. "Yes, ma'am, I'm hoping you can. You see my sister called for a cab a few days ago and I'm trying to locate where it took her."

"Oh?"

He splayed his hands on the counter. "She's sick with the diabetes and needs her insulin, which she took off and left at home. And I can't for the life of me get a hold of her to find out where she is."

The woman was watching him closely, but she didn't seem convinced.

Gary nodded like he understood. "I just don't know what I'm going to do if I can't find her. She's got to be getting sick by now."

"Well, hopefully she'll get to a hospital or something."

"Hopefully. Say, I don't suppose you could tell me if she was dropped off at the hospital, can you?"

"No."

"Can you just check? Please? I'm really worried. I won't even ask which one. I just need to know she's safe and getting care."

She stared at him for a long moment before sighing. "Oh, alright."

Gary gave her Jenny's name and address which she typed into the computer. Her eyes narrowed as she searched the screen.

"No, she wasn't dropped at a hospital."

"No?"

"Huh-uh."

"I sure hope she's okay. She's got to be real sick. Can you at least tell me if she's somewhere safe?"

The door jingled behind him and the woman looked past him to a man entering the office. He had a sucker in his mouth and was humming something to himself as if he didn't have a care in the world. Gary wanted to sock him one right in the mouth to shut him up. He couldn't handle his carefree mood at the moment.

"Please, I just need to know she's safe," he tried again. "She really needs her medication. And she's…hurt. She was in an accident recently and I'm afraid that maybe her memory has been affected from her hitting her head."

"Then you should call the police. Have them help you," she said.

"You looking for someone?" the man with the sucker asked, plucking it from his mouth with an audible pop.

"My sister." He didn't want to take the time to fill this asshole in. He turned back to the woman.

"You said she's hurt?" the man asked from behind.

"Yes."

"I drove a woman a few days ago. She looked real messed up. Paid me cash."

Gary faced him, suddenly very interested in what he had to say. He fished out his wallet and pulled out a photo of Jenny. One he kept with him at all times to look at when he pleased.

"This her?"

The man nodded and stuck the sucker back in his mouth. “Mm-hm. Except she looked a lot worse for wear.”

“Where did you take her? It’s real important that I find her.”

He pondered for a moment, using his tongue to volley the sucker from cheek to cheek. “Darn if I can remember.”

Gary dug in his wallet and pinched out some cash. It wasn’t more than forty bucks, but it was all he had at the moment. He handed it over. “Please,” he said. “It’s all I have.”

The man took it hesitantly but then nodded again. “Truck stop,” he said.

“Sorry?”

“Truck stop. The one just off the highway a ways.”

Gary tucked his wallet back into his pocket and shook the dumbfounded man’s hand. “Thank you,” he said. “Thank you.” He bounded out the door quickly and hurried to his truck where he climbed inside and started the engine. He peeled out of the parking lot and turned toward the highway.

“I’m coming for you, Jenny. And this time, when I find you, you’re not going to get away.”

CHAPTER ELEVEN

Saying goodbye to Floyd had been hard. Harder than she'd expected. She'd hugged him for a long minute, crying into his broad chest like a child leaving her father. He'd patted her on the back, told her it was going to be okay, and made her promise to call him, to let him know she'd got settled okay.

Then she'd gone off with Scottie, who was just as friendly and eager to talk as Floyd had been. He'd offered to take her to her final destination, which he'd asked her about, but she'd politely declined, not revealing that information.

She'd been very careful thus far, not using a cell phone, and not calling ahead to Cliffside to make sure she was welcome. She needed to be untraceable. And thankfully, no one knew about Cliffside. Only her great-aunt, who'd passed away. She'd been the one to tell her about her friend in Cliffside and Jenny had kept that to herself, refusing to even tell Ken.

She'd hoped she'd never need to go, but something had told her that she might want to someday. If, at the very least, to get away for a while. Now she was glad she'd kept it a secret and she silently thanked her aunt for the information and the wisdom.

"This is it, sprite," Scottie said, setting the brakes. "End of the line. Less you changed your mind about me taking you further?"

"No, this is good, thanks." She gathered her belongings and Scottie helped her get out and unload. She had her coat, which she had on, her piece of luggage, and a couple of grocery bags of goods. It wasn't anything she couldn't handle.

"Here," Scottie said, taking the bags from her. He quickly fashioned them to the rolling luggage and then handed over his plaid cane.

"What's this?"

"It's for you."

"But you need it," she said.

"I got another in the truck. 'Sides, you really need it, sprite. With your bad knee and all."

"Scottie, I—"

"Don't try to argue. Just take it. And use it." He grinned his lopsided grin and she embraced him. She didn't cry like she had with Floyd, but she came close.

"Now, now," he said, drawing away. "Don't get sappy on me. You'll make me cry. And the Coyote don't cry."

She laughed. "No, he doesn't."

The cab Scottie had called for her ahead of time pulled up in front of the café.

Scottie saw it and frowned. "You'll be okay?"

"I will."

He nodded. "Alright, then. You take care now, sprite."

"You too, Coyote."

He gave a little howl, and she walked away, turning once to wave goodbye to him before she reached the cab. Then, after conferring with the driver, she climbed inside and waited while the cabbie put her things in the back.

Scottie watched them drive away, still waving at her, and she kept her head craned to watch him, until he finally disappeared behind them.

❖

The ride to Cliffside was peaceful. The driver said very little, seemingly happy with his sizable fare. He asked her once what her business was there, but she simply said she was just passing through on her way to the next town and she wanted to see the sights. He left it at that and she relaxed and this time did sightsee out the window.

The deep green statuesque trees were enveloped by a heavy fog, but eventually the fog dissipated enough for her to see the row of colorful little shops and restaurants that made up the small seaside town of Cliffside.

"This is good," she said, leaning forward.

He pulled to the side of the road in front of a crystal and gem shop whose beautiful wind chimes stirred in the cold salty breeze. She stood at the trunk and took her things from him before paying him cash for his fee. He seemed pleased at the tip and thanked her before he climbed back inside and sped away.

She inhaled the ocean air, listened some more to the chimes, and then stepped inside the quaint shop. It smelled of incense and the woman behind the counter greeted her as if she were surprised to have a customer.

"Welcome," she said and brushed her long, silver braid behind her shoulder. "Can I help you?"

Jenny leaned against the counter, grateful for the respite for her knee, which was smarting. Scottie's cane was a big help, but she figured there was something about the moist air that was causing her bones to hurt more.

"I hope so." She dug in the front pocket of her luggage and pulled out a photo of a seaside house to slide across the glass. The woman studied it carefully, her brows knitting together as she did so.

"Do you know it?" Jenny asked.

"I do."

"Do you know how I can get to it?"

She slid the photo back to her. "Well, that depends. What do you want to go there for?"

"I'm looking for an old friend."

"And?"

"Her name is Abigail. She's a family friend and I've come to see her."

The woman stared at her, obviously sizing her up. "Abigail's not up for visitors."

"I'm not a visitor. I'm hoping to—stay." She hated giving the woman any information, but she felt she had no choice.

The woman's brow raised curiously at that, and she leaned away from the glass top counter.

"You here to help her?"

Jenny blinked. "Yes."

"Well, it's about time somebody showed up." She walked out from behind the counter and waved for Jenny to follow her out the door. Then, to Jenny's surprise, she turned and locked the door and crossed the sidewalk to open the door to her small Volkswagen Beetle. "Normally, I'd say walk, but you look like you're struggling, so I'll take you myself."

"Thank you," Jenny said, settling inside while holding her luggage and bags in her lap.

"I'm Violet."

"Uh—hi—I'm—Kiera."

"Kiera, you got a last name?" she asked as they pulled out onto the road to head toward the cliffs.

"Davenport." Her aunt's last name.

"Welcome to Cliffside, Kiera Davenport. You won't find much in the way of excitement here this time of year, it being the off season and what not. But the locals are friendly and they'll be glad to know that someone has finally come to care for Abigail."

"I'm glad I could help."

"She might not be glad to see you, though. Old Abigail is pretty stubborn. And she likes being alone in that old house of hers. She's a bit of a recluse."

"I understand that," Jenny said. "I'm an introvert myself."

"Well, you two should get along splendidly then."

They drove past more colorful shops and a few sprawling two-story homes to eventually slow and make a right-hand turn just before the cliffs. Then they went downhill, parallel to the crashing sea, partially hidden in the fog.

"It's beautiful," Jenny said, in awe.

"That's nothing. Wait until you see the summer sunsets off the water."

They wound down the road until they came to another sizable hill. Violet slowed and turned left and followed a narrower, dirt road down to a house sitting off to the left as well, not far from the sea itself. The house was also two-storied, and at one time, had probably been beautiful, as in the photo. But as it stood now, it needed new paint and several noticeable repairs.

"We keep trying to get her to move into the cottage over there," Violet said, pointing, back beyond the house. "But she won't hear of it. Maybe you can convince her."

Violet pulled up in front of the porch and Jenny set her belongings on the moist grass before she crawled carefully from the car.

"Thank you," she said. "I really appreciate the ride."

"No sweat." She put the car in gear. "Tell Abigail I said hi." She smirked as if she knew it wouldn't be well received, and drove away, leaving Jenny alone to climb up the porch steps and knock on the weathered wooden door.

She stood quietly, balancing her weight on her good leg, hoping for a nice cup of hot coffee or tea. She was cold and damp and exhausted. What she wouldn't give for a real bed.

The door creaked open and an old face peered out. "Who are you?"

"I'm—Kiera. Kiera Davenport."

"I don't want to buy nothing." She closed the door.

Jenny knocked again. "Abigail, I'm not selling anything."

The door creaked open again, and she narrowed her beady eyes at her. "The townsfolk send you? I told them, I don't need no damn nurse wiping my ass."

Jenny blinked, a bit shocked. "No, they—no one sent me." She shook her head. "Wait. That's not true. Someone did send me. Someone you haven't seen in a long time."

Abigail opened the door a little farther.

"My aunt. My great-aunt. Her name was Ruby Davenport."

Abigail stared at her for a long moment. "Ruby, you say?"

"Yes, ma'am. She passed away a year ago, but before she did she told me that if I ever needed help, that I could come here. That you, Abigail, would help me. That you two were old friends and that you—owed her a favor."

Abigail worried her lips. "I'm afraid I won't be of much help to ya. I'm old. Don't get around too good."

"I don't need anything from you, other than a safe place to stay."

"I don't like people staying with me."

Jenny panicked. "What about that cottage? Back there? Is it empty? I could stay in it and help you out around here."

Abigail finally nodded before slamming the door closed in her face. Jenny stood confused, wondering what she'd meant, when the door pulled open again. Abigail thrust a key into her hand.

"Ain't nothing in there in the way of food. So, you'll have to come back over here for supper. That's if you're hungry, which I assume you are by the look of ya."

"Yes, ma'am. And thank you. Thank you so much."

"Hurry back now. I ain't got all evening to wait on ya. Supper's nice and hot."

"Yes, ma'am." Jenny left the porch as quickly as she could and limped across the damp ground to the cottage. When she unlocked and opened the door, she was greeted by the deep, musty scent of a place that hadn't been lived in in years. She coughed at the dust that stirred from shutting the door. She moved her things into the living room and noted the dingy coverings on the furniture. She'd have to remove all of them and air the place out. But for now, she wanted to return to Abigail.

She left her luggage and walked back across the grass with Scottie's cane. Her knee was killing her, and she wished that Abigail would just let her stay the night in her house, but she knew she had to respect her wishes.

So, for tonight, she'd dine with Abigail and hopefully get to know a little bit more about her before trying to clean the cottage a bit before bed. But as things were, she knew she'd be lucky if she didn't just pass out on the couch soon after returning to her new digs. Cleaning, and for that matter, getting to know the intensely private Abigail, might just have to wait.

Chapter Twelve

The truck stop wasn't very busy when Gary pulled in to park in front of the restaurant, which surprised him. But a quick glance at the clock seemed to explain. It was three o'clock. Well after lunch and before dinner. The truckers that were there were either refueling or resting. Not many appeared to be in the café.

He walked farther into the coffee-smelling dive and made himself comfortable on a seat at the counter. He rested his elbows on the countertop and waited for the waitress to turn and question him about what he wanted, while the man two seats over scraped his fork along his plate, trying to sop up his fried eggs.

Gary nodded politely at him, and the man returned the nod and then refocused on his food. The waitress finally turned, after Gary cleared his throat, and raised a well made-up eyebrow at him.

"Help you?" She eyed the menu filed between a napkin holder and container of sweeteners. He grabbed the laminated menu and perused it quickly.

"I'll have toast and coffee please."

"What kind of bread?" she droned.

"Wheat. Please."

"That all?"

"Yes." He only had what was in his pocket as far as money at the moment, and it wasn't much, having given most to the cab driver. He'd have to stop at an ATM if he was to continue after Jenny. Especially if she left the state. But doing so would be risky. The cops would be able to trace his movements. So, if he was going to do it, he only had one shot.

The waitress put in his order and filled him a cup full of coffee.

"You want cream?" she asked.

"Please."

She gave him a handful of chilled cream containers. Seeing his chance, he lightly rested his hand atop hers. She froze like a deer in headlights.

Gary spoke quickly. "I'm hoping you can help me. I'm looking for someone."

She retreated and held her own hand as if his touch had burned her. Not a good sign.

He kept his voice low and calm, trying to come off as non-threatening.

"She would've been in here about ten days ago. She was injured. Noticeably so. Her name is Jenny, and I'm very concerned for her."

The waitress kept her dead stare, but a brief flicker of recognition had come across her face as he'd spoken.

"Nope, haven't seen her." She walked away.

Gary cursed under his breath before speaking again. "I'm worried for her safety," he said loud enough for her to hear. "She's hurt."

The waitress didn't respond.

"I just need to know where she's gone. It's urgent that I find her. She needs help. She's—not well."

The waitress moved on to clean some nearby tables. He swiveled on his stool to try to appeal to her again. But the man next to him shook his head, as if warning him not to. Then he slid a piece of paper over to him. Gary plucked it up. It was torn from a small notebook, the kind one carries in their back pocket. He pressed open the fold and read. He met the man's eyes, confirming what he'd just read. The man nodded.

Gary thanked him, paid his tab, and slid off the stool to head for the door. He felt the waitress's eyes on him as he went, but he no longer cared about her. He didn't need her.

He read the words on the paper again as he climbed into his truck.

He had all he needed right here.

Chapter Thirteen

Jenny awoke to banging. Caught between sleep and reality, she thought it was the rhythmic noise of the old, loose shutter on Ken's house. The one that had woken her the night of his murder. She groaned and turned over, but the banging grew louder, and a muffled voice accompanied it.

She opened her eyes and forced herself up, trying to recall where she was. Her surroundings were dim and musty and nearly everything was covered with cream-colored sheets. She rubbed her eyes and slowly stood. Someone was at the door. Her heart rate kicked up. Could Gary have found her already?

"You in there, kid?" More banging.

It was Abigail.

Jenny hobbled to the door, her knee more sore than ever. She unbolted the door and found Abigail holding a picnic basket.

"'Bout time." Abigail shoved her way inside. "Did you have a nip of the good stuff before bed or something?"

"Sorry?"

"Did you drink too much?" she asked as she crossed slowly to the kitchen. Though she seemed to move without a hitch, Jenny noticed that her back was curved and her hands were withered and gnarled, gripping the basket firmly.

"Here," Jenny said, taking it from her to set onto the table that Jenny had uncovered the night before.

Abigail seemed relieved and settled onto one of the chairs. "I used to have a nip or two myself at night. To help me sleep."

"Oh, no, I don't usually drink. I just—was really tired."

"Humph. I thought you'd gotten into the whiskey in the pantry."

"No, ma'am. I went straight to bed."

They'd had canned corn chowder the previous evening, heated on a worn pot on the stove for dinner, and spoken very little. Turned out that Abigail was more private than she'd thought, sharing very little about her current life and none at all of her past. She was even tight-lipped about Ruby, stating only that they had been friends. Good friends. And that she was happy to help Jenny out if it meant doing a favor for Ruby. Even if she had already passed away.

"I reckon you were tired. With your traveling."

Jenny grew restless. She'd yet to tell her about Ken or Gary. She'd only told her about her riding with Floyd and Coyote, and surprisingly, Abigail hadn't asked many questions. She seemed to sense that Jenny was holding something back, something she wasn't ready to share, and she respected that. Perhaps it was because Abigail was too. Maybe they both had secrets.

Abigail shifted on her chair, as if searching for comfort. She grimaced.

"Would you like to sit on the sofa?" Jenny asked. "It's a lot more comfortable than that kitchen chair."

"No, kid. What ails me ain't gonna be made better by no sofa." She shoved the picnic basket toward Jenny. "I'm not staying long. I just came to bring you some things for breakfast."

Jenny sat and opened the lid to the basket. Inside was a warm handkerchief full of freshly baked corn muffins, along with two single-serving containers of strawberry yogurt, as well as some spoons and two bottles of chilled apple juice.

"Thank you so much, Abigail. You didn't have to go to all that trouble."

"I didn't," she said abruptly. "I wanted some muffins, so I stirred up the mix and baked 'em. Had some left and brought 'em to you. End of story."

"Still, it was very nice of you." She dug out a muffin and took a bite. "Would you like one?"

"Nah. I had my fill."

She looked around, searching the dim interior with her dark but stirring eyes. "You need to let some light in. Dark as the devil in here."

Jenny rose and pulled open the curtains to the two living room windows as well as the ones in the nook where the table was. Bright light spilled in, illuminating the dust motes floating casually in the air.

Jenny squinted as she settled back down to finish her muffin and sip her juice. She was still rather hungry, even though she'd had her fill of the corn chowder the night before. Her body was healing, she supposed, and she'd neglected it of food for too long. Now it was demanding she make up for it.

"You eat like you ain't had food in a dog's age."

"Mm." She covered her mouth as she chewed, a little embarrassed. "I just haven't felt much like eating until recently."

"Why's that?"

Jenny swallowed, surprised she'd asked. "I—uh—was hurt."

"That how you got those bruises?"

"Yes. I was in a car accident and I—was in a lot of pain. I'm still healing."

"Well, healing takes time. But I reckon you'll be okay. I got to see the doctor here soon. He'll be coming out to the house for a visit next week. You should stop by, let him take a look at you."

Jenny smiled, unsure how to respond. "I might do that."

Abigail pushed herself up. "And I get my groceries delivered from the local grocery store every Thursday. Henry, the owner's son, brings 'em by. He might do the same for you since you're about as lame as I am."

Again, she wasn't sure what to say. So she merely nodded. Abigail moved to the door.

"Come by at noon for lunch," she said as she turned to face her. She pointed at the pantry door in the kitchen. "Broom and stuff is in there. Anything else you need you'll have to come by and get. But don't come between ten and eleven. That's when I have my nap and I don't like being disturbed."

Again, Jenny nodded. She stood to see her out the door, but Abigail waved her off.

"I can see myself out."

"Thank you, again," Jenny said just before Abigail closed the door behind her.

Jenny watched out the front window to make sure she handled the steps okay and was able to walk back to her house. She moved slowly but surely and grabbed hold of her stair rail to ease up her own porch steps. Then she disappeared into the house.

"What a mysterious woman." Jenny returned to the table to finish her breakfast. She had one of the yogurts and put the other in the old fridge, along with the second bottle of juice. Thankfully, the empty fridge worked, though it hummed loudly. After she re-wrapped the muffins and placed them back in the basket, she began cleaning.

The first thing she did was open up all the windows and doors. The windows took some elbow grease to loosen, but she had no problem with any of the doors. She found the cleaning supplies where Abigail had said and removed the remaining covers from the furniture. Then she dusted and swept with a bandana tied around her nose and mouth to help protect herself from the dirt. She moved carefully and slowly, taking much needed breaks often, especially with the sweeping.

Next, she started in on the kitchen sink and counter space, giving it all a good scrub with some simple white vinegar she'd found in one of the cabinets. By the time she was finished with that, she was exhausted, and her knee was crying out in pain.

She sat on the sofa and dug through her bags until she found the Aleve Floyd had bought her. She popped two and relaxed with another muffin and the rest of her juice.

Realizing she needed a longer break than first intended, she eased her legs up onto the couch and began to read her book. She'd already devoured it once, but she hadn't had a chance to dust off and explore the ones she'd seen in the study, so she decided to read it again. She didn't mind, really. It had been a good read. And she often found new little hidden gems when she reread books. She hoped that would be the case this time as well.

When she finally put the book down and checked her watch, it was close to noon. She winced as she stretched and slipped on her shoes to walk to Abigail's. She still had a lot of cleaning to do at the cottage, but she wanted to talk to Abigail again, and she honestly didn't know how much cleaning she'd be able to do the remainder of the day, considering how badly she was hurting.

The Aleve had helped a little, but she'd have to take more to hold her over if she continued to clean. Maybe she should take Abigail up on her suggestion and see that doctor. Floyd had warned her about getting the knee taken care of. He'd said the sooner the better, and she knew he was right.

She felt relatively safe now with a new name and new beginning. Talking to a doctor couldn't hurt, could it?

She knocked on Abigail's door after struggling up the stairs.

"Come in, kid!"

Jenny stepped inside and walked to the pot-bellied stove to warm herself. Abigail was setting the table and Jenny tried to offer her help. But Abigail once again told her she didn't need it.

"Go on and sit," she said, as she moved to the fridge. "You want something other than juice?"

"Juice is fine."

"Good. It's about all I have till Henry comes again."

"Is the tap water safe to drink? At the cottage?"

"It should be."

Abigail offered her some ice water in response to her question, but she politely declined. She was chilled enough from airing out the cottage, and the breeze blowing off the sea was quite brisk this afternoon. She hoped that when she returned to the smaller house, that it would've warmed up a little, seeing as how she'd closed everything up before settling down to read. There was also a stove. She just needed to carry some wood in from the porch. She'd do that when she got back and hopefully sleep warmer tonight.

Abigail brought the juice and sat down across from her in front of her own plate. "I hope you like tuna salad sandwiches."

Jenny glanced down at her plate. "I do. Thank you."

"Well, dig in then."

Jenny did, along with Abigail, and they ate in silence for a while. The sandwich was good, really good, and the bread perfectly toasted.

"This is excellent, thank you again."

"It weren't no trouble."

Jenny smiled, noting that Abigail was uncomfortable being helped and thanked. She wondered what else made her uneasy. Though she was private, she was decent company and she knew how to converse when she chose to. So she wondered why she preferred to hide away down here on the hill away from everyone.

"Do you get many visitors?" she asked. "Other than Henry?"

Abigail chewed for what seemed longer than necessary. "I see the doc from time to time. And that girl, Lizzie, the doc's nurse, she insists on coming by to check on me now and again. Afraid I'll up and croak on her, I think." She snorted. "I may up and die, but I'll damn well do it right here, where I belong. Not in some crazy home for old folks. Nuh-uh. Not me. No sir."

"Do you ever get into town?"

"Town? Now why in the world would I want to do that? I got everything I need right here."

She tore off another piece of her sandwich and ate it with a trembling hand. Jenny watched her, wondering exactly how old she was. Aunt Ruby had passed away in her early nineties. She likened Abigail to be close to the same age.

"So, how did you know my aunt Ruby?"

She set her sandwich down. "You sure do ask a lot of questions. That's why I don't let people in my house. All they do is ask questions."

"I'm sorry. I was just trying to make conversation. I didn't mean to offend."

"I know ya didn't." She sighed. "I just don't like questions. And I get the feeling you don't either."

"I don't."

"Well, there you go then. We won't ask each other any personal questions."

"Okay."

Abigail smiled at that and dotted the corners of her mouth with her napkin. "I think I'm about finished. Made too big of a sandwich for me. You want the other half?"

"I can't," Jenny said, holding up her hand. "I'm stuffed."

"Well, take it home with you. For later." She wrapped it in a napkin and then rose to get a sandwich bag. She handed it all over to Jenny who put the sandwich away.

"Would you like for me to go now?" Jenny asked, not wanting to outstay her welcome.

"You probably should run off. Take care of that cottage before sundown. You got plenty of firewood and such?"

"I believe so."

"You can help yourself to mine if you need it."

"I appreciate that." She stood. "And thank you for lunch."

"Don't run off just yet." She ambled over to the kitchen and came back with a plastic grocery bag. "There's some soup in there and some more muffins and yogurt. So I reckon I won't be seeing you until sometime tomorrow."

"Right. Okay. Thank you, Abigail."

"You don't have to keep thanking me." She rested her hand on her back and escorted her to the door. "Just keep that cottage in good condition and don't have no wild parties or riffraffs over and we'll call it even."

Jenny chuckled. "Yes, ma'am."

"You go on now. Have yourself a good afternoon."

"You too, Abigail."

Jenny stepped out into the cold ocean air and allowed it to play with her hair for a moment before she walked down the porch steps to head back to the cottage. And though her knee ached and her body begged for more rest, she smiled into the wind, feeling content with where she'd landed. Abigail was generous and kind in her own way, and Jenny had a cozy little place to stay. All in all, things were okay. She was incredibly fortunate, and she glanced up to thank Aunt Ruby once again. And she swore, not for the first time, that she felt her presence with her.

CHAPTER FOURTEEN

"Hellooo!"

Gianna removed her sunglasses as she walked up the paved, greenery-lined path to the back side entrance of her new home. The cheerful voice called out again, and as she neared the open door, a bountiful, bubbly woman, whom she knew as Lizzie, came bounding out with her arms wide open.

"Welcome, welcome, welcome!" She enveloped Gianna in a huge hug and giggled like a schoolgirl. "We're just so thrilled to have you here. Just so thrilled."

"Thank you," Gianna said with a laugh, trying to hold her at arm's length. "I'm happy to be here."

"Then you'd better get used to me and my hugs." She embraced her again and bounced on her feet before drawing away.

"A happy, hugging nurse. I guess every doctor should have one," Gianna said.

"That's right." She punched Gianna's arm and it actually stung a little. Lizzie didn't know her own strength. "Old Doc Benfield never appreciated my hugs. But the patients sure do."

"You—hug the patients?"

"Well, of course! This here's a family practice. Heck, I've known many of these folks since they were knee-high to a grasshopper. And Doc B, well he personally delivered nearly half the town. Of course, you got a lot of these younger folks going into the cities to have their babies these days. I think it saddened the doc. It's one of the reasons he retired. All the folks heading into the cities for medical care."

"Oh."

"But you don't have to worry. We still have plenty of patients. And they're excited to meet you. Many of them have never even seen Doc B before. But they heard about you and immediately made appointments. Got two dozen or so newbies lined up already. Pushed the appointment book out three weeks. That's a record for this town."

Gianna was surprised at the sudden interest. It was good news. "That's great. No pressure, though. Right?"

Lizzie laughed and led her inside. "You're a doctor, you're used to pressure." They entered the waiting area, where a row of seats lined the walls, and two small end tables were illuminated with softly glowing lamps. A shiny, tasteful coffee table sat on a new maroon rug holding neat stacks of magazines. The room was cozy and smelled clean, like sanitized wipes and furniture polish.

"As you can see, we've got the place all ready for you. Even replaced some things."

Lizzie continued on through the door and into the small hallway where there were three open doors. Two, Gianna knew, were exam rooms, which Lizzie quickly showed her, and the other was where she would have her office, along with Lizzie, who doubled as her receptionist. It contained two large wooden desks and several empty heavy-looking bookshelves.

After having a quick look at the office, they moved in the other direction, past the exam rooms to the hallway that led into the main house, her living area. It too, was recently cleaned, ready for Gianna to move right in.

Lizzie closed and locked the door to the medical office and opened up the double doors that bordered the kitchen, which had a gorgeous view of the backyard and the tranquil town of Cliffside beyond.

"My son, Charlie, and his friend Henry are on their way over to help move you in."

"Oh, I was going to just hire someone to help," Gianna said, not wanting to put anyone out.

"Nonsense. The boys don't mind. And if you feel so inclined you can buy them some pizza. That'll suffice, trust me."

"Got it."

"We might as well get started with the boxes in the meantime," Lizzie said as she secured the doors open with stone doorstops. Gianna joined her and they walked down the decorative path through the woodsy backyard where the ocean breeze shook the pines and silenced the singing birds.

"It's getting chilly," Lizzie said. "Might have to do chili instead of pizza." She winked. "I make a mean chili. Four-alarm. Charlie loves it."

"Sounds wonderful."

"I could whip some up real quick. Let it cook on the stove while we move you in."

"I don't mind if you don't."

"I'll have to see if Henry can bring the ingredients. He works at the market." She plucked out her phone and sent a text that took a couple of minutes to type. Then she helped Gianna unlock and open the trailer door. "Shoo, you sure do have a lot of stuff packed in here, don't ya?"

"I've got more in the SUV." She shrugged. "I didn't want to drive the big U-Haul truck."

"I understand that. Those things hurt my rear end." She rubbed her backside as if she were having phantom pains just thinking about it.

She and Gianna started in on unpacking the boxes. They made small talk as they worked, carrying load after load back to the house. Lizzie filled her in on Dr. Benfield. He'd left two days before, heading for Scottsdale with his wife and their two little dogs. She said he was ready for some sunshine. Gianna hoped he knew what he was getting into. Lizzie also shared more about herself, telling Gianna that she was divorced going on ten years and that she and Charlie lived alone and liked it that way. She loved her job, loved Doc B, but she was ready to work for someone new. The patients were, as she said before, like family to her and she cared about each and every one. She even accompanied Doc B on the house calls, and sometimes even made calls on her own for blood draws, etc., for the residents that can't get to the office, of which there were a few.

She asked about Gianna, asked about a husband, and Gianna laughed and told her there wasn't one and wasn't going to be one. Lizzie thought that was funny, assuming Gianna was fed up with men. But Gianna clarified, telling her she was a lesbian. A happily single lesbian, to which Lizzie stopped and stared at her, box in hand.

"No kidding? Huh. I never would've guessed. Guess my gaydar needs work."

Gianna breathed a sigh of relief, thinking that would be the end of it, but Lizzie kept on, pressing her for more info.

"So, when you say happily single…"

"As in, I'm not looking to date anyone anytime soon."

"Because…" She set down the box marked "books" and then carefully sat on it to catch her breath.

Gianna joined her on another and took a swig of water from her water bottle. Thankfully, she'd had a small cooler in the SUV full of water and snacks. She opened the cooler and handed an icy bottle to Lizzie who thanked her. She took a hearty sip and eyed Gianna, wanting her to explain about her desire to remain unattached.

"I'm coming off a bad breakup."

"I'm sorry to hear that." Lizzie screwed the lid back on her water. "So, you left her behind, did you?"

"Back in Chicago, yes. It felt good to get away, to start over fresh somewhere new."

"Was it, you know, a mutual breakup?"

"Not exactly. She didn't want things to end, but she didn't give me much of a choice if you know what I mean. She, uh—was unfaithful."

"Ah. I had to deal with infidelity myself. It's awful."

"It was, yes. But looking back, I think the relationship was slowly dying. I had just been too busy and naive to notice. I wasn't really happy. I just didn't realize how unhappy I'd been till I left."

"I get it. I felt so free after I left Richard. Free as a bird." She waved her hands out at her sides, simulating bird wings.

Gianna laughed. Lizzie was too cute and the most friendly person she'd met in a long time. She was looking forward to working with her and she could see why the patients adored her. She must make everyone feel at home.

Lizzie started to speak again, but an old beat-up Ford truck pulled in in front of Gianna's SUV.

"There's my boy," Lizzie said.

The truck backfired as it was turned off and Lizzie jerked and grabbed her chest. "Dang it, I never get used to that." She giggled. "Scares the tar out of me every time."

Two young men emerged from the truck and grabbed sacks of groceries from the bed to head up the dirt path.

She and Lizzie both stood to greet them.

"Hey, handsome fellas," Lizzie said as she took a paper bag. "I want you to meet our new doctor. This is Dr. Walford. Dr. Gianna Walford."

"Gianna, please," Gianna said with a smile as she also relieved one of the boys of a paper bag.

"Nice to meet you, Doc," the young man, whom she assumed was Charlie, said. "Can I call you Doc?"

"Sure."

He set the bags on the kitchen counter and came to offer his hand. "Charlie. But my friends call me Chaz."

"Chaz. I like it."

Lizzie rolled her eyes. "He loves it. But I think it makes him sound like an old time gangster or something."

Charlie laughed. "Whatever, Mom."

"I'm Henry," the other boy said as he placed his groceries on the counter. "Just Henry." He also shook her hand. He was the taller of the two and had darker hair than Charlie, who was fair-haired like his mother.

Both were young and strapping and seemed to be polite young men. She put their age at around eighteen or nineteen.

"Thank you for coming to help," Gianna said.

"Don't mention it," Charlie said.

"Yeah, don't mention it," Henry said. "Where would you like us to start?"

"You can move the furniture out of the trailer if you don't mind."

"We cleared the way," Lizzie said. "Moved all the boxes." She flexed her muscles. "Because we're beasts like that."

Charlie groaned but then laughed. "My mother. The funny woman."

"That's right," Lizzie teased him. "I'm a woman of many talents."

The boys walked back to the trailer and Lizzie got busy preparing the chili while Gianna organized the boxes depending upon their labels. By the time she could smell the chili beginning to cook, she was directing the boys on where to put what. Soon the kitchen contained a small table and chairs and the living room had its furniture. They all took a break and lounged on the couch and love seat, sipping the cold water from the cooler. The boys munched on her snacks, which Lizzie protested about, but Gianna insisted that they could. They were young and hungry and helping her out. As far as she was concerned, they could have as much as they wanted.

"Your furniture's beautiful," Lizzie said. "Is this leather?"

"It's fake leather."

"It's so soft."

"Yes, it's very nice," Gianna said. "I had a friend who had couches like these and I knew I had to have some for myself."

"Are they brand-new? They seem brand-new."

"I've actually had them for a couple of years. Just was rarely home to use them I guess."

The room grew quiet. Finally, Lizzie spoke. "You were very busy in Chicago?"

"Oh, yes."

"Well, you'll be busy here too. But you'll still have plenty of time to break in these nice couches." She winked. "And you'll have us to help you do it. Your new friends."

"I'd like that," Gianna said. "I'd like that very much."

"Careful," Charlie said. "Mom will never leave if you encourage her like that."

Lizzie swiped his chest with the back of her hand and he howled. "I was just kidding."

"She doesn't know that," Lizzie said.

Henry laughed. "It's true though. You practically live here."

"That's because Doc B needed lots of help toward the end. But Gianna here is a different breed. She's young and vibrant and she needs plenty of time to settle in. I intend to give that to her. So don't you boys go scaring her."

Gianna laughed. "I'm sure I'll want lots of company as I settle in. This house is too big for just one person. I might get lonely at first."

"It is big," Lizzie said, glancing around. "You've got a whole upstairs to contend with as well. Speaking of which, why don't you boys stop stuffing your faces and go get that mattress and box springs moved in?"

"On it," Henry said, hopping up to crinkle his empty chip bag.

Charlie followed suit and after they deposited their trash on the counter, they were out the door and headed back to the trailer.

"They're good kids," Lizzie said after them.

"Yes, I can see that they are. It's really nice of you all to help me move in."

"Well, that's the thing about Cliffside. We're nice around here. Help each other out. I think, if you give it a good chance, you'll like it."

Gianna looked out the window at the town nestled between the ocean and the thick pines. "I think you're right, my new friend. I think you're right."

CHAPTER FIFTEEN

Gary groaned as the banging on his front door commenced, keeping him from his sound slumber. He rolled over and covered his aching head with a throw pillow.

"Go away," he mumbled into the couch cushion. He was in no mood for visitors after the way he'd drank last night. No mood at all. He just wanted to sleep.

More banging ensued. "Mr. Hollister? Open up. It's the police."

Gary groaned again, but this time sat up to try to get his bearings. The room spun and he grabbed his head, trying to make it stop.

"Just a second," he called out. "Give me a damn minute."

The fucking police were back. Damn it, why hadn't he just left town? Then he remembered. It was because he was looking for a trucker called Mayweather, waiting for him every damn day down at the truck stop café. And that waitress, she was no help. In fact, he was sure she was keeping information from him. That bitch. She knew more than she was saying.

The banging started up again. "Mr. Hollister. Come to the door."

"Alright, alright. I'm coming." Slowly, he stood and stepped into his dirty jeans. He didn't bother with a shirt, and he didn't turn off the television. He just stumbled to the door rubbing his two days' worth of stubble, cursing under his breath.

He fumbled with the doorknob, which always seemed to stick, and yanked open the door. The bright sunlight stung his eyes, and he winced at the two detectives standing on his stoop.

"Yeah?"

"May we come in?" the bigger of the two said. Damn it, if he couldn't remember their names.

"It's not a good time," Gary said.

"We need to talk, Mr. Hollister. It's either right here, right now, or we do it down at the station. Which do you prefer?"

Gary sighed and pushed the door open farther and waved the men inside. They entered quickly and walked directly into the living room. The smaller one switched off the television like he owned the place.

"Make yourselves at home," Gary said with sarcasm as he closed the front door and joined them. He flopped down on the couch and ran his hands through his wild hair. He knew he must look a sight, but he really didn't care. These fuckers were just there to harass him. He'd bet his truck on that.

"Mr. Hollister," the bigger one said, easing down onto the end of the couch. His gaze lingered over the numerous empty beer cans and chip bags strewn all over the coffee table. He couldn't seem to hide his disgust. Gary wanted to laugh.

"We still haven't been able to locate Ms. McAllister."

"Is that so?"

"We were hoping you could help to shed some light on that."

These idiots. He already had a solid lead on her and it had taken him less than a week. Why couldn't these assholes do the same? He'd be damned if he was going to do their job for them. Besides, he and Jenny? They needed to have words.

"Well, I'm sorry to hear you still can't locate her, but like I've said a hundred times before, I ain't got no inclination as to where she is."

That much was true. He would take a polygraph to prove it.

The smaller one, the one who was wiry with a gaunt face, seemed to have read his mind.

"Are you willing to take a polygraph, Mr. Hollister? To help eliminate you as a suspect?"

Gary laughed. "Ah, hell, boys. You ain't got nothing better to do than harass me over this?"

"When it comes to Ms. McAllister, all roads keep leading back to you, Mr. Hollister," the bigger one, the one whose face looked like it had been gone over with a cheese grater, said.

"That's not my problem," Gary spat.

"Actually, it is. If we can't eliminate you, we're going to keep investigating and questioning you."

"You mean, you'll keep harassing me? Showing up at my house unannounced?" He scrubbed his scruffy jaw and reached for his crumpled pack of cigarettes. "Fine. I'll take the damn test. But only if you swear to leave me alone afterwards." He lit his smoke and inhaled.

The bigger one smiled but he could tell he didn't appreciate Gary smoking. "Let's see what the test says, Mr. Hollister." He stood, and the smaller one followed suit. They both handed him their cards, as they did each and every time he saw them. Gary tossed them into the scattered trash on the coffee table. He didn't bother to stand to see them out.

"Be there tomorrow morning at nine sharp," crater face said. "And sober up. You can't be impaired."

"What if I'm busy?"

Again, the smile. "We both know you're not working, so you should be available."

Gary glared at him. The asshole was right and he had no excuse to not attend. Might as well go and get it over with because he really didn't know where Jenny was. He should pass the thing with flying colors. He couldn't wait to throw that in their faces, just like he had with the fake alibi he'd used for his brother's murder. They'd backed off big time after that.

"Nine sharp," Gary said. "I'll be there."

The detectives left without a goodbye, closing the door shut behind them, leaving in their wake the strong smell of the smaller one's cologne. It lingered and he rose to open a window. What kind of man wears that much cologne? Jesus.

He paced in front of the TV as he smoked, shook up by the visit. They were still looking at him for Jenny's wherabouts. Fuck. It wasn't good. He had to shake them off. Especially if he found Mayweather and discovered Jenny's destination. He'd have to leave town and he didn't want the law pursuing him.

"I've just got to find Jenny and silence her. Then I'm home free." He stopped, ran his hand through his hair again, and sat to sip on some tepid beer. He had to find Mayweather. But who knew how long that would take. He wished he had his real name. But the truckers, they weren't saying, like it was some kind of code. They looked out for each other and he'd been lucky to get what he'd gotten to begin with. Now he was on his own. Watching and waiting. The police hounding him constantly didn't help matters any. They were throwing a wrench in his surveillance.

He would handle that though. All he had to do was pass that polygraph.

He chuckled as he drank some more.

That should be no problem.

No problem at all.

CHAPTER SIXTEEN

Thursday came and there was a soft knock on the cottage door. Jenny rose from the couch and checked out the front window to see who it was. Though she doubted that Gary would ever find her in Cliffside, she still had nightmares about him doing just that. Not to mention the nightmares she still had about him killing Ken and running her off the road in an attempt to kill her.

A young, dark-haired man stood on her porch and she breathed a sigh of relief. He had a rolling cart full of grocery sacks.

Her food had arrived.

She opened the door and welcomed him. "Come on in," she said. "I'm Kiera."

"Henry," he said. He shook her hand.

"Abigail has told me all about you," she continued as she led him into the house.

"Really?" He blushed and pushed the door closed behind him. "She's—funny."

"That she is."

He walked to the table as if still embarrassed and unloaded the bags. After a brief silence he spoke. "She's told me very little about you. You new to the area?"

He seemed far more curious than Abigail. She answered without hesitation, feeling safe enough to do so. "I am. Just needed a change of scenery, you know?"

"We just got a new doctor who said the same thing."

"New doctor?"

"Mm-hm. She's from Chicago. Supposed to be really good. She's really nice too. I've met her." He watched her as she ambled over to the table with her cane.

"She can probably help you with that," he said. "She was like head of emergency medicine or something in Chicago."

"No kidding?"

He finished with the bags. "You want me to help you put the food away?"

"If you don't mind." She was enjoying the conversation. Henry was easy to talk to. And after spending days struggling with what to say to Abigail, who mostly preferred silence, it was a welcome change.

She grabbed a couple of food items and told him where to put things. They worked well together, weaving around each other like a well-practiced dance, with Henry telling her more about the new doctor and how his best friend's mother worked for her as her nurse.

"Oh, is that the nurse who comes to check on Abigail?"

"Lizzie?" He nodded.

"Good, I hope I'll get to meet her."

"I'm actually surprised you haven't already. She usually checks in on Abigail once a week or so. But I guess she's been busy with the new doc."

"I think Abigail is supposed to see the doctor tomorrow. But she referred to the doctor as a he not a she."

Henry closed the refrigerator door and grinned. "I'm guessing she doesn't know about her then. Either that, or she's forgotten. She forgets things a lot."

That explained an awful lot. Like how she had to keep reminding her that they'd already eaten dinner or that she'd already tended to the fire.

"That's why she's always so quiet," he continued. "It frustrates her to hear that she's forgotten something. Makes her real mad. So she mostly sits and listens."

Henry folded up all of the paper sacks. "You want to keep these?"

"Yes, please." He placed them on the table and rolled his cart to the door.

"Is it dementia?" she asked, following closely behind him.

He shrugged. "I'm not sure. I haven't really asked."

She wondered if the doctor would tell her. With privacy laws she doubted it. She'd probably have to get it from Abigail herself and that would be like pulling teeth.

"Well, thank you so much for the delivery, Henry. It was nice to meet you."

He gave her a two-fingered salute. "If you need anything else, just let us know."

"Will do."

She showed him out and watched him walk away into the strong ocean wind. She came back inside and tended to the fire in the potbellied stove and finished organizing her groceries. She had food and her own warm, safe place to stay. She couldn't believe it. She had successfully escaped.

"Try and find me here, you bastard," she said as she made herself a cup of hot honeyed tea. She relaxed on the couch to drink it and sat staring through the front windows at the churning sea. The breaking white caps almost lulled her to sleep, as did the hot tea, but she fought it and lifted the old black telephone receiver instead. She spun out Abigail's number on the rotary dial and waited as it rang.

"Yello?"

"Abigail, it's Kiera."

"Kiera?"

"Yes, er—it's the kid." She'd already called her a few times in the past few days, but each time she seemed to need reminding of who she was.

"Oh, kid. What do ya need?"

"I would like to make you dinner tonight."

"You want to make me supper?"

"Yes, ma'am. How does that sound?"

"Well, that depends on what you're making."

"How about homemade vegetable soup and French bread?"

Silence.

"I reckon I can come by."

"Great. Be here at five. I know you like your dinner then."

"Alright."

Click.

Jenny held the phone up to her face and stared at it in confusion before hanging it up. "Guess she's not good with goodbyes either."

She chuckled and finished her tea and then went to start the soup. She sat down to dice all the vegetables and hummed along to an imaginary song. She thought about taking a trip into town to buy a few more things. One of them being a radio, something to listen to the news on and maybe to sing along with. She also needed a few personal items, like underwear and socks, things Floyd had been too embarrassed to get for her.

Which reminded her, she needed to call him to let him know she was safe. She'd try to find a pay phone in town. She knew she could trust him and she didn't have to let on that Cliffside was where she was staying for good. Regardless of what she said in regard to where she was, she needed to assure him that she was safe. He deserved to know that much after all he'd done for her.

She finished with the vegetables and dumped them in a big pot of water, which she seasoned and added a large dollop of Better than Bouillon to. Then she covered it and got to work on straightening the place up. She started in the living room and made her way into the kitchen, and then on into the bedroom. She didn't have proper bedding for the queen-size bed, so she was still sleeping on the couch with a heavy blanket, close to the stove. Hopefully, she could find some decently priced bedding on her trip into town, along with a warm pair of pajamas. Her money situation was still adequate, thanks to her savings and what Floyd had generously given her.

She walked into the study and began sliding the books she'd dusted back onto the shelves. She kept a few out, too excited about reading them right away to even return them to their place. They were older of course, most from the 1970s. But she didn't care. The older the better as far as she was concerned. She opened one up and inhaled the scent of aged pages. It made her smile, but then another scent caught her attention. The soup.

She carried the books into the kitchen, set them on the counter, and stirred the colorful concoction. It smelled heavenly but it was missing something. She quickly opened a can of both tomato sauce and tomato paste and poured them in. She gave it a good stir and re-covered the pot to set the table. Next, she set the books on the coffee table and lit a couple of lamps. The sun would soon be setting and Abigail would be coming. But in the meantime, she wanted to relax and crack open a book.

She chose one at random and settled in to read. Almost an hour later, she saw Abigail crossing the grass to the porch. Jenny opened the door and went to assist her up the steps, but Abigail gave her a stern look, quickly reminding her to leave her be. Jenny held the door open for her in welcome and Abigail slowly walked up the steps to enter.

"It's hotter than the devil's dick in here," she let out.

Jenny cracked both front windows. "Sorry. I like it warm."

"I reckon so. At this rate I'll have to have Henry out here delivering wood every damn day."

"I told you, I'll gladly help pay for the wood."

"Nah. No need. Just don't burn it all up in a day's time."

Jenny didn't respond. She'd talk to Henry about it privately. She couldn't keep the cottage as cold as Abigail kept her home. She'd be miserable. It was going to be bad enough tonight with letting in the brisk air through the windows. She'd probably never get it warm enough for herself by bedtime.

Abigail turned to look at her. She threw up her arms. "Well, where do you want me?"

"The table is fine," Jenny said. "Here, let me take your shawl."

Abigail shrugged it off and sat at the table. "You need cushions for these chairs. I got some extra at my house you can use."

Jenny poured them both some iced tea. She asked Abigail about a slice of lemon, but Abigail interrupted her.

"You got any of that whiskey?"

"Sorry?"

"In the pantry. There should be some there."

Jenny checked the pantry. She found two bottles of whiskey and brought them both out.

Abigail pointed to the one that was less full. "That 'un."

Jenny retrieved an empty tumbler and poured a little in.

"More," Abigail said.

Jenny poured some more. Abigail finally signaled for her to stop at halfway. Then she raised the glass and took a hearty sip.

"Ah. That's a good burn now."

"What's the occasion?" Jenny asked as she got the soup bowls to fill with their dinner.

"Thursday."

"Thursday?"

"I don't need a damn occasion. I just wanted a drink."

Jenny carried the bowls to the table, serving Abigail first. Then she remembered the bread.

"Oh shoot! I forgot to warm the bread. Just a minute." She turned on the oven and popped the French loaf Henry had brought her inside. "Shouldn't take long."

She placed her own bowl on the table and sat.

Abigail sipped her whiskey. "Don't worry about it none. Soup's too hot to eat anyhow."

Jenny glanced down at her own steaming bowl. She drank from her glass of iced tea. She'd wanted tonight to be perfect, to thank Abigail for allowing her to stay. But she'd messed it up with the bread.

"I should ask you the same," Abigail said.

Jenny looked at her in confusion.

"What's the occasion? For this supper?" Abigail asked.

"Oh. I just wanted to thank you for letting me stay. And for all the help you've given me."

"I told you, I don't need no thanks."

"I know but—"

"I owe Ruby. You wanna thank somebody, thank her."

"I have," Jenny said softly. "Every night before bed."

"Then we're even Stephen. Now stop looking like you just wet the bed. This here's a good meal, don't ruin it with your sourpuss."

Jenny sipped her drink again. "I just wanted it to be perfect."

"Perfect is boring. I despise perfect. You'd be wise to do the same. Because life, it's full of curveballs, kid. Ain't no perfection there. No, sir."

"Yes, ma'am." She set her glass down. "You've had a lot of curve balls in your life?"

Abigail closed her mouth and pressed her lips together. "I've had my share."

Jenny waited to see if she'd elaborate but she didn't. She just kept sipping her whiskey.

"You wanna check on that bread?" she asked.

"Oh, right." Jenny slid out the bread and set it on a dish towel on the table. She carefully sliced a thick piece for Abigail who asked her to butter it for her.

"My hands is hurting today."

"No problem. Happy to do it."

"Don't get used to it. I don't usually need any help."

"I know."

"Good."

She handed over the bread and Abigail carefully served herself a bite of soup, blowing on it before she slipped it into her mouth. "Mm, that's good, kid. Real good."

"You think so?"

"I said so, didn't I?"

Jenny laughed. "You did."

"Then take me at my word. I ain't gonna bullshit you."

"Yes, ma'am."

Jenny fought more laughter as she spooned her own bite to blow on. She was enjoying Abigail, even if she was grumpier than usual. She had a way about her. A no-nonsense but genuine personality that Jenny found quite endearing. She knew her heart was good. So it didn't matter what all she griped about.

Abigail had helped her and was keeping her safe and sound. Her, with her false identity, a complete and perfect stranger.

You couldn't get any kinder than that.

Chapter Seventeen

Gianna swiped the screen on her tablet as Lizzie quietly drove. The late afternoon was gray and drizzling with rain. The wipers moaned against the windshield, trying to entice her to nap, and Gianna was glad that this was their last patient of the day. Supposedly, anyway. It wouldn't surprise her to see another lingering patient back at the house once they returned, however. Someone always seemed to need care, day and night. Just like at the hospital.

She didn't mind though. The people were kind, grateful and genuine. And each had their own personal story to tell.

"Rhydian Hill," Gianna said, reading the address. They turned just before the foggy bluff and were driving slowly downhill, where the fog seemed to grow thicker. They made a left-hand turn onto a dirt road and soon the angled roof of a house came into view, along with the slate gray sea, which seemed to be churning rather angrily.

"Yep, this is old Abigail Rhydian's house."

"Old Abigail?" She didn't appreciate the description.

"It's just what she's known as."

"Well, let's not refer to her as such, okay? She's our patient. So, it's Mrs. Rhydian."

"Ms."

"Ms. Rhydian."

Lizzie laughed.

"What?" They stopped close to the porch and Gianna cracked her door, ready to grab her medical bag and hurry up the steps to escape the rain.

"Ms. Rhydian. She's not exactly a warm and fuzzy type of patient."

"No?"

"Just wait, you'll see."

They climbed out, grabbed their gear, and trotted up the steps to knock on the door. Gianna brushed her hair back from her face and smoothed down her heavy sweater and khaki slacks. Dots of rain decorated her clothing and dampened her hair, but there was nothing she could do about it. She hoped she still looked professional enough.

A voice growled from behind the door. "Who is it?"

"It's Lizzie and the doc, Abigail," Lizzie said.

"Ms. Rhydian," Gianna quietly corrected her.

Lizzie covered her mouth and then spoke again. "Ms. Rhydian. We're here for your appointment."

The door creaked open, and a pale but weathered face peered out. "Why in the hell are you calling me Ms. Rhydian?" She turned and walked away, further into the house, leaving them to fend for themselves.

Lizzie entered first and Gianna followed. The house was open but dim with the overcast light from the storm. It was warmer than outside, but not by much. Yet Ms. Rhydian wore nothing but an old shawl over a long-sleeved knit shirt and black knit pants with tattered house slippers.

A tea kettle whistled from the stovetop and Ms. Rhydian went to tend to it.

"You want some tea?" she asked with her back to them.

"I would love some," Lizzie said, setting their bags on the coffee table. The house was roomy and pleasantly aged. The furniture being just as old and worn in. Several colorful knitted blankets were strewn across the couch and chairs and the lamps were Tiffany-style with stained glass shades. At one time, the home must've been quite beautiful.

"You have a lovely home, Ms. Rhydian," Gianna said, opening her bag to pull out her stethoscope.

"There you go again with the Ms. Rhydian." She turned with two cups of tea in her red-knuckled hands. "Why in the hell are you calling me that?" She looked up and locked eyes with Gianna. Her eyes grew big and then instantly slitted.

"Who in the hell are you?"

Gianna looked to Lizzie whose eyes had also widened.

"I'm Dr. Gianna Walford."

"Dr. Gi—who? Where's Doc B?"

Lizzie stammered. "Now, Abigail, we told you last time we were here that Doc B was retiring."

"No, you didn't."

"We did, sweetie. And he's gone now. Moved down to Arizona with Trixie and the dogs. But Dr. Walford is taking his place. She's—"

"Get outta my house," she barked.

Gianna blinked, shocked. "But, Ms. Rhydian—"

"I said, get outta my house!" She threw the teacups to the ground, shattering the ceramic and spilling hot tea all over the kitchen floor.

Gianna jerked and moved to gather her things, but Lizzie shook her head at her, causing her to halt.

"Now, Abigail, is that any way to act toward our new doctor?"

"I don't give a good goddamn."

Lizzie gently led her around the mess on the floor to a well-worn chair in the corner of the living room. She eased her down with Ms. Rhydian slapping at her hands in defiance.

Gianna quickly cleaned up the mess on the floor with paper towels. The teacups weren't salvageable so she had to toss them, but she was able to get all the pieces and the tea up without issue.

She washed her hands in the sink and returned to the living room where Lizzie sat in front of Ms. Rhydian, gripping her hands, trying to convince her to calm down. But she kept fussing, insisting on seeing Doc B.

Gianna spoke. "Ms. Rhydian, I know this must be quite a shock, but I'm only here to help."

She glared at Gianna with dark brooding eyes. "My name is Abigail. Get that through your thick skull, young lady."

"Yes, okay. Abigail. Can I call someone for you? Someone who can come be with you while we're here?"

Lizzie spoke. "She doesn't have anyone. She's all alone." She looked back to Abigail. "This is why you need to let us treat you, Abigail. You don't have anyone else to care for you."

"The hell I don't." Abigail yanked her hands away from her and reached for the phone on the end table. She lifted the receiver, glanced at a small notebook full of handwritten phone numbers, and dialed. Lizzie seemed perplexed. She shrugged at Gianna as Abigail ordered someone she called "kid" to come to the house right away. She hung up with a grumble and crossed her arms.

"She'll be here any second."

"Who will?" Lizzie asked.

"My new caretaker."

"But sweetie, you don't have a caretaker."

"I do now. She moved into the cottage next door."

Lizzie straightened. "What? Someone is living in the cottage?"

"That's what I said."

Lizzie seemed distraught and Gianna couldn't figure out why the news seemed so concerning. Hearing that Abigail had someone to look after her, someone so close, sounded like good news.

"Who is it? How do you know this person?" Lizzie asked.

"She's the niece of a good friend of mine and that's all you need to know. Now quit going on about it."

There was a soft knock at the door. "Abigail? You okay?" The door eased open and a woman stepped in, leaving Gianna speechless. It wasn't just the fact that she was breathtakingly beautiful, it was the fact that she'd seen her somewhere before.

The woman blinked at her, reddened, and then turned like she was about to leave.

"Kid, come on in," Abigail said. "And close the door."

Slowly, the woman did as instructed. She limped to the couch and stood awkwardly with her cane.

That's when Gianna remembered. She'd seen her back in Flagstaff, leaving a restaurant with an older man who'd seemed rather possessive of her. Their brief encounter had first intrigued her and then left her quite alarmed. Who was she? Why was she so scraped and bruised? And why was the man so possessive?

"This is…" Abigail started.

"Kiera," the woman finished. But she still wouldn't look at Gianna.

She remembers me too.

"I told you I had someone," Abigail said, interrupting Gianna's thoughts. "Now you all can leave. I'm fine. Kiera will take good care of me, won't you, kid?"

"Yes, ma'am."

"You're her caretaker?" Lizzie asked in disbelief.

Kiera hesitated. "Yes."

"Then you won't mind convincing her to let the doctor examine her."

"Doctor?"

Gianna stuck out her hand. "Dr. Gianna Walford."

"Oh. Right."

They shook hands and Gianna stared into her golden eyes as she finally looked at her.

"Do I know you from somewhere?" Gianna tried. Maybe if she broke the ice, Kiera would relax.

"Me? No."

"Hm." *Damn it, no dice.* She wasn't going to admit their encounter, leaving Gianna to wonder why. "Never mind then."

"I'm Lizzie," Lizzie said, from her position in front of Abigail.

"Nice to meet you, Lizzie." Kiera smiled, but Gianna could tell she was still nervous.

"Abigail," Lizzie said. "Will you please allow Dr. Walford to take a look at you? It's just a check-up. Nothing invasive."

"I don't want to answer no questions," she said.

"Okay," Lizzie said, trying to appease her. "No questions. Just an exam." She stood and nodded at Gianna who began her examination, taking everything very slowly. She found Abigail's vitals to be strong, especially her heart, and her breath sounds were clear. She had her stand and walk for her, which she did with a grumble. She seemed to have decent mobility, even with a severely curved back.

Gianna wanted to ask her questions, to get a better feel for how she was doing, but she knew she should wait.

"Thank you, Abigail," Gianna said. "That's all for now."

"How about I make you some more tea?" Lizzie said. "While the doctor gets to know Kiera better?"

"I reckon, if you're hurting to do it," Abigail said and she and Lizzie walked into the kitchen and began making more tea.

Gianna pulled out her tablet and made notes, reminding herself to thank Lizzie later for distracting Abigail. She sat on the couch and asked Kiera to join her. "How's she been doing?" she asked softly.

"Pretty good, I'd say."

"Any mobility issues?"

"She struggles with the stairs. But she manages."

Gianna turned to look at the staircase. It concerned her. "Her bedroom is upstairs?"

"Yes."

"Is there any way she'd allow someone to move that downstairs for her?"

"I doubt it. She's rather stubborn."

"I don't like the idea of her walking up those stairs alone."

"Oh, I'm usually here when she goes up for the night."

"Are you? That's good."

"We eat dinner together almost every evening, and I make it a point to stay as she goes up to bed. Then I lock up and leave."

"I'm glad you do that. But still, I'm concerned. She will get to a point, probably in the not-so-distant future, where she won't be able to manage them. So try to hint to her that moving her bedroom downstairs might not be such a bad idea."

"I'll try."

"How about her sleep? Anything unusual?"

"She naps once a day and turns in early, not long after dinner."

"How's her appetite?"

"Mm. I'd say small to okay. She tends to eat the most at dinner."

Gianna pulled up her history and gave it another quick read. "Her memory? Better, worse, the same?"

"I don't really know how to answer that. I haven't been here very long."

Gianna met her gaze. "Have you noticed anything as far as memory issues?"

Kiera glanced back at Abigail as if to make sure she wasn't paying attention. Then she explained the things she'd noticed and Gianna nodded and continued to take notes. When she was finished, she pushed out a breath. "That too, I'm sad to say, will continue to progress." She eyed Kiera's cane.

"And how are you doing? Is this an old injury?"

"My knee? No, it's recent."

"Has it been looked at?"

She reddened again. "No."

Gianna sensed her anxiousness and decided to push very gently. "Why don't you call the office on Monday and make an appointment to come see me?" She smiled, hoping to put her at ease.

But Kiera turned away and cleared her throat.

"You appear to be struggling when you walk," Gianna said. "Are you in any pain?"

"Some."

"All the more reason to come see me." She handed her her new card. "Please, call on Monday."

Kiera took the card and stared at it. "How much? To see you?"

"Is money a concern?"

"Right now, yes. I don't have insurance."

Gianna searched her face, hoping to find answers to her silent questions. But there was only fear and sorrow. It tugged at her heart.

"Would it be okay if I examined you now, then?"

"Right now?"

"Would that be okay?"

She seemed to think a moment. Then she nodded.

"Great." Gianna slid the coffee table away from her and knelt. "Is it okay if I push up your pant leg?"

Kiera visibly swallowed but nodded once again.

Gianna gently slid up the leg of her pants and carefully examined her knee. She felt the soft tissue and the patella and then had her extend and retract as best she could. She definitely was in pain and the injury needed more attention as there was difficulty with movement and some extensive swelling.

"I'd say it's very irritated," Gianna said. "How exactly did you hurt it?"

Kiera stared at her. "I—uh—it was a car accident."

"Oh, I see." She wanted to ask her more about that but she refrained, not wanting to scare her off. "Well, you've definitely hurt yourself, Kiera. Probably just a strain, but I can't say for sure right now. You need to come to the office for an X-ray. We won't worry about a charge. Okay?"

"I can't let you do that."

"You can. Just this once." She winked at her and gently patted her thigh before lowering her pant leg. "But let's not tell anyone, okay? I've got a reputation to build." She stood.

Kiera smiled slightly.

"So, you'll call?" Gianna asked. "To make an appointment for that X-ray?"

She nodded.

"Very good. In the meantime, take an over-the-counter painkiller and anti-inflammatory like Advil or Aleve. Keep the knee elevated and alternate ice and heat. Fifteen minutes at a time, a few times a day. Sound good?"

"Yes."

"Do you need any help in caring for Abigail?"

Kiera once again looked back at the kitchen table where Abigail and Lizzie sat chatting and sipping hot tea.

"I don't think so. Not yet anyway."

"So, you're saying that right now, she doesn't really need much one-on-one care?"

"Correct."

"Then why did she insist that you're her caregiver?"

Kiera shrugged. "Maybe she's trying to reassure you, so you'll leave her alone. She doesn't like interference when it comes to her life."

"Yet, she let you in. Why is that?"

Kiera blinked at her. "I really couldn't tell you."

But Gianna didn't buy it. There was more to the story there, she was certain. Just like she was certain that Kiera had been in some kind of trouble. But, she supposed, those were questions for another day.

"Be sure to call us if her care becomes too much for you to handle," she finally added.

"I will."

Gianna packed her bag and motioned for Lizzie, letting her know she was ready. Lizzie gave Abigail a quick squeeze, which Abigail grumbled about, and then joined Gianna at the door.

They said their goodbyes and headed for the car in the cold, drizzling rain.

"So what's her story?" Lizzie asked, referring to Kiera.

They climbed in the SUV and Lizzie started it up while Gianna wiped the damp from her face.

"I don't know," Gianna said. "But there's definitely one there."

And I intend to find out.

CHAPTER EIGHTEEN

Gary wished he could say the test went off without a hitch, but he couldn't. He'd become unusually nervous as he'd entered the police station earlier that morning and he hadn't been able to calm himself. The questions the polygraph examiner had asked him before the test had really set him off and he realized that he might not do as well as he'd originally thought. He'd had to admit his feelings for Jenny in order to explain the information the police had about how he'd previously behaved around her as well as some of the things he'd said to his family in regard to her. None of it looked good, but he'd tried to explain it all away.

He'd eventually taken the test and done the best he could, but now he was wondering if it was good enough as he sat in the small interrogation room biting at his cuticles. He'd been waiting for over an hour and it was freezing in there. He swore they kept it cold on purpose. They wanted to make him uncomfortable.

At last the door opened, and Gary dropped his hand as if he'd been caught playing with himself. He pushed out a breath, trying to force himself to relax, but it did little good. His nerves were on edge and crater face the cop…well, Gary couldn't read him. So he sat and waited while the big man positioned himself on the seat across from him.

"I've got good news and bad news," he eventually said. "Which do you want first?"

"Whichever," Gary said, attempting to sound nonchalant.

The detective kept his seriousness. "Okay, I'll start with the good." He riffled through some papers and cleared his throat before he read aloud. "As pertaining to the question, 'Do you know the whereabouts of Jenny McAllister?' You did not show deception."

Gary exhaled and blinked. He leaned forward in his chair and waited for the bad news.

"As pertaining to the question, 'Did you cause harm to Jenny McAllister?' You did show deception." He slapped the papers on the table and stared into him. "What do you have to say to that?"

Gary just sat there, mouth agape. He had no words. He'd failed to pass the exam with flying colors. How could he have been so naive to think he could've? Of course he'd harmed Jenny. Just not the way they were thinking. He blinked some more and closed his mouth to force down a swallow.

"I, uh—it's not what you think."

"Then what is it? Because as of right now, Mr. Hollister, you're our number one suspect in her disappearance." He drummed his thick fingers on the table. The sour cherry smell of the cough drop that was tumbling around in his mouth was turning Gary's empty stomach. "Know what my partner is doing right now, Mr. Hollister?"

"No."

"He's outside, examining your truck. Know why?"

Gary tried to swallow again, but it was difficult. He ended up coughing. "No."

"Did you run Ms. McAllister off the road in an attempt to harm her?"

"No." His voice caved and he sounded weak. He clenched his eyes, needing to get a hold of himself. He should've had a shot of whiskey before he came. It would've calmed him and given him the control he so badly needed. They wouldn't have known. Why hadn't he done that?

"We have evidence, new evidence, that suggests otherwise."

Gary's heart thudded. He waited. Crater face said nothing. Just chewed up his cough drop.

"Am I under arrest?"

"I don't know. Should you be?"

"We're impounding your truck, Mr. Hollister, for forensic analysis. If you'd like to leave you're free to do so, but you're going to need a ride home. And I'd suggest you stay home. Don't leave town."

Gary slowly stood. He was inexplicably dizzy as he headed for the door. He waited for the click, the sound that it was unlocked, and walked out. Numerous cops with closely shaved heads stared at him coldly as he went. Their thoughts weren't hard to read. They thought he'd killed Jenny and hidden her body somewhere. And once they matched his truck's paint to her car, they'd really think so.

Fuck.

What was he going to do?

He had to find Mayweather. One way or another. And he had to get out of town. It was only a matter of time before they arrested him and he'd go down for a crime he didn't even completely pull off.

How fair was that? Jenny was alive and well somewhere and they wanted to put him away for her death, not Ken's.

The fucking irony.

He walked outside and lit a cigarette. He sucked on it hard as he fumbled with his phone. He texted a friend and asked him for a ride. He had to wait twenty minutes before he'd be there. Voices came from his right. He followed them and saw several men surrounding his truck as a wrecker pulled up to attach it.

Fuck.

They were really taking it away.

Why hadn't he cleaned it better? Just scraped off all the evidence of Jenny's car?

He massaged his temple. How could he have been so stupid in all this?

Ken. It was all Ken's fault. If he'd just loaned him that money…but no, Ken had to fight him on it. Had to call him names, like lazy and no good. He had to cut him deep. So deep that Gary had lost all control and brandished the gun, just to shut him up. To show him that he was in control. But Ken hadn't apologized. He'd just froze, hands up, face contorted like Gary was the devil incarnate. He'd started begging him to drop it. Like Gary was a crazed killer or something. Started begging for his life. Like a little bitch.

All of it had spun around and around in Gary's mind in a split second and he couldn't take it anymore. He couldn't take any more of Ken's bullshit. Couldn't take any more of Ken having the better life, the better girl, the better business.

He'd told him to shut up and he'd fired. He'd killed him.

And he'd never felt such a high. Such a feeling of power and vengeance. It had been intoxicating. But now those shots were coming back to haunt him. Causing all kinds of trouble.

Damn it.

His friend pulled up in his rickety old truck and screeched to a stop. The cops standing around Gary's truck glanced over at the noise. Gary gave them a dirty look and crawled inside.

"What's up, man? You get arrested again?" Billy asked.

"Just drive." He turned in his seat to watch as his truck was loaded up onto the wrecker, taking his future right along with it.

Chapter Nineteen

The pain in Jenny's knee grew worse over the weekend. She figured it was due to all the chores she'd been doing around the cottage and Abigail's place, like hauling wood and cleaning, which Abigail only fussed about. She still insisted she didn't need any help, but it was obvious that she did. So Jenny swept and mopped her floors, as well as polished her furniture and tidied her bedroom and bathroom. She also made her a big pot of chicken soup and stored some in the freezer for her so she wouldn't have to cook every night. And though Abigail complained about all the help, she did seem somewhat grateful. Relieved even, as she sat in her chair and quietly watched while sipping her tea.

She even looked at Jenny long and hard with watery eyes after Jenny said goodbye to her on Sunday evening. But she still didn't offer her thanks or appreciation. It seemed too difficult for her to do. Like expressing herself was painful. Jenny knew she was grateful though. She didn't need to voice it.

Now it was Monday, and Jenny was paying the price for all the hard physical work she'd done over the weekend. She had put off calling Dr. Walford's office, however, too concerned about seeing her again. The doctor had recognized her, which wasn't good. In fact, it downright scared her. Her only hope was that she wouldn't pursue it. So she wasn't going to give her a chance to, which was why she was going to avoid her.

She couldn't, however, stop her mind from reliving the moment Dr. Walford had examined her. Jenny had felt a rush of hot adrenaline when the doctor touched her and stared into her with those hypnotic eyes. She'd struggled to even breathe with her close proximity and she'd hoped Dr. Walford hadn't noticed. Regardless, Jenny didn't want a repeat, so it was best to stay away for more than one reason.

Instead, she was going to go into town to do a little shopping, despite the pain. She'd buy the proper supplies for her knee, like a heating pad and a cooling gel pack, as well as more Aleve. The bag of frozen peas she'd been using just wasn't cutting it. And as for heat? She had nothing, other than positioning herself closer to the wood stove, which wasn't working too well either.

She had other things to purchase too, so it was off to town for her.

She walked out the door with her purse and her cane as the taxicab pulled up in front of the porch. She waved to Abigail, who was looking through the window, as she crossed to the car, having already called her to ask if she needed anything from town. Abigail had said no, asking only that she return before dark so she wouldn't worry about her.

Jenny had agreed and she rode in the back of the cab in silence, speaking only when giving directions. She told the driver to drop her across from the crystal and gem shop at the home goods store. She headed inside and found the store to be too expensive for her pocketbook, so she walked back outside and headed down the sidewalk to the thrift shop. She found all sorts of neat things in there, but most of it she didn't need.

She exited the thrift shop and looked up and down the street, trying to decide where an appropriate store was for her bed linens and pajamas, as well as the supplies for her knee.

Thunder cracked overhead in the afternoon sky.

"Wonderful." She couldn't seem to find the right store and it was going to storm. Didn't the sun ever shine in the winter on the Oregon coast?

She searched for a nearby pay phone, but there didn't seem to be one of those either. She sighed, frustrated, and thunder growled louder this time. How was she going to call for a cab?

I need to get a pay as you go cell phone.

But where?

Most of the shops in town were for tourists. So where did everyone get their necessities other than groceries?

An SUV pulled up alongside her and slowed. The window eased down, and she saw Dr. Walford leaning in her seat toward her.

"Kiera," she said. "How's the knee?"

Jenny felt herself heat under her intense stare. What was it about this woman that got her heart racing? Was it the fact that they'd recognized each other and seemed to lock eyes and share a thousand words without uttering a single one?

Yes, that must be it.

"It's fine, thanks."

"Really? Because you're moving like you're in an awful lot of pain."

"Well, it hurts some. But I needed to do some shopping, so…"

"You having any luck with that?"

Jenny looked down at her empty hands. "Not really."

"I find that I have to drive out to the Walmart to find most of what I need," Dr. Walford said.

"There's a Walmart?"

"A few miles outside of town. You need to go?"

She could get everything she needed there. "I do, actually. But I need to call for a cab. Could I borrow your phone?"

"Don't be ridiculous. I can take you. Hop on in."

"Oh, no, Dr. Walford. You don't have to do that."

"I know. I want to. Besides, I'm headed there myself." She smiled.

Jenny hesitated. She desperately needed to go and get supplies, but she was concerned about being alone with her. Dr. Walford caused reactions in her body she just didn't understand and if she questioned her about Flagstaff… "I don't know," Jenny said.

"Come on. I won't hurt you." She winked and Jenny's heart fluttered. "Promise. And you don't want to get caught in this storm, do you?"

Jenny's heart pounded yes while her head screamed no. Her heart won out. "You sure it's no trouble?"

"Positive. And please, call me Gianna."

Jenny climbed carefully into the SUV and they drove slowly down the street, bypassing all the little shops as the rain began to fall.

"You got in just in time," Gianna said. She made a right turn at the end of the street and headed away from town. "Can't believe it's raining again."

"It seems to do that a lot here."

"You from somewhere else?" Gianna asked.

"Mm." She quickly turned the question back to her, even though she knew the answer. "How about you?"

"Chicago," she said. "Although I'm originally from Arizona."

That explains why I saw you in Flagstaff.

"What brings you to Cliffside?" Jenny asked.

"I needed a big change."

"I understand that."

She laughed. "Oh, yeah?"

"Definitely."

"So, tell me more about this car accident you were in."

"What do you mean?"

"Well, for starters, why weren't you treated for your injuries?"

Jenny stared out the window, growing uncomfortable. She was trapped. Inside the car with Gianna. There was no escape. She'd either have to ignore her and give her the silent treatment, flat out lie, or just tell her the truth. She wasn't very good at giving people the silent treatment and she hated lying. So she decided to be truthful. As much as was safe anyway.

"I didn't go to the hospital."

"Why's that?"

"I was alone. Out in the country. And I didn't think my injuries were that bad."

Gianna was quiet. "What about now? It's obviously pretty bad, yet you didn't call and make an appointment for the X-ray."

"I needed to shop."

"And that took precedence?"

"Yes."

"I'm not trying to nag, but you really should come in. At the very least I could fit you with a good brace and give you some better painkillers. I wouldn't charge you. I just want you to get some help with it."

She glanced over at Jenny, waiting.

Jenny shrugged. She had no argument. She couldn't very well tell her that she was attracted to her and worried she'd figure out who she was now could she?

"That sounds okay."

"How about we do that after Walmart?" Gianna asked.

"Tonight?"

"Sure."

"I need to be home before dark. Abigail, she might worry."

"I'll have you home in time."

They drove on in silence and when they got to Walmart, Gianna insisted Jenny use a motorized cart. She fought it at first, but soon gave in and they shopped rather quickly, finding everything she needed easily. Gianna helped her choose a heating pad and two cooling gel packs, as well as some bandage wrap to secure the cooling packs with. Then Gianna selected a few grocery items for herself, and they checked out and loaded up the SUV to drive back to the doctor's office.

Once there, Gianna unlocked the main door and put her goods away. Then she led Jenny into one of the exam rooms and had her sit on the exam table as she rolled the portable X-ray machine into the room.

"New purchase," she said.

She placed a slide beneath Kiera's knee and positioned the X-ray machine over the top to take the X-ray. Next, she took one from the side, and then she had Jenny bend her knee and one from there.

"All finished," she finally said, wheeling the machine out. When she returned, she had a tablet in her hands which she used to view the X-rays.

"The good news is there's nothing here that looks overly serious. But there is some swelling and excess fluid from the sprain."

"What does that mean?"

"It means you need to baby it a lot more than you're obviously doing."

"But I have things to do. Things that can't wait."

"Like shopping?"

"Yes."

"We can have someone run your errands for you. That won't be a big deal."

"What about household chores?"

"Just do the minimum for now. The major stuff, Henry and Charlie can help out."

"I don't want to trouble anyone, Gianna."

"You've got to heal, Jenny. And the only way to do that is with rest. You're going to have to let people help you."

She stood before her. "Promise me you'll rest."

Jenny got lost momentarily in the depth of her kind and stirring irises. "Okay," she muttered, completely helpless not to.

"Good. Now let's find you a brace. Be right back." She left the room and returned a few minutes later with a knee brace. She tore the plastic wrapping encasing it and removed the brace. "You're a small, I think." She motioned for Jenny to stand as she unstrapped the Velcro and knelt to secure it on her knee. She then tightened the straps and straightened. "How's that feel?"

Jenny took a few steps.

"Does it feel better with that support?"

"It does."

"Wonderful." She smiled. "Wear that when you're not icing or heating, okay? Now, let's see about getting you a stronger pain killer." She pulled out her prescription pad.

"No," Jenny said. "I mean—I don't need it. I'll be fine with the Aleve."

"You sure?"

"Positive."

"If you change your mind…"

Jenny nodded. "What do I owe you for all this?"

"Not a thing."

"I really should give you something."

"You did. Your company." Her smile was soft, genuine, and once again, Kiera's heart fluttered and this time she was left speechless.

Gianna led her out of the office and into the main house, which was large yet cozy feeling, with soft accent lights and comfortable but expensive-looking furniture. Gianna had good taste, very good taste.

"It's not much to look at yet," Gianna said, catching her gaze. "I'm still unpacking and getting things situated."

"It's beautiful," Jenny said. "Just as it is."

"You think so?"

"Yes, I wish the cottage looked like this."

Gianna raised her brow. "Do you have everything you need for it?"

"Oh, yes, I'm fine. It's just rather eclectic at the moment."

Gianna nodded as if she understood. Then she glanced out the window. "We better get you back. The sun has set."

Jenny followed her out to the SUV and climbed inside.

The rain had stopped and the air had a crisp, moist feel to it, the earth smelling freshly cleansed and alive.

"Thank you again for all your help," Jenny said as they pulled onto Rhydian Hill and slowed before the cottage.

"Don't mention it. I was just glad I could help."

Gianna killed the engine and crawled out to unload Jenny's shopping bags from the hatch. Jenny hurried as best she could to her side to try to take them.

"I've got them," Gianna said. "You just go get the door."

Jenny ambled up the steps, her heart racing. Gianna was about to come inside her place. The mere thought sent her head spinning.

She opened the door and allowed Gianna inside.

"You can just set it all on the kitchen table."

Gianna did and stood with her hands on her hips, taking in the tiny cottage.

"I like what you've done with the place."

Jenny laughed. "It's not as nice as your place, but thanks."

"No, you've done very well."

"I just—don't have much." She rubbed her forehead.

"It's nothing to be embarrassed about, Jenny."

"It is though. I'm—starting over and—"

"Hey." Gianna walked up to her and rested her hand on her arm. "It's okay. We all have to start somewhere."

Jenny held her stare as long as she could before glancing away. She could feel the heat of her hand radiating right through her jacket and she realized with a start, that she wanted to feel Gianna's hands on her bare skin.

She flushed profusely and cleared her throat. She moved to the door.

"Thanks again."

Gianna watched her, as if confused, but then joined her at the entryway. "No problem." She studied her closely and then gave her a warm smile. "You take care now." She left and Jenny closed and bolted the door. She sat on the couch and watched her drive away, taillights disappearing in the growing darkness.

It took several minutes for her heart rate to slow, and when it did she groaned.

"What is wrong with me? Crushing over a woman I have no business crushing over?" She palmed her forehead and rose to go to the kitchen where she poured herself a small glass of Abigail's favorite whiskey.

She took a hearty sip, winced at the burn and the taste, and stared back out the front window, knowing that only the sea was out there churning in the darkness, but wishing that Gianna was still there too.

CHAPTER TWENTY

"Okay, bud, I've almost got it. Just sit real still for me, okay?" Gianna angled the young boy's head so that she could better see up his left nostril. Blaze, as the boy was called, trembled slightly but did as she instructed. She adjusted the light strapped to her forehead and inserted the thin metal tongs to grab the obstruction.

Blaze scrunched his face and made a noise of discomfort as she withdrew the object from his nose and held it up before him.

"One honey roasted peanut extracted," she said with a smile.

His mother, Nancy, clapped from behind Gianna. "Oh, my God. Thank you so much."

Gianna discarded the peanut in a small jar and screwed on the lid. She handed it to Blaze.

"Keep it. As a reminder of what NOT to do with peanuts."

He giggled and eyed the peanut through the jar, as if fascinated.

"I wanna see!" Blaze's younger sister, Willow, cried.

"No way, it's my peanut."

"Blaze, let your sister see," Nancy said, rolling her eyes at Gianna. "I swear they're gonna be the death of me."

"Kids are a handful," Gianna said, having seen many in the ER with all sorts of strange ailments and problems. Peanuts up the nose included.

"You're telling me. I've got two more at home. Older than Blaze, but still, a handful."

Gianna laughed and led them out of the exam room. She had them check out with Lizzie, and then went on to tidy up the waiting room and prepare to lock up. It was the end of another long day and though she was tired, she felt rather good. Working in Cliffside was nothing like it had been in Chicago. For starters, she actually had some free time, and she called it quits most nights before sundown, which allowed her to call home frequently to check on her folks and on Lauren.

She wiped down the table, chairs, and magazines with Clorox wipes and then did the doorknobs as soon as Nancy and the kids left.

"Well, that was a new one," Lizzie said with a laugh as she watched her lock up.

"What, the peanut?"

"Now why in the world would he stick it up his nose?"

They wiped down the exam rooms next and then headed into the main house for their customary after-work drink.

Gianna washed her hands and poured the wine. It was a nice zinfandel, and as she sipped it she started thinking about dinner.

"He said he wanted to see if it would fit," Gianna said as she sipped her wine.

"Crazy kid," Lizzie said. "I guess it's better than swallowing a penny. I did that when I was young."

Gianna laughed. "I can see you doing that."

"Shut up, you can not." She took a drink of her wine and shook her head. "Charlie used to pick his nose, not stick objects up it."

"You were lucky then."

"I guess. If you call having to clean boogers off his bedroom wall lucky."

"Eww."

"That's a boy for you."

"God, I'm glad I don't have kids."

Lizzie sat at the kitchen counter and carefully spun her wine glass around. "You ever think about having a family?"

"Me? No. Never."

"Why not?"

"I was married to my career."

"Well, what about now? I know a few lesbians in town who'd gladly date you." She winked. "They've even said so."

"No, thanks. I'm fine with the way things are right now." She wagged a finger at her. "And I told you, no fixing me up."

"I'm not fixing you up. I'm just feeling things out a little around here for you."

"Well, don't. I'm not interested."

Lizzie took another drink and arched her brow. "I don't believe that. I saw the way you were with that young woman at Abigail's. What's her name? Kiera?"

"I was helping her." She set her glass down and began searching through the pantry to make something for dinner. She didn't like where Lizzie was headed with this conversation.

"Right. Just like you were *helping* her when you took her shopping and brought her here after hours for an exam? Which you didn't charge her for."

Gianna cringed and grabbed a box of whole wheat spaghetti. "I was just trying to get her treated."

"Uh-huh."

"Hey, she's a patient. Er…sort of. End of story." She emerged from the pantry and put a pot on to boil. "You staying for dinner?"

"No, I gotta get home to Charlie to make sure he's not burning the house down trying to cook."

"That's sweet, him trying like that."

"Ha. You haven't eaten what he cooks." She stood from the barstool and took one last sip of her wine before slinging her purse over her shoulder.

"You know, if Kiera refuses to see you again as a patient, it wouldn't exactly be a bad thing."

"How's that?"

"Because you'd be free to date her."

Gianna closed her eyes. "I'm going to pretend you didn't say that."

"Why? It's true. She didn't pay you for your help and you said yourself she didn't even really want it. So it's safe to say she won't come back. Therefore, you'd be free to date her."

Gianna opened her eyes. "What makes you think I want to?"

Lizzie chuckled. "Please. You're not very good at hiding your attraction to her. Nor is she good at hiding hers to you."

"Wait. She's attracted to me?"

"You two are ridiculous. Yes! Open your eyes, Doc. She's into you."

"But you just said yourself she didn't even want me to treat her."

"Probably because she's attracted to you. I mean, come on. She was blushing so hard the other day at Abigail's when you examined her, I thought she might pass out."

"Really?" She'd thought that had been because they'd recognized each other. But maybe not. Maybe it was something more.

"You know, for a highly trained physician, you sure are clueless." She opened the back door. "You really should work on that."

Gianna tossed a cloth napkin at her. "Get outta here, will ya?"

"Night, Doc."

"See ya."

Lizzie left and Gianna put the pasta on to cook and then heated up some marinara before taking her wine to her laptop to look up Kiera Davenport.

She didn't want to think about all that Lizzie had said, mainly because she'd been right in every aspect. But she didn't want to admit that to her. At least not yet. Because as of right now, she still considered Kiera a possible patient. That didn't stop her from being curious, however. Especially since she'd seen her before, back in Flag.

She typed in her name and the town of Cliffside and did a basic search. Nothing came up. Next, she did a nationwide search, including Arizona, and several matches showed, but none of them were around Kiera's age. There also didn't seem to be any social media presence that matched her either, which was very unusual.

"What the hell?"

She tried a more exclusive search, one she had to pay for. Still, nothing that matched. It was like she didn't exist at all.

She closed her laptop and ate her dinner at the table in silence, thinking about Kiera, trying to figure out who she was. And more so, trying to figure out why she cared so much about a mysterious stranger?

Was it her beauty, or the enigma surrounding her?

"Both."

And who was the man she'd seen her with? He'd seemed overly protective, even possessive. Could he have caused all those marks on her body? While he did seem a little old to be the culprit, she did wonder. After all, she'd seen many unbelievable things in the ER. Things far worse than a peanut up the nose. Human beings…they could be downright vicious to one another. So if the man hadn't been the one to hurt her, who was he? And where was he now? Had he driven off in his semi-truck only to return later? Kiera hadn't said as much. But then again, she did seem rather private.

Gianna figured she'd find out soon enough if the man returned. It would be difficult for Kiera to hide him in Cliffside. With Henry delivering her groceries and Gianna and Lizzie making house calls to Abigail, she wouldn't be able to hide him for long. Someone would see him and the rumor mill would start.

She hoped, for Kiera's sake, that the man hadn't been the one to cause her injuries. She didn't want to imagine someone hurting her like that. But there were further questions. For instance, why didn't Kiera get treated for her injuries after the supposed car accident? She didn't buy her story about not being hurt enough to go in. Mainly because if the accident was reported, the EMTs would've definitely told her she needed to be seen and even tried to insist she let them take her. And what about the police? They would've told her the same and called the EMTs themselves. Something wasn't adding up. Could it be that maybe the accident itself wasn't reported? If so, why not? Or maybe there was no accident at all? Maybe someone really had caused those injuries to her?

Gianna pushed her plate away, unable to finish her meal. She rinsed and deposited the plate in the dishwasher and poured herself another glass of wine. She sat on the sofa and draped her arm across the back to stare out beyond her yard to the backdrop of Cliffside. The lights twinkled against the dark, serrated pines, trying to illuminate the gray cliffs guarding the sea. It really was breathtaking. And for the briefest of moments, she wished she had someone to share the view with. Someone to cuddle up with and just take in the twinkling lights together as they relaxed at the end of a long day.

Her eyes drifted closed as she imagined it. Then Tiffany crossed her mind and she winced from the internal pain the memory of her caused. Try as she might, sometimes she just couldn't shake the image of her locked in an embrace with that other woman no matter how hard she tried. She knew it was because it had been such a shock to see that, that her brain was still working to put it in its place. But it hurt nevertheless, and it made her want to drink all the wine in the world so she wouldn't have to see that image ever again.

She finished what was left in her glass and eyed the bottle on the kitchen table. She could have more. She could numb herself to oblivion tonight. But what would that solve? Not a thing. Besides, she knew better. And she refused to become dependent on alcohol over Tiffany. That woman had caused enough pain. She wouldn't allow her to cause anymore.

Speaking of which, Gianna slid her phone out of her pants pocket and checked the recent calls. Tiffany had called again earlier, while she was with patients. She hadn't left a voice mail, but she had left another text. She was still wanting to see her, wanting to talk things through.

Gianna scoffed and returned her gaze out the window. Tiffany was calling, but only during the day, when she knew she'd be with patients. And she wasn't even courageous enough to leave a voice message, preferring instead to send a text. It wasn't saying much for her, that much was true. And what was it she wanted to say? That she'd made a mistake? That it had meant nothing? Gianna had heard it all before and she knew it was bullshit. Tiffany was just sorry she'd got caught. Plain and simple. And her lover had probably ended things, so Tiffany had no one to warm her bed at night. And everyone knew how Tiffany hated being alone.

Gianna laughed a little at that. Tiffany would just have to get used to it. She'd just have to lie in the bed she'd made. Alone.

Just like she had to.

Here in Cliffside.

Her new home.

CHAPTER TWENTY-ONE

There wasn't much Gary could do without his truck. So he sat around home for a couple of days, waiting anxiously for the cops to come and arrest him. He tried to drink himself into a stupor, but it wasn't enough to kill his worried thoughts. It only slowed them down, which made them all the worse. Because then he couldn't work out any answers, or figure out what he was going to do.

So on the third day, he kept what little beer he had left in the fridge and sat at his tiny kitchen table with a paper and pen to write out his plans. But as soon as he picked up the pen to write, it struck him. There was only one thing he could do. He had to leave town. He absolutely had to. Otherwise, he'd be trying to locate Jenny from a jail cell.

He held his head in his hands and cursed. How the hell was he going to escape when he had no vehicle?

He'd have to borrow one, or steal one. There was no other option.

He could borrow Billy's truck, no problem. But it was old and rickety and it wouldn't get him far. But still, Billy was just dopey enough to lend it to him without question, and it could at least get him to a different county where he could hopefully find another means of transportation.

He pulled out his phone and texted Billy. Said he needed to borrow his truck to run a quick errand. Billy responded right away, with various misspelled words and no punctuation. Gary wasn't a damn English teacher or anything, but he had something on Billy, who acted like he'd barely passed the first grade. Nevertheless, he'd been a good friend and he'd been a hard worker on those construction sites they'd worked together. Gary sure needed a friend now and it seemed old Billy was going to come through once again. He said he'd be home in an hour and that Gary could come by and get the truck.

Perfect.

Gary went straight into his bedroom where he threw some strewn about clothes into an army duffle bag, along with a carton of cigarettes, some snacks from the pantry, and a couple of disposable lighters. He didn't have much else to consider taking with him, so when he finished packing, he checked his place for anything the cops might find that could be used against him. Thankfully, he'd done that, because he'd found a map under the mess on the coffee table with notes on it about where to search for Jenny. He folded that and stuffed it into his bag. Then he showered quickly, put on the same clothes, and left the house unlocked to begin the walk to Billy's, who lived about a mile down the road. While Gary rented a small bungalow apartment, Billy lived in the nearby mobile home park, so the walk wasn't far. Gary smoked a cigarette as he walked, pondering where he'd go next. He had to find Mayweather, but he'd had no luck so far at the truck stop café, and he knew, just knew, it was because of that waitress. She was like a gargoyle, guarding that place like it was her castle. Giving him the evil eye every time he stepped foot in the door. And the man that had given him Mayweather's name to begin with? He'd up and vanished. Gary hadn't seen him since.

So what was he to do?

Again, the words *get out of town* ran through his mind. Yes, first and foremost, he had to get out of town and out from under the cops' mighty grasp. He figured he'd head west, into the neighboring county. That was the direction Jenny had most likely gone. They were already on the coast, so she couldn't have gone east. So west it was. He'd drive as far as he felt comfortable in Billy's truck, ditch it somewhere off road, and then try to find a new ride.

His hot-wiring skills were old but reliable, but cars these days? They had fancy starters and computer chips and GPS. He'd have to stay clear of those. What he needed was an older model car, one that would get him somewhere, one that was in much better shape than Billy's old truck.

He entered the mobile home park and made his way past a loose and roaming friendly dog to Billy's rusted trailer. He walked up the steps and knocked on the door. Billy answered quickly, with a wide grin on his boyish face.

"Hey, man."

"Hey, Billy."

Billy jangled his keys. "You need these?"

"I do."

Billy pushed open the screen. "Here you go, brother." He dropped them into Gary's hand. "Bring her back in one piece, okay?"

His long crucifix earring reflected the sunlight as he held his goofy grin and Gary felt a small pang of guilt at taking advantage of such a gullible guy. But then he remembered what being in a jail cell felt like and he squashed that guilty feeling quickly.

"You got it." Gary clenched the keys in his hand and nodded. "I really appreciate it, Billy."

"It's no trouble, man."

Gary turned to walk back down the steps.

Billy spoke from the edge of the front porch. "Say, what's the duffel bag for?"

Gary stopped, thought quickly, and faced him with a smile. "Just doing some laundry."

"Oh, okay. Well, take good care of her. She's my baby."

Gary gave another nod and climbed in the truck. The door squeaked as he pulled it closed. How this old piece of crap could be anyone's baby was beyond him. But whatever. He started the truck up, revved the hesitating engine, and waved at Billy as he drove away. Billy watched him go, seemingly pleased to be helping him out. Another pang of guilt came, but Gary lowered the window to let it and the strong scent of the pine freshener go, leaving him to inhale the fresh air of freedom as he sped down the road.

CHAPTER TWENTY-TWO

Jenny woke early and sat at the edge of the bed. The dawn was gray and wispy with fog as she looked longingly out the window. Slowly, she stood, putting pressure on her knee. She grimaced as the pain registered, but she continued regardless and dressed in warmer clothes. She walked down the short hallway to the kitchen and made herself some instant coffee with a quick pour of almond milk to stir in. She sipped it carefully and crossed the living room to look out at the churning sea. The white caps were angry and crashing onto the shore like they had a fierce battle to fight on land. She wondered if the battle would be won, or if the sea, like everyone else, would have to realize that not all battles could be won.

She cupped the hot mug in her hand and settled on the couch. She covered herself with a blanket and continued to watch the angry sea as best she could through the settling fog. Eventually, the fog would dissipate and the sun would shine through. She hoped anyway. But here lately, the sun seemed to hide away, leaving the town of Cliffside to contend with the gloom of gray and foggy days.

"At least it isn't raining," she whispered. She nearly choked on her coffee when a gust of wind came off the shore and splattered light rain drops across the windowpane.

So much for that.

She cuddled deeper beneath the blanket and nixed the idea of going out to walk along the soft shore where the waves crashed with their mighty swords drawn. She'd yet to take that walk and she was yearning to do so. Her knee had kept her away, and she couldn't wait for it to heal. So she'd been doing as Gianna instructed. She'd been resting as much as she could, walking only to go to Abigail's for dinner to see how she was. Abigail, of course, fussed about it. Wanting her to stay at home to rest her knee completely, insisting that she didn't need anyone checking on her. Jenny had merely agreed and told her that she enjoyed their dinners and wouldn't miss them for the world. Hurt knee or not.

Abigail had nothing to say to that, so the matter was settled. The cleaning was on hold, with Jenny doing what little she could to straighten up at Abigail's after Abigail climbed the stairs to go to bed after dinner every night. The rest would have to wait because Abigail refused to let Henry come in and help. Nor anyone else for that matter. So Henry did what he always did. He brought in her groceries, helped her put them away, and kept them both in plenty of firewood.

He did, however, help Jenny out. She was more than willing to let him help her with some necessary chores when he stopped by. She also enjoyed getting to know him. He was a kind young man. Thoughtful and generous with his time. And he always seemed to talk about Gianna, which she really enjoyed.

Apparently, Lizzie shared a lot of details with Charlie, who in turn told Henry. And, as it turned out, Lizzie had told Charlie that she was hoping to set Gianna up with some of the women in town. That little bit of information had sent Jenny absolutely spinning. Gianna was gay. She liked women. Was that why Jenny was so affected by her? Because she'd sensed that and found her attractive? Or was it something else entirely? Whatever it was, Jenny couldn't seem to get enough information about her, and the thought of her dating someone, anyone, left her feeling sick to her stomach, which confused her all the more. She wasn't gay. Had never been interested in a woman before. So why all these feelings over a woman she hardly knew?

Jenny didn't know and the more she thought about it, the crazier she felt. She wished she had someone to talk to about it with, but Abigail didn't exactly seem like the right person. And after her, there was no one else. She would be far too embarrassed to talk to Henry about it and he'd surely tell Charlie, who would then tell Lizzie and Gianna would certainly find out. So, no, she had no one.

She'd just have to keep her thoughts and feelings to herself. Figure it out on her own. Which she really needed to do because she was equally as confused with her feelings over Ken. She hadn't been crying as much over his loss at night, and she didn't understand why. The shock and pain of his loss was still there, but the deep, stomach-churning ache was gone. Now she just had anger. Anger at Gary and what he'd done. He'd ruined her life and taken Ken's. All for some unknown, no doubt ridiculous reason. If she wasn't so afraid of him, she'd want to confront him, hurt him even. Pound on him until he told her why. Why he'd done all this and hurt so many people in the process.

She finished her coffee and rose to make more. When she finished, she sat at the table and picked up the ink pen she'd purchased at Walmart and started writing in the composition journal she'd also bought. She'd decided, since she had no one to share her feelings with, that she'd put pen to paper and work things out in her mind that way.

It wasn't perfect, and she wasn't much of a writer, but it helped and that was all that mattered. So far, she'd written about Ken's death, how she felt about it, and her journey out west with Floyd. Whom she still needed to call.

"Wait. No. I'll just write him."

She smiled and turned to a blank page. She spent the next twenty minutes filling him in on her well-being, careful to leave out exactly where she was, and thanked him again for all his help.

She asked after his wife, hoped she was well, and promised she'd write again soon. Then she sealed the letter in an old envelope she'd found in a drawer and addressed the front. All she needed now was postage. She'd have Henry bring her some.

She smiled, sipped her coffee, and relaxed. She felt better already. Ready to start her day.

But a knock on her door startled her. Her heart leapt in her chest as she stood and peeked around the wall of the kitchen to look out the front window. She saw Gianna's SUV parked in the drive. Her heart leapt some more, and she swallowed hard as she walked to the door to unlock it and ease it open.

"Good morning," Gianna said with a broad smile, standing there in a thick waterproof coat and beanie snug on her head. She held out a box. "I brought you some donuts from Glenda's in town. They're the best I've ever had and I bet you've never tried them."

"No, I've never tried them," Jenny said, offering a smile in return. She took the box, unsure what else to say. She was overwhelmed, both by her presence, and by the thoughtful gesture. "I—thank you?"

Gianna laughed. "I know my visit is unexpected and I apologize. I just assumed you'd tell me no if I called first, so I took a chance." She smiled again, as if waiting for Jenny to respond.

Jenny struggled for words. "Yes—I—you didn't need to do this. It's so nice of you. Would you like to come in?" The house wasn't as tidy as she would've liked it to be, but she knew inviting her in was the polite thing to do.

"Oh no, I can't stay. And I wouldn't want to intrude. I just—" She looked down at Jenny's legs. "How's the knee?"

Jenny lifted her leg as if in offering. She lowered it quickly though due to the pain.

"Still hurts, huh?" Gianna asked.

"Some. But it's feeling a little better. I think all the rest is helping."

"That's good."

Gianna shoved her hands in her jacket pockets. Her breath came out in white puffs. "I should probably get back to the house. I have patients arriving soon. You'll keep me posted on the knee?"

Jenny nodded.

"Okay then. Have a good day, Kiera."

"Thank you, you too."

Gianna turned and walked down the steps to cross the frosty grass. Jenny called out to her as she reached her truck.

"It was nice to see you!" She waved.

Gianna beamed at her and returned the wave before crawling into her SUV and backing down the drive. Her taillights disappeared in the fog, leaving Jenny all alone at her front door.

The cold began to seep into her skin as she stared after Gianna in the swallowing fog, forcing her to eventually close the door. She slipped on her shoes and her coat and reemerged out front, this time to walk to Abigail's with the donuts. The rain sprinkled down on her head, prickling her face with its icy tease and the sea sent a gust of wind, nearly freezing her as she walked up the steps to the front door to knock.

Abigail hollered for her to come in and she did, glad to be inside the semi-warm home. Abigail was in her favorite chair by the window, drinking from a coffee mug.

"Who was that paying you a visit so early in the morning?" she asked, obviously having seen Gianna drive up.

"Dr. Walford." Jenny sat on the sofa and opened the box full of goodies.

"Who?"

"You know, the doctor who came to see you with Lizzie."

She appeared confused but quickly replaced the look with one of indignation. "What did she want?"

"She brought donuts."

"Donuts? From Glenda's?" Abigail asked. "I won't eat any other donut."

"They're from Glenda's." She rose to get plates and napkins and returned to offer the box to Abigail, who chose the one she wanted right away. "I like the pink ones," she said, like an excited child. She plucked it out with a shaky hand and plopped it on her plate. She didn't take a bite until Jenny had returned to her place on the couch and selected a donut of her own. She chose a chocolate cream filled and bit into it. Surprisingly, it was still a little warm and it nearly melted in her mouth it was so good.

"Mm," she said, closing her eyes. "This is delicious."

"Yes, sir," Abigail said. "Glenda's are the best."

"They absolutely are." She opened her eyes and smiled over at Abigail, who was taking a small bite of her own.

"It's no wonder that place has been in business some fifty years now," Abigail said. "They know how to make a good donut. Yes, sir, they do." Her gaze fixed out beyond the window. "Hard to believe it's been fifty years," she said softly. "Time…it just gets away from us, doesn't it?"

Jenny swallowed. "Yes, ma'am, it does."

Abigail continued to stare for a moment, looking out at the fog-covered sea. Then she blinked and took another tiny bite of her donut. "Is that all that doctor wanted? To deliver donuts?"

"She asked about my knee."

"Hmph. That's a rather nice house call, don't you think? Coming out all this way without an appointment to deliver donuts and check on you?"

Jenny blushed. "I think she's just really concerned about my knee."

"Then you should probably make an appointment. Save her the trouble of having to come out here so early in the morning just to check on you."

Jenny was silent. Too embarrassed to respond.

"Course, I reckon you can just see her when she comes to see me. No harm in that."

"You're going to keep seeing her?" Jenny asked.

"Well, yes, why wouldn't I?"

"You didn't seem too happy about her replacing Doc B."

Abigail looked at her in confusion again. "Don't be ridiculous. A doctor's a doctor."

Jenny set her donut down, needing a break.

Abigail continued. "I wouldn't turn away a doctor. Especially if she keeps bringing treats." She laughed as if she'd amused herself.

Jenny sat back against the couch and clasped her hands together. It *was* rather unusual for Gianna to show up unannounced to give her donuts and check on her. It was nice, but unusual nonetheless. Jenny didn't know what to make of it. Was Gianna really that concerned over her knee? Or could there be something more to it?

She blushed again as she considered the possibility that Gianna might, just might, feel like she did. But just as quickly, she chided herself, knowing it was crazy and she was just fantasizing once again.

What is going on with me?

She was all mixed up inside and couldn't discern right from left. One minute she was thinking about Ken, the next Gary, and then the next Gianna.

There was definitely something going on with her. Maybe she really was losing her mind. After all that happened, it wouldn't be that farfetched.

"What's eating at you?" Abigail asked, causing her to climb back out of her head.

"Hm? Nothing."

But as she halfway listened to Abigail carry on, she knew that was a lie. Because the real answer was *everything.*

CHAPTER TWENTY-THREE

"Dr. Walford?"

Gianna glanced up from her desk to see Lizzie looking alarmed, standing just inside the office door.

"What is it, Lizzie?"

"Your next patient is in two." Her normally jovial face was ashen and bleak with concern. Gianna immediately stiffened.

"And is something wrong?" She pushed away from her desk and stood.

"Well, he's uh…"

"He's what? Lizzie? Is he hurt?"

She shook her head. "Oh no, nothing like that. He's just—you'll see."

She handed Gianna the new patient file as Gianna bypassed her to head into exam room two.

Gianna skimmed through the papers quickly, recognized the last name, and entered the room after a brief but friendly knock.

"Mr. Haas, good afternoon," she said with her best smile. But the hulk of a man sitting in the chair next to the exam table stood with a scowl that made her stop dead in her tracks. She hesitated to shut the door behind her.

"You her?" he asked. "The *doctor*?"

"Yes. I'm Dr. Walford." She extended her hand. He didn't take it. Instead he stalked up to her and spoke directly in her face.

"Where's Doc B?"

She'd dealt with irate patients before. Plenty of times in the ER back in Chicago. She knew how to handle them, so she was careful to keep her composure.

"He's retired."

"I know that," he spat. "But *where* is he? I want to see *him*."

"He's in Arizona. Scottsdale."

The man, whose name was Derek Haas according to the file, took a step back and rubbed his hard-looking jaw.

"Who am I supposed to see, then? You?" he said, his voice retaining its sharp tone.

"I'm the one taking over for him."

"But you're a woman."

Gianna forced a smile. "Yes. But I can assure you, I'm a doctor just the same." She gently closed the door with the palm of her hand. "Why don't we have a seat and discuss things, Mr. Haas?"

"I don't want to see a woman. I want Doc B."

"Well, I'm afraid he is no longer in practice. But if you like, you can go into the city where you will find plenty of other doctors to choose from. I'm sure many of them will be male."

He sank down onto the chair and pointed a finger at her. "You treated my boy. Not that long ago. Had a peanut up his nose."

"Yes."

"My wife brought him in. Didn't ask me first. Just brought him to you. She shouldn't have done that. I could've taken care of it."

Gianna eased onto her stool, careful to keep her guard up. The man was huge and volatile. While she didn't really think he'd do anything violent, she had to remain prepared just the same. Thankfully, Lizzie was aware of the situation. Which was why she'd been so alarmed. She must've sensed his attitude.

"He needed treatment, Mr. Haas, and I provided what was expected of me. As for the rest, you'll have to discuss that with your wife."

"I did. And don't you concern yourself with it. She won't be coming back. We don't need the help of any woman doctor."

He stood again, and this time his face contorted in pain and he grabbed at his lower back.

Gianna watched him, upset at his words, but worried about his obvious distress and pain. "Mr. Haas, why don't you let me take a look?"

"No." He continued to wince.

"Then why did you come in? If you knew I would be the one treating you?"

He ambled toward the door, and she rolled her stool out of the way.

"It was a mistake," he said. "A big mistake."

"You're obviously in pain—"

He opened the door.

"Mr. Haas." She rose to follow him out. "Mr. Haas, please. It will only get worse. Please get treatment somewhere."

He pushed out the door into the waiting room and beyond, leaving her feeling dumbfounded.

She sighed and slapped the file against her leg and brought the door to a close. She walked back into the office where Lizzie stood waiting next to the desk.

"He bite your head off?" she asked.

"Yeah, thanks for the warning." Gianna tossed the file onto the desk and rounded it to sit.

"You always say to speak about our patients with respect, so I wasn't sure what to say."

"You say whatever is necessary. If we have a hostile patient, I need to know about it."

Lizzie nodded solemnly. "He's always had a big chip on his shoulder, but today he seemed worse."

"He's in pain. And apparently, he isn't fond of female doctors."

"Sorry, boss."

Gianna waved her off. "Let's forget about it. It's over."

Lizzie brightened. "Well, you're sure to smile at who you see next."

Gianna glanced back up at her. "Oh?"

"Mm-hm. I'll go get her." She left the room and Gianna heard her open the waiting room door and call someone back. She waited for Lizzie to tell her which exam room to go to, but instead, Lizzie surprised her by returning to the doorway.

"She's right here," she said, moving to the side.

Gianna blinked. It was Kiera. Lizzie showed her in and closed the door, leaving them alone.

Kiera had a basket in her hands and she was bundled up in a bright blue puffy jacket, white scarf, and beanie, and wore her knee brace over her jeans. She didn't have her cane, which was a good sign.

"Kiera, hi." Gianna started to rise, but Kiera stopped her.

"No, please, don't get up. I just dropped by to bring you these." She held the basket out and approached. She still limped but she wasn't acting like she was in great pain. She deposited the basket on the desk.

"They're blueberry," she said. "Made fresh with the freshly picked blueberries Henry brought us."

Gianna peeked in the basket and saw a dozen or so muffins, sprinkled with sugar.

"What's the occasion?" Gianna said, smiling up at her. "Is it someone's birthday and I'm not aware?"

Kiera smiled bashfully. "No, it's just a thank you. For the donuts. And for coming to check on me."

"It was my pleasure, Kiera. You certainly didn't have to do all this."

"We wanted to."

"We?"

"Abigail and I. I shared the donuts and she was more than happy about that. She's a big fan of Glenda's."

"Who isn't?" Gianna chuckled. "Gosh, these smell so good. May I?"

"Please."

"Would you like one?"

"Oh, no, I've had my fill. But you go ahead."

Gianna plucked a thick muffin from the basket and sank her teeth into it after peeling down the wrapper. "Mm. Oh, my God. That is so good."

Kiera laughed. Then she touched at her lip. "You've got a little blueberry on your mouth."

Gianna raised her hand to her lips. "Did I get it?"

"No, it's—" She came closer and lightly skimmed Gianna's lower lip with her thumb. "Right here."

Gianna stiffened at the gentle contact. She hadn't felt such a sensual touch in a long while. In fact, she couldn't remember when. Tiffany had stopped all affection well before she'd caught her in the affair.

Kiera backed away as if she'd touched a hot flame. "Sorry."

"Don't be," Gianna said, standing. But Kiera was already at the door. "Kiera, wait."

"Thank you again," Kiera said as she pulled open the door. "For your kindness." With that she was gone, walking past Lizzie, who had remained suspiciously close to the door.

Gianna sank back down in her chair with a sigh. Great. She'd scared her off. *Why did I react like that? Like a woman so hard up for touch I nearly jumped out of my skin?*

Because she hadn't been touched in ages. And because it was her. Kiera.

The realization hit her hard, like a lineman slamming into her from behind. She wanted Kiera's touch.

"So what was that all about?" Lizzie asked as she strolled up to her.

"Huh?" Gianna had to refocus. She could still feel the burn of Kiera's touch on her mouth. "Oh, she brought us muffins." She shoved the basket toward her.

"Us?"

"Yeah."

"You mean, you."

"Whatever. I'm going to share them with you."

"Not the same, friend, not the same." Nevertheless, she selected one for herself and bit into it and groaned. "Damn," she said, mouth full. "That's a good muffin."

She chewed and swallowed. "What was the occasion?" She grinned like the Grinch sneaking in to steal presents.

"Nothing, silly. She just wanted to thank me."

"For?"

"Will you stop with the grin?"

"Not until you tell me."

"I stopped by her house the other day to check on her, alright?"

"You did?"

"Yes."

"And? What happened?"

"Nothing."

"So she made you muffins?"

"I brought her donuts from Glenda's. So I think she felt the need to bring me something in return."

"I see," Lizzie said, chewing and swallowing another bite. "But that doesn't explain the raging blush she left here with."

Gianna pushed out a breath and stood. "Do I have another patient waiting?"

"Mm-hm. Room two."

"Good." She rounded the desk and walked toward the door.

"Hey, Doc?" Lizzie said, turning to look at her.

Gianna halted.

"You might want to get rid of your blush too."

CHAPTER TWENTY-FOUR

Things hadn't exactly gone the way Gary had wanted. First of all, he'd had to ditch Billy's piece of junk truck just inside the neighboring county when the damn thing starting hitching and making crazy noises. So that had been the end of that.

He'd left it on the side of the road, door wide open, an offering to the next jackass that might come along and try to use it.

Good for nothing Billy. He should've known better than to depend on him for anything. The guy didn't know his head from his ass, and he no longer felt any sort of guilt when it came to him. Billy was lucky he didn't storm back there and beat his ass, teach him a lesson about screwing over a friend with a deadbeat vehicle.

Billy. Fucking idiot kid.

Gary kicked at a stone before he crossed the street from the gas station. He hitched his thumb as a car whizzed by, but it didn't stop. Whatever. He'd catch the next one. He'd been walking the back roads for days now, catching rides whenever he could, sleeping out under the stars, eating greasy gas station food and snacks. He opened a bag of Funyuns and shoved a handful in his mouth. He didn't want to waste his Sun Drop on that horrible aftertaste, so he lit up a cigarette instead.

The man in the gas station had told him it was four o'clock. That meant he needed to find some place suitable for the night and soon. He thought about checking into a cheap motel, but he wasn't sure if he really wanted to spend the money. He was saving a ton right now by not needing gas, but eventually he hoped to steal a car and get going for good. He still needed to hit the truck stops to try and find Mayweather. It was his only solid lead on Jenny.

He'd been thinking about her a lot. The cops already assumed he'd killed her, and they were probably going to put him away for it. So why chase her and kill her?

Because as soon as I'm arrested, she'll come back and testify against me about trying to kill her. And I'm as good as toast then too.

He also had it in for her and it was time she paid the price for all the rejection. He hadn't deserved that kind of treatment. All he'd ever done was love her, worship her, promise to give her the world. And what had she done? She'd pretty much spit in his face. Told him no. Never. Not in a million years. She loved Ken, wanted Ken, was with Ken. Ken, Ken, Ken. Christ, it was enough to drive a man mad. And he thought it finally had. Nothing else could explain his actions recently. His family was up in arms about the cops and their questions. They had even called him themselves, asking why the cops were asking after Jenny. Even his grandmother had asked. He didn't know why they cared. As far as he knew they didn't even really like Jenny. So what did it matter if she was missing? But that was just like them to change their minds and try and blame him for something. They didn't love him. They had no loyalty or respect for him. Just Ken. It was always about fucking Ken.

If the situation had been reversed, they'd never do that to Ken. They'd never ask if he'd done something to Gary's girlfriend. Because Ken was just perfect. And him? Well, he might as well be the mud on the bottom of their shoes because that's how they treated him.

He tossed the Funyun wrapper in the ditch along the side of the road and hitched his thumb at the next vehicle. It was a small pickup truck, with a mismatched back end. It slowed and pulled to a stop.

Gary leaned on the door. "Howdy."

"Hola," the man said. He motioned toward the bed of the truck.

"Thanks." Gary slung his bag over the side and hopped in. The man pulled back on the road and continued west.

Gary wasn't sure where he would sleep that night, or the next. But he knew one thing. It wouldn't be in jail.

Chapter Twenty-five

The morning breeze was cold, blowing the mist from the sea into Jenny as she limped along the shoreline. It was the first morning she'd made it out to walk along the water, to inhale the salty air and breathe in the sea spray. Though the walk was difficult with her sore knee, it still felt wonderful to be outside.

She stopped and closed her eyes and faced the water. She took in the sound of the crashing and hissing waves. The calls of a distant seagull. She couldn't believe she had made it. She was in Oregon, on the opposite end of the country, back where she belonged. With the sea.

What would happen from here? Would she continue to build her life, alongside Abigail, with the hopes that Gary would never find her? Was there anything else she could hope for? It wasn't likely. Nevertheless, she was grateful. So eternally grateful. For Abigail, and for Ruby, who had led her to safety, even from beyond the grave.

Thinking of Abigail, she turned and walked across the soft sand to her front porch where she carefully climbed the steps to knock gently on the front door.

"Abigail?" she called when she heard nothing from inside.

She knocked again and waited. She heard something, something faint. It sounded like Abigail and she sounded distressed.

Panicked, Jenny opened the door and rushed inside. "Abigail?"

"Here."

Jenny hurried into the kitchen where she found Abigail on the floor, splayed on her side, wearing her nightgown and a bathrobe. One foot was bare, while the other was covered with a worn house slipper.

Jenny knelt to examine her, worried she was injured.

"What happened?" she asked. "Are you okay?"

"I just lost my footing, kid. Damn slippers. I need to get new ones. Here, help me up." She gave Jenny her hand and Jenny eased her up as best she could. She steadied her and held onto her as she led her over to the kitchen table where she sat.

Jenny knelt in front of her and brushed wayward strands of her silver hair away from her face. "Do you hurt?"

"Course I hurt, kid. What do you think? I'm ninety-four years old."

"I meant from the fall."

"Nah. I'm fine. Just a little shook up." She swatted at her. "Go on now. I'm fine. Go sit."

But the kettle whistled from the stovetop, startling them both. Jenny moved it from the burner and made them both some tea.

"I had forgotten I put the kettle on," Abigail mumbled.

Jenny brought her a steaming mug and placed it on the table in front of her. Then she settled in across from her.

"You sure you're okay? I think maybe I should call the doctor to get you checked out."

Abigail gave her a stern look. "Absolutely not. I told you, I'm fine. And that's the end of it. I don't want to hear about it anymore."

"But you could've fractured something, Abigail. Sometimes with hairline fractures, you aren't even aware of them."

"What did I just say?"

Jenny clamped her mouth shut.

"If you keep on, I'm going to ask you to leave," Abigail said.

"You would do that?"

"Damn right I would. I don't need you fussing after me."

"I care, Abigail. That's all."

"Well, I don't need you to." She hugged her mug with her arthritic hands and lifted it to her mouth. A bit of tea splashed from the mug from her trembling. She cried out briefly and wiped the hot tea from the back of her hand. "Dagblasted." She wagged a finger at Jenny. "Don't you say a word now."

"I wasn't going to."

Abigail lifted the mug again and this time took a tentative sip. It seemed to please her because she sighed and sat back in the chair.

Jenny watched her closely, worried for her. But she couldn't let on. Abigail was eyeing her, just waiting for her to voice more concerns. It was obvious she was overly sensitive about her well-being.

But she had fallen and she was fortunate that Jenny had happened to stop by. Otherwise who knows how long she would've remained there on the floor with the stove on? The thought frightened Jenny. More than frightened her. But what could she do about it?

Abigail wouldn't even discuss things with her. She was in total denial and downright combative about it.

Jenny continued to sip her tea in silence, trying to work out what to do. Was there anything she could do? Other than drop by more often? Was this the first time something like this had happened?

What really had caused the fall?

She wished she had answers, but none were forthcoming.

After a while, she rose to heat up the remainder of her tea. She offered to heat Abigail's as well, but she shook her off, still a little touchy about the morning's happenings. Jenny opened the microwave and did a double take. Something was in it. It was the remote control for the television.

What the hell?

She removed it and turned to Abigail. "Have you been looking for the remote control to the TV?"

"Yes." She perked up. "Why?"

"I just found it. It was in the microwave."

"The microwave? What in the world was it doing in there?"

"You must've put it in there."

"Oh, I did not."

"Abigail—

"I wouldn't do something so ridiculous."

"But—"

She stood. "Don't you even suggest it." She bored her dark eyes into her. "I wouldn't do something so stupid as to put a remote control in the microwave. So don't you even suggest it."

She took her tea and walked into the living room to sit in her chair. She fixed her gaze out the window.

Jenny poured her tea down the sink and went to sit next to her on the couch.

"Abigail?" she said softly. "Do you need help getting back up the stairs to dress?"

It was pushing nine o'clock and Abigail was always up and dressed and ready for the day by eight. Had she been unable to get back up the stairs and that's why she decided to put the kettle on while still in her gown and bathrobe?

Abigail didn't even bother to look at her. She didn't answer her either.

"Abigail?"

A tear formed and slipped down her wrinkled face. She wiped at it like it was a nuisance. "What if I do? You going to think I'm some sort of helpless invalid?"

"What? Abigail, no. Of course not."

"'Cause I'm not. I can still get around. Do for myself."

"I know. And yes, you can, and you do. But there's nothing wrong with needing a little help. Nothing wrong with that at all."

Abigail remained silent. Jenny waited. Eventually, Abigail set her mug of tea aside and breathed deeply.

"I reckon I do," she said. "So you going to help me or what?" She pushed up from her chair and Jenny hurried to her side. Together they made their way up the stairs and into her bedroom.

Jenny sat her on the bed and began picking up the clothes that were strewn all over the floor and settee. It looked like Abigail hadn't been able to do laundry in some time. Jenny felt awful. How could she not have noticed?

"Do you need to wash up?" Jenny asked, again, keeping her voice low and soft.

"I reckon."

Jenny left her to go into the bathroom. Abigail had a bathtub/shower combination, so she'd have to step up to get into the tub. Jenny wasn't sure if she could manage. She returned to the bedroom.

"Can you get in the tub to shower?"

"I brace myself on the wall and get in."

"Okay, do you want to do that if I get everything ready for you?"

"I reckon."

Jenny turned on the water, adjusted the temperature, and set out some towels. Then she helped Abigail into the bathroom where she slowly undressed and stepped into the shower.

"I'm going to sit right here," Jenny said, sitting on the closed commode.

"Okay," Abigail surprised her in saying.

Jenny pulled her phone out of her back pocket to look up the phone number for Gianna's office. She created a new contact and made a note to call her as soon as she was alone. She was more concerned than ever now, and she needed some advice. She'd quickly scanned Abigail's body as she'd undressed and she'd seen the beginnings of bruises from her fall. Abigail needed to be examined and some changes needed to be made and fast. Jenny just wished that Abigail would be more open-minded to discussing things and possibly getting some help.

Jenny hoped that maybe Gianna would be willing to talk to her and that Abigail would at least listen to her.

The shower water cut off and Jenny stood to hand Abigail her towel. She helped her from the tub and wrapped her in her bathrobe to lead her back into the bedroom where she eased her onto the bed.

"What would you like to wear today?"

Jenny opened the closet and stood looking at the gaping hole where clothes should be. A lone shirt hung on the right, the rest of the clothes no doubt had been on the floor. Jenny plucked the shirt from the hanger and walked to the dresser.

"Your pants and things in here?"

Abigail nodded.

Jenny opened the drawers, found one of the last pairs of clean underwear, a pair of pants and a cable-knit sweater. She set them all on the bed and helped Abigail dress. Thankfully, Abigail didn't protest. Jenny figured she was too sore and too cold to do so.

"There," Jenny said when they had finished. "All dressed." She grabbed the towel and handed it to her to dry her hair. "You want your hairbrush?" Again, she nodded. Jenny returned with it and watched as Abigail brushed her long silver locks and then twisted them up into a tight bun. She asked for the hair tie on the dresser which Jenny got for her.

"Do you feel better?" Jenny asked with a smile.

"I reckon."

"How about some more tea?" She offered Abigail her elbow and then led her back down the stairs to her chair. Jenny covered her with a blanket, reheated her tea, and then left her to go gather the clothes from upstairs. When she returned with an armload, she found Abigail watching her.

"What are you doing?" she asked.

"I was just going to start some laundry for you."

"You don't need to be doing that."

Jenny stood at the bottom of the stairs, arms full. "Actually, Abigail, I do. You're out of clean clothes. So no fussing allowed. I'm doing your laundry."

Abigail stared at her, opened her mouth to speak, but then seemed to change her mind. She turned to stare back out the window and sip her tea, leaving Jenny to do as she pleased.

Jenny put a load in the washer and then went back upstairs for another armload. While she was there, she went into the bathroom and closed the door. She dialed Gianna's office number and waited.

Lizzie answered on the third ring and Jenny tried to speak. Her voice caved however, as all her concern and worry for Abigail came pouring out. Lizzie listened intently, calmed her down, and said what Jenny had been hoping to hear.

She told her that they'd stop by later that afternoon.

CHAPTER TWENTY-SIX

"Sounds like she's going to need more care than she's getting now," Gianna said as Lizzie steered them down toward Rhydian Hill.

"Mm-hm."

"And Kiera said she's being stubborn about even discussing things?"

Lizzie laughed. "She did. But honestly, Doc, Abigail Rhydian is one of the most stubborn people I've ever known, so that doesn't surprise me in the least."

"We've got our work cut out for us."

"No doubt we do, Doc. No doubt we do."

Gianna readied her medical bag and tablet as Lizzie pulled up the drive and parked in front of the porch. When she killed the engine, Gianna climbed out into the partial sunlight and headed up the steps. Lizzie followed and Kiera greeted them right away, opening the door before they even had time to knock.

"Thanks so much for coming," Kiera said softly, with a concerned smile.

"Does she know we're coming?" Gianna asked, sensing her quiet demeanor.

"I just told her the doctor was stopping by."

"Oh."

"She's not happy about it." Kiera showed them inside and Gianna smiled broadly as she took in a scowling Abigail.

"Abigail, it's good to see you," she said, placing her medical bag and tablet down on the coffee table.

"Who in the hell are you?" Abigail asked, causing Gianna to stop dead in her tracks.

Lizzie looked at Gianna with alarm. Kiera knelt in front of Abigail and took her hands. "Abigail, this is Dr. Gianna Walford. Don't you remember her?"

"I told you, I don't need no damn doctor."

"Abigail, you fell. You're all bruised up. You need to be examined."

"Where's Doc B? He's my doctor." She caught sight of Lizzie. "Where's Doc B? Why isn't he with you?"

"Doc B retired. Moved down to Arizona. Dr. Walford has taken over his practice," Lizzie said. "She's real nice, Abigail. And she's one hell of a doctor."

Abigail scoffed. "I'll be the judge of that."

Gianna kept her smile. "Does that mean you're willing to give me a chance?"

Kiera squeezed Abigail's hands and looked at her hopefully.

"I reckon," Abigail said.

Kiera beamed and straightened.

"She's all yours," Kiera said as she backed away.

Gianna brought her bag and tablet over to Abigail and politely offered her hand in greeting. Abigail took it and Gianna held it dearly, with both hands. "Thank you for giving me the honor, Abigail."

"Uh-huh," Abigail said.

Gianna opened her bag and retrieved her stethoscope. She listened to Abigail's heart, which sounded nice and strong. Next, she took her blood pressure, which was a little low, which could've explained her fall.

"Have you been feeling dizzy?"

"I've had a spell or two."

Gianna handed the tablet over to Lizzie who began entering in all the information as Gianna continued to question and examine her. Abigail complied, even when Gianna asked to see her bruises. She just mumbled under her breath and occasionally cursed, but she allowed Gianna to do what was necessary. When Gianna finished, she thanked Abigail and left her with Lizzie while she stepped outside on the porch with Kiera.

"So, what's the verdict?" Kiera asked, sliding into her jacket and crossing her arms. "Is she okay?"

"She's not seriously hurt. Just bruised. But as for the rest…"

"Yes?"

"Without getting into her medical condition, which I would need her permission again to do…Kiera, I think she now needs full-time care."

Kiera's face crumbled and she turned away to face the roaring sea.

Gianna lightly touched her shoulder. "Hey," she said. "It's okay."

But Kiera shook her head. "It's not. It's so not. I have no idea what to do."

"Does she have anything written, expressing her wishes in this circumstance?"

"I have no idea. I just know that she wants to remain at home. She's told me so several times."

"I don't think that's possible without someone with her full-time. The risk is just too great."

Kiera wiped away a tear. "I'll have to talk to her." She turned back to Gianna. "Will you help me? I'm afraid she'll fight me on whatever I say."

"Of course."

"Thank you." She covered her face as sobs overtook her.

"Hey," Gianna whispered.

"I'm sorry. I'm just so—she's been so kind to me—she doesn't deserve this."

"I know."

Kiera continued to cry. Gianna pulled her into her arms and held her, feeling her body shake as she sobbed. "It's going to be okay. We'll figure something out."

Kiera drew away and wiped her cheeks. She stared up into Gianna's eyes. "I don't see how," she said. "I mean, the only thing I can think of is to have her move in with me in the cottage. But I don't think she'll go for that."

"Why not?"

"Because it's not her home. And because she doesn't want to live with someone."

"I'm afraid she's not going to be able to fight that anymore. Like it or not she needs to be with someone. She'll just have to accept it." Gianna studied her. "Why don't you move in here? That way she could stay in her home."

Kiera sighed. "The stairs are a problem. She could barely manage them today. And that was with my help."

"So we move her bed downstairs. Think she'll go for that if it means she can stay at home?"

Kiera threw up her hands. "I don't know."

"Do you mind moving in here?" Gianna asked. "It's asking a lot of you to care for her like this."

"I don't mind. She's helped me, so it's the least I can do."

Gianna wondered what all Abigail had helped her with, but she kept her questions to herself. All she knew was that Kiera had seemingly appeared out of nowhere to live in the cottage and look after Abigail. And according to Lizzie that was highly unusual, as Abigail had kept to herself for years and years.

Gianna patted Kiera's upper arm. "That's very kind of you. You know that, right?"

Kiera blushed. Gianna dropped her hand. "You okay?" Gianna asked.

"Just a little shook up. It's been an unusual day."

"You've handled it very well."

"Really? Because I feel so clueless."

"You're far from clueless. You did exactly what I would've done. You called for help."

"I thought about calling an ambulance, but she would've killed me. And she didn't seem that hurt."

"You did okay, Kiera. If she'd been hurt more seriously, you would've called the appropriate people. But as it is, you did alright."

"Thank you," she exhaled.

"I get the impression that you haven't heard that a lot."

She shook her head. "I haven't."

"Why is that?"

Kiera searched her face as if she was unsure as to what to say. "I—I guess no one has thought so, that's why."

"Who's no one?"

"I don't know, Ken, his friends and his brother."

"And who is Ken?"

Kiera froze as if she'd said too much. "Uh, no one."

Gianna watched her closely. Her gaze had shifted and she was uneasy on her feet. "Don't want to talk about it? That's okay. Let's go inside and talk to Abigail, okay? See if we can get this sorted out."

Gianna moved to open the door, but Kiera stopped her by lightly gripping her wrist.

"Wait," she said. "I—thank you."

"For what?"

"For being so kind. And for not making me feel inadequate."

"But you're not inadequate, Kiera."

"I know. It's just—it's been a while since I've heard that and really believed it."

Gianna wasn't sure who Ken or the others were that she'd spoken of, but one thing was for certain, they had done a number on her self-esteem.

"Well, rest assured you'll hear it from me," Gianna said with a smile. She winked and opened the door. Kiera entered first and Gianna closed the door behind them. Lizzie smiled from her seat in front of Abigail, where she'd pulled up an ottoman to sit on.

"You two look comfy," Gianna said.

"We are," Lizzie said. "Aren't we, Abigail?"

"If you say so."

"I was just telling Abigail all about you, Dr. Walford." Lizzie said. "About your time in the emergency department in Chicago and how you ran the whole team there. Abigail said she's been to Chicago. Right, Abigail?"

"Some years back. Had a friend who lived there. She owned a bar."

"Really?" Gianna said, settling on the couch. "Which one? Maybe I know it."

"Nah, it's been too long ago now. She sold it and retired. Passed on, she did."

"Oh, well, I'm sorry to hear that."

"No need to be sorry. It's what happens to us all." Her gaze shifted to the window and she stared longingly out at the sea. Gianna wondered how many hours a day she sat doing just that. She supposed it soothed her and there was nothing wrong with that. After all, who wouldn't be able to relax with that view?

"So, Abigail, Kiera and I have been talking," Gianna said.

"I know." She didn't break her stare out the window. "And I reckon it was about me." She turned and pinned Gianna with a hard look, her jaw set firm. "I'm telling you right now, I ain't going to no nursing home. So don't let me hear it even come out of your mouth. You got that?"

Lizzie grabbed her hand in an attempt to calm her. But Abigail pulled her hand away. "Now, Abigail, let's not get upset," Lizzie said. "You haven't even heard what Dr. Walford has to say."

"I don't care to know," she let out.

"Actually," Gianna said. "You might care. Because it involves a plan to keep you right here at home."

"Is that so?" Abigail said, seemingly unconvinced.

"It is." Gianna looked to Kiera who nodded. Gianna continued. "Kiera has offered to move in here with you for the time being. To help out."

"No," Abigail said.

Gianna smiled, hoping to disarm her a little. "Abigail, it is my recommendation that you receive full-time care. And Kiera is willing to provide that full-time care right here with you, in your home."

"I don't care. I don't want it."

"But you need it, Abigail," Lizzie tried.

"Otherwise, I'm afraid you'll need to either hire someone to come in and stay with you, or you'll need to move into a facility where you can be appropriately cared for."

Abigail set her jaw again and looked from Lizzie to Gianna to Kiera.

"You're ganging up on me and I don't like it. Don't like it one bit."

"We're trying to help you, Abigail," Kiera said. "We only want what's best for you and we all agree that what's best is to do as you wish and keep you right here at home."

"Malarky. I'm fine. You can keep coming to check on me like you've been doing."

Kiera walked over to her. She knelt beside Lizzie and took her hand. "Abigail, look at me. Please." Abigail did. "You need help. You need someone here. You fell today. And God only knows how long you would've been stuck on the floor had I not stopped by. That's scary. And it's not okay or something we can ignore."

"It was an accident. Those blessed slippers—"

"And what if another accident happens tonight, Abigail? Or tomorrow?"

She seemed to have no answer for that.

"Please," Kiera said. "I just want you to be safe. I want you to be okay."

"You do?"

Kiera smiled. "Of course, I do. So, let me help you, Abigail. Let me stay with you. I'll stay out of your hair as much as I possibly can, I promise."

"You won't yammer on and on and talk my ear off?"

"No." She laughed. "I promise."

Abigail again looked to Lizzie and Gianna. "You think this is what's best?"

"We do," Gianna said.

Abigail sighed. "Oh, alright. Do what you must do."

Kiera hugged her, which caused her to groan. Then she planted a big kiss on her forehead. "Thank you, Abigail."

"Yeah, yeah. Just quit kissing on me, will ya?"

Gianna packed up her bag and placed her hands on her hips, truly relieved that Abigail agreed to the help. "Okay, now that that's settled, it's time to talk about your bedroom."

Abigail whipped her head up to look at Gianna who couldn't help but laugh.

It seemed the battle wasn't over just yet.

Chapter Twenty-seven

Gary crept along the overgrown weeds in the dark, crouched low, moving as quietly as he could. When he reached the older Ford F150 pickup truck, he cracked the unlocked door, froze to listen for any sounds that someone in the house had awoke, and then climbed inside when he heard nothing but silence. He remained low, and covered his small penlight with his palm as he flicked it on.

He again stilled, listening for any signs of disturbance. He heard nothing and he proceeded, shining the light solely on the steering column which he managed to crack open with the flathead screwdriver he retrieved from his back pocket. Working quickly, he exposed the necessary wires and traded his screwdriver for his knife which he used to splice the wires. Then, holding the penlight in his mouth, he touched the two wires together, once, twice, three times until the engine sparked to life. Quickly, he twisted the wires together and raised up in the seat. He put the truck in drive, careful to keep the headlights off, and drove slowly over the overgrown lawn to the road. With one brief look in the rearview mirror, which showed nothing but darkness back in the house, he pressed on the gas and pulled out onto the pavement.

He gained speed gradually and switched on his lights and finally allowed himself to breathe, removing the penlight from his mouth. Sweat ran down his forehead and he palmed it away and tossed the penlight onto the seat next to him. He'd gotten himself a vehicle. A rather nice one at that. Even if it was a model from the early nineties. It was pretty well taken care of and he knew it would be missed, so after he checked the gas gauge to make sure he had plenty of fuel, he pulled into the first busy restaurant he saw and switched out the license plates.

He worked quickly, like he had before with hot-wiring the truck, and no one seemed to see him. He climbed back into the truck and headed out, feeling much better. Now all he had to do was put some miles between him and that house. He'd drive the truck all night long, stopping at a couple of truck stops along the way, hoping to find Mayweather. Once he found him, he'd be on to Jenny.

And he couldn't wait to find her.

Chapter Twenty-eight

The next couple of days seemed to fly by as Henry and Charlie came to help move Abigail's bedroom downstairs and to move Jenny into the big house. Lizzie and Gianna stopped by when they could, in the evenings, to check on things, which was nice. Jenny enjoyed seeing Gianna again, and she was more and more impressed by her compassion for Abigail and her kind and giving nature. She made sure Abigail had everything she needed for a smooth transition downstairs and even suggested that they order her a reclining bed. Abigail fought it at first, but Gianna convinced her, ensuring her that insurance would most likely pay for it, since it was medically necessary. Abigail had trouble getting out of bed without assistance, something she hadn't wanted to admit. But Jenny had discovered it the first morning she'd awakened at the house and went into Abigail's room to check on her. She'd found her in her bed, struggling to sit up and she'd told Gianna about it, who had then suggested the reclining bed.

Once they got that settled, things seemed to fall into place rather quickly. Jenny was moved in and Henry was just getting ready to follow Charlie out the door after they'd done a quick run to bring back some groceries.

"Say, Henry?" Jenny said, as she followed him out the door.

"Yeah?" His prominent Adam's apple bulged as he swallowed. A soft downy mustache marked his upper lip and she smiled, assuming he was trying to grow in some facial hair. He and Charlie really were just boys. But they were good boys. Polite young men, and very helpful.

She handed him an envelope. "Can you mail this for me next time you're in the city?"

"Sure."

"Thanks."

She'd made sure not to put a return address and she hoped with the postmark being from out of Cliffside, that it wouldn't pinpoint where she was. For all Floyd knew she could be in any of the numerous areas surrounding the city. Not that it would matter much. Floyd wouldn't come looking for her. She knew that without a doubt. Still, it was better to play it safe.

Henry gave her his trademark salute and trotted down the stairs. She watched him and Charlie drive away in the loud pickup truck and then went back inside to escape the chill. Abigail was settled in her chair, and the fire was crackling in the wood stove, gently heating the house. It was a peaceful moment and the home felt welcoming, cozy even. Like the cottage, which Jenny knew she was going to miss. But there were perks to living at Abigail's. For one thing, everything was bigger. The kitchen, her bedroom, the living room. So there was plenty of room to breathe and stretch out without stepping on Abigail's toes. The only downside she could foresee was the temperature Abigail kept the house at. She liked it considerably cooler than Jenny, so Jenny had taken to wearing layers to stay warm, which was mostly effective, so it really wasn't any big deal.

"Would you like some tea, Abigail?" Jenny asked her.

"Hm?" She broke her trance from staring out the window.

"Tea?"

"I reckon."

Jenny put the kettle on and sat at the kitchen table. Henry had brought her the newspaper from the city and she perused it carefully, searching for anything about the case in North Carolina. But there was nothing. Just as she figured. What she really needed was a computer to do an online search. But Abigail didn't have one and she wasn't sure where to find one.

She perked up.

The library. Surely there must be a public library somewhere.

She'd have to ask the boys or Lizzie or Gianna when she saw them again.

Adrenaline shot through her as she thought about searching for her hometown online. Were the police looking for her? Was she considered just missing, or was she a wanted woman? Or had they wised up and arrested Gary for Ken's murder? If not, then where was Gary? Was he looking for her?

Chills ran down her spine as she recalled the way he'd sat watching her in his truck after she'd crashed into the tree. He'd tried to kill her and his cold, dead stare was one she'd never forget or hoped to ever see again.

She refolded the newspaper and shoved it aside. She'd offer to read it to Abigail, along with the gossip magazines she favored. Jenny might not watch much television or keep up with the popular gossip, but Abigail sure did. And she made sure to watch her "stories" daily. So Jenny had taken to watching the soap operas with her and she'd found it quite easy to pick up on the storylines and become engrossed.

Jenny glanced at the clock as the kettle whistled. It was nearly time for the next soap. She quickly made their tea and carried the tray over to the coffee table. And after setting Abigail's mug on the table next to her, she settled on the couch and flicked on the TV with the remote. She carefully sipped her own tea as she and Abigail watched the drama unfold for the next hour. It was nice to get lost in something other than her own problems for once. So much so, that she nearly fell asleep she was so content and relaxed. She fought the fatigue, however, and eventually rose to make their lunch. Abigail liked to help, so they worked together making tomato soup and grilled cheese sandwiches, which they ate at the table.

"Ruby loved tomatoes," Abigail blurted.

Jenny paused, spoon held halfway to her mouth. "Pardon?"

"Ruby," Abigail said, louder this time. "She loved tomatoes."

"Did she?" Jenny wondered how much Abigail knew about her great-aunt. "I didn't know that."

"Course you didn't. You're just a young thing. Probably were too young to remember much about her likes and dislikes. But she did. She loved tomatoes. Used to make her own tomato juice even."

"No kidding?"

Abigail set down her spoon and smiled. "She did. She'd grow those tomatoes, pick 'em when they were just ripe, and squeeze them into a jug and add plenty of salt. She loved it. Would sip on that for days and just grin like the dickens. Hell, I've even seen her eat a tomato like an apple. Just bite into the side of it and let the juice run down her chin."

"Wow," Kiera said, imagining it. "She really did love tomatoes."

"I wouldn't lie, kid. I'm telling ya she did." Abigail grew quiet and her smile faded. "She also loved Doris Day. Would play her records for hours at a time. Even tried to fancy her hair like hers at one point. But that didn't last long. Ruby never was meant to be blond."

"Ruby went blond?" Jenny said, dumbfounded. "I would've loved to have seen that."

"I got a picture of that somewhere around here."

"Really?" Jenny brightened.

"Somewheres."

"We'll have to find it."

"I got loads of pictures in a box under one of them beds somewheres."

Jenny wanted to get up immediately and search, but she refrained. They had a meal to finish and the photos weren't going anywhere.

"So how did you know my aunt Ruby again?" Jenny asked.

Abigail's face drew in as if somebody had pulled a thread to tighten her eyes and mouth. "I told you. She was a dear friend."

"I know, I just wondered how you met. How you knew her."

"I didn't always live here, kid. I grew up in North Carolina."

Jenny nearly choked on her grilled cheese. "You did?"

"Yes, sir. Born and raised. Didn't move out here to Oregon until fifty-some years ago. When I was in my forties."

"Gosh. I had no idea, Abigail. What made you move?"

Her face drew tighter. "That's enough of that now. Finish your sandwich. We got washing up to do."

"Then we'll look for the photos?"

She shifted in her seat as if suddenly uncomfortable. "If you're that determined to see them."

Jenny smiled. "I can't wait." She wanted to learn about Ruby, and about Abigail. Who was she? Who had she been? And why was she so secretive?

Jenny considered her own life and her own secrets and wondered if Abigail's life was anything like hers. She shook the thought away, knowing how unlikely it was that Abigail had dealt with anyone like Gary coming after her. Or had been witness to a murder, for God's sake. Whatever her story, Jenny was sure it wasn't as crazy as hers.

She's probably just a private person. That's all.

Jenny finished her sandwich and cleaned up their dishes in the sink, with Abigail drying with her trembling hands. It seemed no matter how badly she felt, Abigail still insisted on trying to help or to do things herself. Jenny had learned rather quickly to stop fighting her on it, because it was pointless and an argument she could not win. Abigail was determined and that was all there was to it. She was going to do things and Jenny figured it was probably good for her to move about. Sitting in a chair all day long couldn't be healthy, even if Abigail was older and a bit frail.

Jenny didn't see the harm in letting her do what she pleased around the house. After all, she was right there with her, making sure she didn't hurt herself or take a spill. So, it was working out. They were falling into a daily routine, working as a team, and for the most part, Abigail seemed to enjoy having her around.

She'd only bickered about it for the first few hours after Jenny had moved in. But then she'd seemed to let it go and embrace the new arrangement.

Now they worked together, had long spells where they both seemed content to be silent, and then spent some time talking, discussing the soaps or the weather or what they needed Henry to bring by from the store. All in all, things were going okay and Jenny was relieved.

So when they finished the dishes and wiped down the table and pushed in the chairs, Jenny began looking for the box of photos, leaving Abigail in her chair by the window, sipping more hot tea.

Jenny went from one bedroom to the other, looking beneath the beds until she found what she was sure was the correct box. It was a hard, glossy one with a flower pattern and a secured lid. She slid it out, dusted it off, and pulled off the top. Inside were dozens and dozens of photos. Jenny ran her hand through the loose piles and plucked one up that caught her eye.

She sat back on her haunches as she examined the old black-and-white photo. It was one of Ruby, her great-aunt, whom she recognized right away, regardless of the short blond hair. But there was someone next to her, someone she was embracing. It was a woman, but she was wearing men's clothes and had her hair pulled back in a tight ponytail. Jenny lifted the photo closer for a better look. Then she reared back with true shock and surprise.

The woman holding her aunt Ruby was Abigail.

CHAPTER TWENTY-NINE

Lizzie hung up the phone as Gianna returned to the office after having seen her sixth patient so far that day. Gianna sighed, feeling physically drained, and went to sit at her desk where she sipped on her cup of tepid coffee and searched her drawer for a fun-size Kit Kat bar.

"Don't you think it's strange?" Lizzie asked as she watched Gianna tear into the small candy bar.

"What?"

"That Kiera Davenport doesn't have a cell phone."

Gianna cocked her head as she chewed. "Was that her on the phone?"

"It was. And I just think it's weird that she always has to call from Abigail's landline instead of just sending you or me a text."

Gianna swallowed. "Maybe she can't afford one?" She knew Kiera didn't have a lot of money.

"One of those little burner phones don't cost much, do they? She could buy only as many minutes as she needed."

Gianna sat perplexed. She'd seen Kiera checking out the phones at Walmart, but she'd left them just as soon as Gianna had walked up next to her.

"It's weird, Doc. This day and age…"

Gianna was silent for a moment, thinking. It was rather odd. Why wouldn't she have a phone? It would be so much more convenient. Especially in contacting her or Lizzie about the bed they'd ordered for Abigail. Or about anything really.

"I don't know," Gianna said. "I guess she just doesn't want one."

"Yeah, but why? I can't think of any reason why someone wouldn't want one."

Gianna shrugged. "Maybe she's got a thing against technology." It was possible. But then why check out the phones at Walmart at all?

Lizzie shook her head. "Whatever the reason, it's weird."

"Okay, enough with the weird talk. You've got more patients to call back."

Lizzie made a face at her and left to see to the waiting patients, leaving Gianna alone with her thoughts.

Lizzie was right. It was a bit strange. So was the way she'd just appeared and moved in at Rhydian Hill. According to the woman who owned the crystal and gem shop, Violet, Kiera had literally walked in her store one day and asked where to find Abigail's house, perplexing her and eventually, the entire town. No one knew who she was or where she'd come from, and Abigail hadn't had any visitors in decades.

The only clue to who Kiera Davenport was what Gianna knew. She'd seen her in Flagstaff at that little restaurant. She was certain. But she couldn't seem to get any more info than that. Kiera wasn't listed in Flag, or Arizona for that matter. Wasn't listed anywhere. She knew because she'd checked and checked some more. So who was she? And why was her identity such a mystery?

Was she in some sort of trouble? She had been with a man who'd seemed to usher her away and help her into a big truck. Were they related somehow? Or maybe…she'd just been along for the ride?

Gianna straightened in her chair. Truckers were known to sometimes give people rides. They weren't supposed to, but that didn't stop them from doing it. She rubbed her temples and tried to remember the trucking company written across the door of the cab.

Damn it, she could see the blue cab, see the neon green lettering, but she couldn't recall the words.

She opened her laptop to search for trucking companies with blue cabs. But Lizzie popped her head in the door before she could type anything.

"Patient in two is ready."

"Thank you." She closed the computer and stood to stretch and take another swallow of coffee. "Will you go in the house and get me a Diet Coke from the fridge? Get yourself one too, if you like."

Lizzie disappeared down the hall as Gianna knocked and slid into room number two. As she listened to and examined her patient, her mind kept drifting back to Kiera. Would she ever find the answers she was seeking about her? Or would she forever remain a mystery?

She hoped not. She'd like to get to know her. But would Kiera ever allow that? There were brief moments when Gianna would see a flicker of interest in her eyes and others when she could swear she saw the flames of desire. Was she just imagining it? Wanting it to be true?

And what am I doing having those kind of hopes anyway? Especially with such a secretive woman?

Maybe I should just flat-out ask her about Flagstaff.

It wasn't doing either of them any good in ignoring the fact that they recognized each other from that restaurant. At least it wasn't doing her any good. She couldn't speak for Kiera.

She refocused on her patient, who'd finally finished filling her in on her grandson, and ended the exam with some advice and a new prescription. She walked her out and headed back to the office. Lizzie was on the phone again as she entered. She hung up and smiled.

"The bed arrived."

"Abigail's? Already?"

"Yes. It's being delivered and assembled now."

"Excellent." *That'll give me an excuse to stop by.*

She cracked open her icy can of Diet Coke and took a hearty sip. God, it tasted good. More caffeine to the rescue.

"What do you want to do for lunch?" Gianna checked her watch. They should've broken for their meal an hour and a half ago.

"I don't know. How about Mercury's? I could do with a good burrito."

"Sounds great." She liked eating at the local spicy food haunt and the takeout was just as fabulous.

Lizzie gathered her purse. "You want the same thing as before? That 'Hot as the Sun' burrito with chicken?"

"Uh-huh."

"Got it. I'll be right back."

"Anybody else waiting?"

"Not at the moment." She looked at the clock on the wall. "Your one thirty canceled and your two o'clock isn't here yet. So you've got some time."

Gianna sank into her chair and sipped more of her Diet Coke. Lizzie left and Gianna eyed the phone. After a few moments, when she was sure Lizzie was gone, she lifted the receiver and dialed Abigail's number, which she now knew by heart.

Kiera answered right away, sounding breathless. It made Gianna's heart skip a beat.

"Kiera? Hi, it's Gianna."

"Oh. Hello."

"I heard the bed arrived."

"Yes, they're here now, they just walked in."

"Oh, well, that's great news. I won't keep you. I just wanted to maybe stop by later. See how Abigail likes the bed. Would that be okay?"

"Sure. We'd—uh—it would be nice to see you."

"Great. See you a bit later."

"Okay then, goodbye."

"Bye."

Gianna replaced the receiver and opened her personal laptop. She did a search for the trucking company with the blue cabs and got a few hits. She searched images until she found one that looked familiar. She clicked on the image and zoomed in. Yes. That was the one.

Ride Right Trucking. Out of Knoxville, Tennessee. She chewed on her lower lip as she studied the photo. So had the trucker been driving all the way from Knoxville? Probably. But that didn't mean that's where Kiera was from. If she had gotten a ride from him, he could've picked her up anywhere.

She thought back to the way the man had behaved. He'd seemed so protective, like he'd known her better than someone he'd just picked up off the side of the road. Or then again, maybe it had been possessiveness. She wasn't sure. She lifted the phone again and dialed the number for Ride Right Trucking. A woman with a strong southern accent answered and offered her help. Gianna hesitated, unsure what to say at first. Then she spoke.

"Yes, hello. I recently saw one of your trucks driving through Flagstaff, Arizona. Is that a common route for your trucks?"

"Yes, ma'am. They have a pickup not far from there that they get on their way to California."

"They do?"

"Yes, ma'am."

Again, Gianna chewed her lip. "Is there any way I can find out who was driving through Flagstaff on that specific date? The driver was very kind to me. Helped me with a flat tire. I'd probably still be stuck there if it wasn't for him."

The woman was quiet for a moment. "I'm not supposed to give out information like that."

"Well, maybe you can, just this once. He was an older man. Stocky. Broad-shouldered, with gray hair and a gray goatee. He had on a dark blue jacket, and a worn navy blue ball cap. He was very kind."

Silence.

Then…

"That sounds like Floyd. He's been a driver for us for many years."

"Floyd?" Gianna scribbled down the name. "Does he have a last name? Or an address? I'd like to send him a thank you card."

"No, I'm sorry, I can't give you any more information than I did."

"Please, I just need—"

The line went dead. Gianna hung up and tapped her pen on the sticky notepad.

Floyd.

Floyd with Ride Right Trucking.

Shit. How was she going to find out his last name if the trucking company wouldn't give it to her? Worse, she wasn't even sure if he was the right guy.

"Damn it."

She refocused on her computer screen and did a quick search for Kiera Davenport in Knoxville. Nothing. Then she searched the state of Tennessee. She got a hit, but the person was a young athlete. She took another sip of her soda and searched the neighboring state, North Carolina. There she found a few Davenports, but none named Kiera. She searched the images, looking for any sort of clue she could find, thinking that maybe Kiera wasn't really her first name. She froze when she came to one photo in particular listed on an ancestry website.

It was an old photo, a black-and-white, and the woman was strikingly beautiful, just like Kiera. The resemblance was uncanny. Gianna read the name.

Ruby Rene Davenport.

"Ruby." She clicked on the photo and discovered that Ruby had already passed away. She had been considerably older than Kiera but they had to be related. They just looked too much alike not to be.

"It's the eyes. They look right into your soul."

She took a screen shot to keep on file and printed a hard copy for herself. She retrieved it from the printer and slid it into her desk drawer as she heard Lizzie returning with their food.

"One 'Hot as the Sun' burrito delivered right to you," Lizzie said as she deposited the warm bag in Gianna's hands.

"Now, that's what I call service," Gianna said.

Lizzie batted her eyes. "Anything for you, boss."

Gianna laughed. "Quit it." She opened her bag and pulled out her foil-wrapped burrito. "What did you get?"

"Same ol' same ol'."

"The 'Hot as Hell' nachos?"

"Yep."

"I don't know how you can eat those. Good God, they are hot."

"Mm, I know. I love 'em." She opened her Styrofoam container and plucked out a tortilla chip smothered in cheese and jalapeños and popped it in her mouth. She chewed and swallowed without so much as a flinch.

"You're insane," Gianna said, carefully removing the hot peppers from her burrito. While she loved the flavor, she didn't love the heat. So she made sure to remove the jalapeños before she even took a bite.

"So, what have you been up to?" Lizzie asked nonchalantly.

Gianna blinked. "What do you mean?"

"Your personal laptop is open. You don't usually use that here in the office."

"Oh, you know, just doing some shopping."

"You're a terrible liar, Doc."

"What?"

"You can't lie to save your life. Your face gets too red."

"Knock it off."

"Hey, I'm just saying."

Gianna pointed at her playfully. "You don't need to know everything I do, okay? Boundaries, lady."

"Ha. Yeah right. In Cliffside? Keep dreaming. Besides, I was just curious. You're so private. Everyone wants to get to know you, but you don't make it easy."

"Because you're forever trying to set me up on dates."

"Women like you. Is that so awful?"

Gianna rolled her eyes and took a bite of her burrito. It had just the right amount of heat.

"They like what they see," Lizzie said. "And they want to get to know you."

"Well, they can wait because I'm not ready to date."

Lizzie laughed. "Right. If Kiera Davenport called and asked you out, you'd go. Don't even try to deny that."

"I—" She swallowed some of her soda wrong and coughed. Lizzie laughed again. Gianna shook her head. "You're impossible."

"And you're smitten."

"Oh, I am not."

"Uh-huh. If it means anything to you, I think she is too. Henry says all she does is ask about you."

Gianna chewed and forced down a swallow. "Seriously?"

"According to him. Thought you weren't interested?"

Gianna didn't respond. Her mind was already going at warp speed, thinking about Kiera. Could she really be interested?

Gianna didn't know. But she was very much looking forward to seeing her that evening. Now more than ever.

CHAPTER THIRTY

Gary slowly pulled out of the heavily wooded area and back onto the dirt path that led to the main road. He'd spent the night in the cover of the woods, hoping to stay out of sight in his stolen truck. He'd taken a risk and kept it for a couple of days, careful to stay on back roads, traveling through numerous small towns in central North Carolina. He knew it was time to get a new vehicle, but he had one more stop to make. It was another stop that truckers favored, just outside of town. He drove straight there, tossing his paper map aside, and parked in the back of the lot, where he planned to abandon the truck.

"You've been good to me," he said, patting the dash. "But it's time to move on."

As he walked up to the truck stop restaurant, he kept his head low, thankful that there hadn't been any kind of news about him yet in the papers. The cops may have an APB out on him, however, so he still had to play it safe. But for the most part, according to the news, everyone was still searching for Jenny. She was still wanted in connection to Ken's murder, which made him laugh. The cops were clueless and he was way ahead of them.

He pushed through the glass door and ordered himself a cup of coffee at the counter. But instead of sliding onto a barstool and keeping to himself, he politely asked the waitress if she knew Mayweather. He said he was an old friend, trying to locate him.

The waitress, who's name was Pearl, raised her brow at him. "You're in luck, partner. Mayweather just walked outta here about five minutes ago. He's probably over at the pumps refueling."

Gary turned to take a quick look out the window. Then he thanked Pearl and hurried out the door. There were three trucks refueling at the moment, and he had no idea which one was Mayweather's. So he put on his best smile and walked up to the first trucker and stuck out his hand. "You Mayweather?"

The trucker seemed surprised. "No, man, I'm not. Who the hell are you?"

"Sorry." Gary left him without an answer and walked up to the second truck. The driver was nowhere to be found. Gary quickly glanced around and climbed up into the unlocked cab. He searched for papers, anything with a name on it. He found a small stack of envelopes and shoved one of them in his back pocket before he exited the cab. He waited for the driver, but then gave up and moved on to the third trucker before he drove away.

"Hey, you Mayweather?" he called up to him.

The driver started his loud, purring engine and motioned toward the convenience store. "He's in there."

Gary thanked him and backed away. As the big truck hissed and pulled away, he slid the envelope from his back pocket and read the name.

"Floyd Barns." He smacked the envelope against his palm and silently read the address, which was in Asheville. He thought about climbing back into the cab and hiding in the sleeper, but he feared Floyd finding him and he didn't want to have to get violent. At least not before he had his information on Jenny.

He crossed the parking lot and scoped out vehicles. Most of them were newer and not obtainable for the skills that he had. So he darted across traffic to a row of popular restaurants and searched there. He found a car almost immediately. An older Honda Accord, black with four doors. He easily popped the lock with his window tool and climbed inside to open the steering column and hot-wire the car. It started on the first try and he drove the car back across the street and sat and waited for Floyd who finally emerged from the store, drinking a large fountain drink.

Gary smiled to himself as Floyd drove away from the truck stop and made his way to the highway. Gary followed carefully, wondering if Floyd was going home to Asheville. He didn't have to follow long before he'd figured out that the answer was yes. They were headed for the mountains of western North Carolina.

It was perfect. Gary not only had Floyd's address, but he had him in sight.

It was only a matter of time before he'd have Jenny in his crosshairs.

Chapter Thirty-one

Jenny studied the old photo of Ruby and Abigail again, still in complete awe at what she was seeing. She had so many questions, and she was dying to know the answers, but she knew she'd have to do it at the appropriate time, otherwise Abigail wouldn't budge an inch and she'd most likely shut down. So until the right moment came, Jenny would just have to study the photo in private and keep her curiosity to herself, happy to discuss some of the other photos she'd found in the box beneath the bed. Abigail seemed okay in reminiscing about those and Jenny was enjoying the stories. She did notice how Abigail's facial expression changed when she came across photos of Ruby though. She'd visibly soften and speak fondly of her, recalling times long ago and mentioning some of the adventures they had together. Abigail made them sound like the best of friends. And perhaps they were. But the photo Jenny had found suggested they were so much more.

A knock sounded from the front door and Jenny quickly tucked the photo back into her dresser drawer and eased it closed.

She hurried out of her bedroom and called out to Abigail who'd been dozing in her chair.

"I'll get it."

Dang it, she hadn't had time to check her appearance. She'd been too caught up in the photo to pay herself any mind. Now she was almost certain that it was Gianna standing on the other side of the door and she had no idea if she looked presentable. A quick glance at her outfit comforted her a little. At least she was in jeans and a sweater rather than sweats.

She pulled open the door and smiled. "Hi."

Gianna's breath came out in a white cloud. "Hi."

"Come on in." The sun had set behind Gianna and the chill in the air was fierce. It was no wonder she was bundled up in her heavy coat and beanie hat, which she quickly slid off as she entered the house.

"Here, allow me." Jenny took her coat and hat and hung them on the hall tree. Then she stood awkwardly, taken aback by Gianna's appearance, like she always was. Today Gianna had on navy blue chinos with a blue-and-white-striped button-down. Her blond hair was twisted up into a loose bun and her wrists were adorned in an oversized silver watch and matching chunky bracelet. She looked professional, yet casual. Like you could have a serious conversation with her and yet feel more than comfortable in doing so.

Gianna rubbed her hands together in an obvious effort to warm them and faced Abigail. "So, I hear you got your bed?"

"I did," Abigail said, adjusting the light blanket on her lap. Her voice was weak and gravelly from sleep. She'd taken to napping for brief moments throughout the day and Jenny wondered how long that had been going on. If she was sitting in her chair, it seemed she was either lost in thought staring out at the sea, or she was dozing off and softly snoring.

"Care to show it off?" Gianna asked.

"Nah, I'll let Kiera show you. I'm going to stay right here in my chair."

Gianna didn't seem to take offense. But rather, she turned to Jenny once again. "I'm all yours."

Jenny felt herself burn with a blush and she moved toward Abigail's bedroom quickly, hoping Gianna didn't see it. She flicked on the light and stood to the side to allow Gianna entry. The reclining hospital-style bed sat with the head centered against the wall and Jenny had already made it up with Abigail's favorite sheets and comforter.

"Does she like it?" Gianna asked.

"She seems to. But you know Abigail, she wasn't about to make a big fuss. She just came in, laid on it, and played with the reclining button a bit. Then she was up and back in her chair in the living room to watch her afternoon soap."

Gianna chuckled. "Well, hopefully having this bed will help her. She can sleep slightly reclined if she prefers, which will help with reflux and snoring too. And she should be able to get up to go to the restroom easier as well. Do you have night lights for her?" She glanced around.

"We just leave on the little lamp in the corner."

"I'll pick you up some night lights. You should have them all over the house for you and her both."

"You don't have to do that, Gianna."

"It's no trouble. I'm happy to help."

Jenny gave her a warm smile. "Well, thank you. You've done so much already."

"Not really. I could do a whole lot more." She shoved her hands in her pockets and acted as if she'd said too much. "I just don't want to make anyone uncomfortable. Abigail…I don't think she's very fond of me."

"Oh, no, she is. She just forgets that she is sometimes. Forgets who you are."

"Her memory problems are getting that bad?"

Jenny nodded. "Some days are better than others. Today's a pretty good day. She remembered you when I told her you were stopping by. And she did okay with the guys delivering the bed."

"That's good." She focused back on the bed. "Will you show me how it works?"

Jenny hesitated. "You just use the remote—"

"Lie down and show me."

Jenny fought another blush and walked slowly to the bed where she lay down and reached for the remote. She pressed the button and showed Gianna how the bed moved up and down.

"See?" she said when she'd finished. "It's nice, isn't it?"

Gianna seemed at a loss for words. She reached for Jenny's hand and helped her to stand. "It is," she said breathlessly.

Jenny's mouth went dry as she looked into irises that seemed to be searching her own. For what, she wasn't sure. But they were searching deeply, thoroughly, nonetheless.

"Kiera," Gianna whispered, brushing her hair back from her brow. "Do you know how absolutely beautiful you are? How kind and endearing? Do you have any clue?"

Jenny was speechless, her heart tumbling over itself in her chest. She was certain that Gianna could hear it, feel it even, as if it were drumming throughout the room.

"I—no," she finally managed.

"Well, you are," Gianna said. "And I just can't seem to wait any longer." She inched closer. So close that Jenny could feel her hot breath. "I so very much want to kiss you. Would that be okay, Kiera? If I kissed you?"

Jenny closed her eyes and swayed with dizziness. Gianna steadied her and when Jenny opened her eyes, she nodded in agreement, wanting nothing more in the world in that moment than for Gianna to kiss her.

Gianna brushed her thumb across Jenny's lips and dipped in for an impossibly soft, warm kiss. It lasted only seconds, but it was enough to nearly knock Jenny off her feet because she swayed again and grew lightheaded and had to be steadied by Gianna.

"Whoa," Gianna said as she drew away to look at her with concern. "You okay?"

"Mm. Yeah." She touched her lips, still able to feel Gianna's against her. She wanted them back, needed to feel them again. She looked up at her in a silent plea for more and Gianna seemed more than happy to comply, but a distant knock sounded, causing her to stiffen.

"Is that someone at the door?" she asked.

Jenny listened. The knock came again, and this time Abigail called out for her to answer it.

"I need to get that," Jenny said, and she and Gianna headed back into the living room. Jenny rubbed her cheeks, hoping to erase the prominent brush strokes of red that she could feel were still there. Abigail's dark eyes were trained on her as she hurried to the door. Could she see the blush? Did she suspect what they'd been up to in the bedroom?

She pulled open the door, feeling exposed and uneasy. She didn't want anyone to know. It was private. Her and Gianna's own little secret. Their own little moment. God, had it really even happened? Or had it been a dream?

"Hiya," Lizzie said with her arms full of shopping bags. "How are you?"

Jenny struggled to speak, truly surprised to see her. "Uh, fine. How are you?"

"I'm just dandy, darling. I went shopping and bought you some things. Some goodies."

"Oh, well, please, come inside."

Lizzie stamped her feet on the welcome mat and then walked inside. She grinned at Gianna. "Saw your car out front. Didn't expect to see you here."

"I stopped by to check out the new bed."

"Uh-huh."

She carried the shopping bags over to the kitchen table and pulled out a new comforter in a see-through plastic bag and brought it over to show Abigail.

"Abigail, I got you some things for your new bed," she said. "It's a new comforter. A heavier one. One that will keep you warmer."

Abigail studied the comforter for a moment. "I like the comforter I got. Keeps me plenty warm."

Lizzie laughed but it was filled with nerves. "But you see, this one is better. It's—"

"I said I'm plenty warm. That's the trouble with all you young people. You don't appreciate what you have. You're always replacing things when they don't need to be replaced."

Lizzie pressed her lips together and turned to face Jenny and Gianna. She looked helpless.

"Abigail sleeps a little cooler than most folks, I think," Jenny said, trying to explain.

"Oh. Well, do you need a comforter, Kiera?"

"No, that's not necessary—"

"Yes," Gianna said. "She does. The one she bought at Walmart in no way can be warm enough for her in this house."

Lizzie seemed pleased. "Good, then I'll just go put this stuff on your bed and you can use it. I got you some flannel sheets as well."

"Lizzie, I…" Jenny started.

Gianna touched her arm. "Just let her. It's not like you don't need it."

Jenny sighed. "You guys are too kind. You really are."

"You're helping Abigail. So we want to help you too."

Jenny smiled but a tear formed in her eye. She wiped it away, hoping Gianna hadn't seen.

"Hey," Gianna said. "No need to cry."

"I'm not."

"Liar."

Jenny laughed. "I'm just so…moved. Truly."

"You deserve this," Gianna said softly, tugging her in for an embrace. "Whatever or wherever you came from, you deserve this right now. Okay? You're safe. You're with people who care."

Jenny felt her heart pound. She drew away and wiped her eyes again. Gianna was referring to her past and she didn't know why or what all she knew, but she didn't like it.

"Kiera, I didn't mean to scare you. I just meant—we've seen each other before, back in Flagstaff and—"

"Okay, you're all set," Lizzie said, emerging from the bedroom. "One new complete set of bed clothes is all ready for you to wash and put on your bed."

Jenny forced a smile at her. "Thank you, Lizzie."

"No sweat." She looked from Jenny to Gianna. "What's going on? Did someone's best dog die or something?"

"No," Gianna said. "Nothing's wrong."

"Well, something's obviously up, but I don't have time to try to find out what. I got Charlie at home cooking so that means I need to get home before the smoke alarm starts going off." She waved to Abigail. "I'll see you later, Abigail."

"I hope not too soon," Abigail said, causing Lizzie to roll her eyes.

"I'll keep that in mind." She shook her head and linked her arm in Gianna's. "Come on, toots. Let's get out of here before we overstay our welcome."

Gianna looked helplessly at Jenny but slid into her coat and hat all the same.

"Thank you again, for all your help," Jenny said, showing them out.

"Don't mention it," Lizzie said, bounding out the door ahead of Gianna.

Gianna turned to Jenny, a look of sadness and concern on her face. "Please take care," she said. "And I'll see you again soon, yes?"

Jenny pressed her lips together for a soft small smile. She nodded, unsure what to say.

Gianna seemed to accept that and she turned and walked away.

Jenny closed the door, not bothering to watch her drive away this time. Because this time she was too worried about what Gianna knew to do so.

CHAPTER THIRTY-TWO

Gianna rolled over in bed as the phone continued to ring and flash, illuminating her bedroom like lightning in a thunderstorm.

"Hello?" she groaned as she answered the call.

"G?"

"Yeah?" She sat up, recognizing the voice but still shocked nonetheless.

"You're asleep?"

"Yes, why wouldn't I be?" Gianna checked the bedside clock. It was six o'clock and the sun had still yet to rise.

"Wait, what time is it there?"

Gianna sighed and ran her hand through her hair. "It's six. What do you want, Tiffany?"

"Oh, shit. I forgot about the time difference. You're usually up early and I just didn't even give the time a second thought."

"I'm in private practice now, remember? So I'm not up as early as I used to be."

"So…how's that treating you? The private practice?"

Gianna flicked on the bedside lamp and slid into her fuzzy slippers. "I know you didn't call me this early to chitchat, Tiffany, so what gives?"

"Actually, I did. I just wanted to know how you were doing and to, you know, see if you missed me as much as I miss you."

Gianna stood. "Are you kidding me right now?"

"No, I'm not. I really miss you, G. Like a lot. You're all I think about."

"Too bad you weren't thinking of me when you were in bed with—"

"Stop. Okay? Don't go there."

"Don't go there?" Gianna headed downstairs, flicking on lights as she went. The house was cold and she'd forgotten to put on her robe, so she stopped to adjust the thermostat before making her way into the kitchen to start the Keurig. "How can I not go there, when you literally did? You invited her into our bed. OUR bed, Tiffany. Do you know how twisted that is? I mean if you want to fuck her, do it somewhere else at the very least."

"Look, I said I'm sorry, okay? I messed up. Really badly. I get that. But I can't make it go away. I wish I could. I wish I could just make it disappear and have you back in my arms right now."

Gianna scoffed. "Not a chance."

"Why not?"

"Are you serious?"

"I've apologized again and again. Begged you to come back. I said I'll do anything and I mean it."

"What's really going on, Tiffany? Did she dump you? Is that it?"

Silence.

"I don't know what she has to do with anything," Tiffany said.

"So, she did. Well, now things make a whole lot more sense."

"What's that supposed to mean?"

"Goodbye, Tiffany."

"Wait. Gianna—"

Gianna ended the call and turned off her phone. She knew Tiffany would keep calling and she wasn't in the mood to deal with her anymore. It was early. She was still half asleep and she was cranky, thanks to that wake-up call.

She made her coffee and sipped on it as she went upstairs to shower and dress. She took her time and languished under the hot spray, letting it work her tight muscles. When she emerged, she wiped the steam from the mirror, combed her hair, and dressed. Then she returned downstairs and nearly jumped out of her skin as a pounding came from the door.

"Doc! Doc, open up!"

It was Lizzie and she sounded frantic. Gianna answered the door. Lizzie made a clamor as she came in, red-faced and breathless.

"What's wrong?" Gianna asked, grabbing her shoulders.

"Your phone. It keeps going to voice mail. I've been trying to reach you—"

"Never mind that. Tell me what's wrong."

"It's Nancy Haas. We have to go now."

Gianna pulled on her coat and hat, grabbed her medical bag, and followed Lizzie outside to her running vehicle. Lizzie peeled out of the drive and Gianna tugged off her beanie to twist her damp hair up into a bun. She pummeled Lizzie with questions, to which she got very limited answers. The truth was, Lizzie didn't know much. Willow, Nancy's daughter, had called her, saying her mother was having trouble waking and that she was scared.

"Where's Derek?" Gianna asked as they sped through town to emerge on the opposite end, where the woods grew dense once more.

"He's working."

"Where? Close by?"

Lizzie shook her head. "He's a trucker."

Gianna cursed under her breath. "Has EMS been called?"

"I was getting ready to hang up and call EMS when Nancy finally woke and spoke into the phone. She begged me not to call an ambulance because Derek would have a fit over the cost. She sounded really bad. It was obvious she was in a lot of pain."

"Shit," Gianna said, aloud this time.

Lizzie braked hard and made a turn down a dirt road. They bumped along until they came to a clapboard two-story house lit up by a single pole light in the front yard. Gianna rushed from the vehicle, followed closely by Lizzie, and knocked on the front door.

It was opened immediately by Willow who stood looking ashen with fear.

"Where's your mama?" Lizzie asked.

She pointed up the stairs. Gianna hurried up them, taking two at a time. She could hear Lizzie close behind her.

"Mrs. Haas?" Gianna called as she cleared the stairs and began peeking into bedrooms. She found her in the one at the end of the hall, huddled in bed with a small bedside lamp glowing next to her, lighting up the sweat coating her skin.

"Mrs. Haas," Gianna whispered as she came to her bedside. "It's Dr. Walford. Can you tell me what's going on?"

She hugged her knees and moaned. "I told Lizzie not to come. Derek will be so mad."

"Don't worry about your husband," Gianna said. "Just tell me, are you in pain?" Gianna touched her forehead. She was burning up with fever.

"I'm fine," she mumbled, but then cried out in agony.

"Tell the doc what's wrong," Lizzie said. "You've got to, honey. It's the only way it's going to go away."

"Is it your stomach?" Gianna asked.

She nodded.

"Can you show me?"

She cradled her knees and cried. "It hurts."

"I need to see, Mrs. Haas. Please. Can you ease onto your back for me? It will only take a moment."

Slowly, Nancy rolled onto her back and allowed Gianna to gently straighten her legs.

"Good, now point to where it hurts."

She did and Gianna palpated the area, causing her to cry out again in excruciating pain.

Gianna turned to Lizzie. "Call EMS. Tell them it's her appendix."

"No!" Nancy gripped Gianna's hand. "We can't afford an ambulance."

"Mrs. Haas, if you don't get into surgery as soon as possible, you could die."

"Then you take me. You drive me. Please."

"You can't even walk. And you need a line put in—"

"Please. I'm begging you. I'm not going otherwise."

"Let's just take her," Lizzie said. "Instead of standing here arguing with her."

Gianna helped her sit up. "I'm going to try and carry you," Gianna said. "It's going to hurt."

Gianna carefully lifted her into her arms, thanked God she was a petite woman, and slowly made her way downstairs while Lizzie gathered up the kids. Gianna settled Nancy into the back seat of Lizzie's car and got in next to her while the children crammed in around her, both in the front and back. Lizzie then peeled out once again.

"Is Mama going to be okay?" Blaze asked, craning his head to look at Gianna from the front seat.

"Shh, let the lady doctor work on her," his older sister said, wrapping her arm around him, encouraging him to face front.

Gianna called ahead to the hospital and apprised them of the situation. She did her best to keep Nancy calm.

"Derek," Nancy said, between breaths. "Someone should call him."

"I'll handle it," Gianna said.

"He doesn't like you."

"I really don't care," Gianna said.

Lizzie spoke up. "I'll call him, don't you worry."

"The kids," she said next. "Where will they go?"

"They'll be okay," Gianna said. "You have my word."

Nancy swallowed. "Thank you." Her eyes drifted closed and Gianna gently shook her.

"Mrs. Haas?" She didn't stir. Gianna called out to Lizzie. "How much further?"

"We're here." She pulled into the emergency bay and skidded to a stop. Gianna pushed open the door and yelled for the staff who came running out with a gurney. They loaded Nancy onto it and Gianna left Lizzie with the kids to give the best update she could to the staff. Ten minutes later, they were wheeling Nancy up to surgery.

Gianna walked slowly back outside and found Lizzie still sitting with the kids in the car.

"What's the word?" Lizzie asked.

"She's in surgery."

"You going to stay?"

"For a while. You'll be alright with the kids?"

Lizzie nodded. Blaze was fast asleep in his sister's arms.

"Is she going to be okay?" The girl wanted to know. She was older than Blaze and Willow and seemed to know the seriousness of the situation.

"She will," Gianna said, touching her cheek. "You just look after your siblings, okay?"

Gianna backed away from the car.

"Keep me posted," Lizzie said.

"I will," she said as she watched them drive away. She headed back inside with her adrenaline finally starting to decrease. The feeling was familiar, though it had been a while. Not since Chicago had she been so keyed up over a patient, and now that she was starting to come down, all sorts of things were going through her mind. For one, she wondered why Nancy was so terrified of upsetting Derek? Two, what had prompted Tiffany to call her again out of the blue? And three…was Nancy already too far gone to make it through surgery?

She hoped not. For the kids' sake she hoped not.

She sank down into a waiting room chair and rested her head in her hands.

It seemed things in Cliffside weren't as peaceful as she'd hoped.

CHAPTER THIRTY-THREE

The manufactured home sat on a two-acre lot all alone in the woods on the outskirts of Asheville. Gary kept a close eye on it and its two occupants from his position nestled back into the trees, parked in the Honda Accord he'd managed to procure. He wasn't parked close so he had to squint to see when Floyd and the woman he assumed to be his wife went out and about, but he was seeing enough to get a good feel for the house and the surrounding property.

He lay in wait for two days before he was satisfied with his plan and ready to carry it out. So on the second day, when the sun set behind the mountains, he crawled from his car with his knife in hand, and walked across the crunchy, frozen grass to the front door. He knocked in a familiar way, like maybe he was a friend coming to visit.

The porch light came to life and the door opened a crack and the woman peered out.

"Who are you?" she said.

Gary smiled. "Floyd home?"

"Yeah, who are you?" she asked again.

"A friend." He slammed into the door, shoving her backwards and onto her rear. She screamed as she crawled like a crab, trying to escape him. He brandished his weapon and kicked the door closed behind him. Floyd emerged from the hallway, bath towel wrapped around his sizable waist and shaving cream dripping from his face.

"Who are you?" he demanded.

Gary laughed. "Is that all you people can say?" He held up the knife. "All you need to know is this, got it?"

Floyd nodded and went to help his wife up off the floor.

"No," Gary said, stopping him. "You go sit on the couch. She can get up by herself."

"But she's hurt."

"She's fine. Aren't you, sister?"

She nodded furiously and scrambled to her feet. She sat on the couch and clung to Floyd as she struggled to breathe.

"What do you want?" Floyd asked.

"I ask the questions," Gary said, strolling into the kitchen to open the fridge. He was ravenous after having sat in the car for two days without so much as a crumb to eat. He found a container of food, opened the lid, smelled it, and then searched for a fork. He found one in a drawer and dug into the cold, flavored noodles. He continued to eat as he came to stand in front of the frightened couple.

"You want some pants?" he asked Floyd, who was shivering worse than his wife.

Gary looked to the woman. "What's your name?"

"Mel," she squeaked.

"Mel, why don't you go get him some pants? And grab a towel while you're at it for his face."

She nodded but didn't flinch, she just clung to Floyd.

"Go," Gary said. "Now."

She stood and disappeared into the bedroom. Gary called out after her. "You call anyone and I kill him, understood?"

Mel was gone for a few seconds and then returned pale-faced and breathless, carrying a pair of flannel pajama pants and a towel. She handed both to Floyd.

"Dress," Gary said, as he shoved more noodles in his mouth. He eased onto the chair across from them and swallowed.

Floyd pulled the pants up under his towel and secured them. Then he wiped the shaving cream from his face.

"Sit," Gary instructed him.

"What do you want?" Floyd asked again.

Gary chewed one last bite and set the container aside. Then he withdrew his knife again. "I'm looking for someone. Her name is Jenny. And you're going to tell me where she is."

Mel cried as she looked to Floyd. "I told you helping those girls like that would lead to trouble."

"Shh," Floyd said.

Gary chuckled. "I know you helped her, Floyd. No sense in trying to hide it. She was with you. So you might as well tell me where you took her. Save us all a lot of trouble."

"I don't know where she is," he said, setting his jaw.

Gary tsked. "See, now, Floyd. I know you're lying. And lying, well, it pisses me off something fierce."

He picked his fingernails with the knife. "And this knife, it's sharp and all. But this here screwdriver, well, it gets the job done too. It's just a lot more painful." He slid the screwdriver from his back pocket and held it up for them to see.

Mel sobbed and buried her face in Floyd's chest. She mumbled as she cried. "He didn't do anything. Didn't do anything but give her a ride."

"Where to?" Gary asked. "That's all I want to know."

"California," Floyd finally said as he comforted Mel. "That's all I know." But his eyes shifted, ever so slightly, to the end table on the other side of Mel. Gary caught it and he knew it was the look of a man concerned about something.

"Something over there?" Gary asked. "Something, perhaps, you don't want me to see?" He set his weapons down on the ottoman and stood to examine the contents of the table. Next to a water glass and lamp, was a pile of mail. Gary grabbed the stack and returned to his seat where he began sifting through the papers. He hummed as he riffled through the envelopes, all of which were open.

"Let's see here," he said. He came to one addressed to Floyd with no return address. He plucked out the letter inside and grinned from ear to ear as he saw the signature at the bottom. "Well, well,

well. Look at what I found?" He held up the pages for them to see and then he began to read aloud. Mel sniffled and Floyd seemed to grow angry, because the veins in his prominent neck bulged and he kept flexing his jaw.

Gary finished reading, enjoying that doing so had upset them. Served them right for lying to him.

He turned the envelope over and noted the postage mark.

He grinned again. "Oregon, eh? I've always wanted to go there." He tucked the letter back into the envelope and stuffed it into his back pocket. He stood again and carried his knife over to the trembling couple sitting on the couch. "Now, tell me exactly where she is and I'll get out of your hair."

"I don't know," Floyd said, his nostrils flaring.

"Come on now, Floyd. Tell the truth. Otherwise, Mel here, well, she's going to bleed. And you wouldn't want that, would you?" He brought the knife closer to Mel and lightly traced it along her cheek.

Floyd bolted up from the couch and tackled him. Mel screamed. Gary had the breath knocked from him and he fought to push Floyd away, but the man was like dead weight. With a loud grunt and a force he didn't know he had, Gary managed to roll Floyd off and crawl to his knees. His hands were coated in blood. Warm, sticky blood. Floyd's blood. And his knife was on the floor. He grabbed it and stood. Mel was still screaming.

Gary tucked the knife into his back pocket and wiped his hands on his jeans. He got right in Mel's face.

"You call the police and I'll come back and finish you. You understand?"

She nodded as she gulped for air from her sobs.

"I mean it," he said. He tossed her the towel. "Hold this to his wound."

He hurried from the house and ran across the yard to his car. He started it and sped away, knowing now exactly where he needed to go.

CHAPTER THIRTY-FOUR

Jenny padded slowly across the living room to the other side of the house where Abigail's bedroom was. As quietly as she could, she cracked the door and snuck a peek inside. Abigail was still fast asleep in her bed with the small table lamp lit in the corner. Dawn had just started to break, sending streaks of dull gray light into the slats of the blinds. She had less than an hour before Abigail would wake.

After pulling the door almost closed, Jenny shrugged into her coat, grabbed her book bag full of goods, and walked out the front door. The ocean air was fresh, crisp and heavy with moisture. She inhaled deeply as she headed down the steps, careful to mind her knee, and crossed the cold soft sand to the shore. Once at the water's edge, she stripped down to her birthday suit, left her clothes and bag in the sand, and waded out into the frigid Pacific. The hungry waves greeted her like a starving being, trying to devour her right away, trying to knock her off her feet and pull her under. It took a moment for her to find her footing, but once she did, she walked with more confidence and merged further into the water. Her teeth were chattering and her breathing was sporadic, but it felt wonderful. She felt awake and alive. She was once again at one with the sea.

Truly happy for the first time in weeks, she held her breath and slipped under an incoming wave. The cold water washed over her completely, leaving her breathless and renewed as she spurted up and arched her back toward the morning sky.

She let out a cry. A roar. A celebratory exclamation. She was here. She was okay. And nothing was going to stop her from living the life she wanted.

She closed her eyes, allowing the waves to push into her bare body as thoughts of Gianna came. Their last conversation had been keeping her up at night, along with that wonderful, earth-shattering kiss. How could a woman so effectively excite her and terrify her at the same time?

Jenny still wondered what all she knew and why she'd said the things she'd said. She couldn't possibly know who she was or where she was from. No way. So what was she so worried about?

Because she looked at me like she knew. Like she could see into the depths of my soul.

Jenny opened her eyes and took one final dip beneath the waves. She rode them to shore and when they pushed her out, she hugged herself and hurried over to her bag and dug out her towel. She wrapped it around herself and brushed her hair away from her face so she could better see the house. A light was on in the kitchen now, which meant that Abigail was up.

Jenny gathered her clothes, shoved them into the bag, and crossed the sand to walk up the steps. Her knee still wasn't completely healed, but it was getting there and swimming in the cold sea had helped to numb the dull ache that so often bothered her.

She was just about to open the front door when she heard a loud shrill noise. A shrieking beep of sorts. Alarmed, she pushed open the door and immediately smelled smoke. It was coming from the stovetop in the kitchen.

"Abigail!" She called, running as best she could toward the flames. She skidded to a stop in front of the stove and stripped herself of her towel. She batted at the flames until they were extinguished, leaving nothing but a scorched oven mitt and some floating ashes. She pried open the kitchen windows and turned, completely breathless, and saw Abigail standing just inside the living room. She was looking at her in complete shock.

"Abigail," she breathed. "You're okay."

The smoke detector finally stopped its shrieking. The silence was deafening.

"Of course I'm okay," Abigail said. "Why wouldn't I be? And why in tarnation are you naked?"

Jenny released a long breath. "You turned on the stove and left the oven mitt too close to the flames. It caught fire."

"Caught fire?"

"Yes. Were you trying to make tea or something?"

"I reckon." She sank down onto a kitchen chair, appearing as dumbfounded as Jenny felt. "I turned on the stove?"

"You must've. I went out for a swim, so it wasn't me."

"A swim? In that cold water?"

Jenny retrieved her clothes from her bag and dressed. Then she cleaned up the mess from the stove and put the kettle on to boil. She needed some tea to warm up and to calm down. Her heart had about beat itself to death at the sight of those flames.

"What were you doing swimming in that ocean?"

Jenny sat down across from her. "I love to swim in the sea. I used to do it all the time back home."

Abigail studied her. "You're like your aunt Ruby. In so many ways. You look like her too."

Jenny smiled. "Do I?"

"She had the same dimple in her cheek and the same sparkle in her eyes. You remind me of her in so many ways."

"She was very special to you," Jenny said, thinking of the photo.

Abigail stared out the front window as if once again mesmerized by the waves. "She was."

"You ever going to tell me how you two met?"

"Lord, no. You don't want to hear that."

"Actually, I do. Especially after seeing all those photos of you two. You looked like you had so much fun together." She didn't mention the photo she had in her dresser drawer. The one where Abigail was dressed in men's clothes and holding Ruby close, like she belonged to her.

"She…well," Abigail started. "I suppose the simplest way to say it is that she ran me over."

"What?"

"She did. She was in her daddy's old Packard, learning how to drive, and she took a turn too fast, didn't see me on my bicycle and she hit me. Knocked me off my bicycle and into the bushes."

"Oh, my God." Jenny covered her mouth, unsure if she should laugh. "That's crazy."

"It hurt, I'll tell you that. I went face-first right into those bushes. Had leaves in my hair, scratches on my face. She had to help me out. And boy, was she torn up about it. She thought for sure I was mortally wounded." Abigail chuckled. "I'm not sure who was more frightened, me or her."

"But you were okay?"

"More or less. Course my daddy wasn't happy about it and he liked to tan my hide over it."

"Why? It wasn't your fault."

"I wasn't supposed to be on that bicycle. It belonged to my brother and I wasn't permitted to ride it you see. Things back then was different. Girls…they weren't supposed to do things that boys did. And my brother's bicycle was bigger than mine and off limits. But I took to sneaking and riding it anyway. Until Ruby up and hit me. After that my daddy was on to me like flies on a horse. Couldn't get away with nothin'. Nothin' that is, except spending time with Ruby. He let me do that. Thought she was good for me. Her being a church girl and all."

"But little did he know just how much trouble we got into." Abigail smiled. "She was the dickens."

"Sounds like you had a lot of fun."

"Oh, heavens yes, we did."

"I wish I had someone like that in my life," Jenny said softly.

"You do, kid. You just got to open your mind a little."

"What do you mean?"

But the tea kettle whistled and she stared off again as if lost in thought.

"Abigail?"

"Hm?"

"What did you mean by that?"

"Mean by what?"

Jenny shook her head. "Nothing. I'll get you some tea." She rose and poured them both a cup of tea. She brought Abigail hers, along with the container of sugar, and sat to watch her stir in her cubes as she sipped from her own mug.

"We got any milk?" Abigail asked.

"Yes. Would you like some?"

"I always take milk in my tea."

Jenny blinked at her. This was the first she'd heard of that. Nevertheless, she got her the milk and sat in silence as Abigail added some to her tea. The house still smelled of smoke, though not as badly, so she left her too-hot-to-drink tea and closed the windows to combat the invading cold. She cleaned up the remainder of the mess at the stove and returned to finish her tea at the table. Abigail was stirring her drink, staring endlessly into the mug.

"What brought you and Ruby apart, Abigail?"

Slowly, Abigail's gaze met hers. "Times was different than they are now."

Jenny waited but she didn't say any more. Abigail shivered and Jenny rose and helped her to her chair where she covered her with her favorite blanket and placed her cup of tea on the table next to her. Then she added some wood to the potbellied stove to warm the house.

She sat on the couch and covered herself with a thick blanket, trying to fight off the chill she felt settling in. Her hair was still damp and her skin still prickly with goose flesh. But she felt alive and free nonetheless.

She knew that she wouldn't be able to leave Abigail alone to swim again. She wouldn't be able to leave her alone under any circumstances and that posed a problem. Abigail was getting worse, things were getting dangerous. And she had things she really needed to do. Like go to the library for starters. She had to know what was going on back home.

So what was she going to do?

She needed help, someway, somehow.

There was only one person she could think to call to ask for it.

CHAPTER THIRTY-FIVE

Gianna stuck her head into the partially open hospital room door. "Knock knock." She stepped inside, made sure the coast was clear, and walked slowly over to Nancy's bed. "Mrs. Haas," she said. "How are you feeling?"

Nancy licked her parched lips as she turned her head to look at her. She attempted a smile. "I'm okay, I think."

"Yeah?" Gianna sat in the chair next to her and inched closer to hold her hand.

"They said you got me here just in time," she said with a raspy voice. "That it had just ruptured."

"We were lucky," Gianna said. "Willow, she saved your life."

A tear formed in Nancy's eye. Gianna squeezed her hand. "You should be very proud."

"I am. I just hate that she had to go through that. Hate that any of them did. I—thought it was just a cramp. I didn't know how bad it was until it was too late. Derek—he gets so upset with the doctor visits and everything because of the cost…"

"Do you not have insurance?" She couldn't remember how they'd paid when they'd come to the office before.

"We do, through his work, but with all of us and the copays and deductible, it costs us quite a bit out of pocket. We just can't afford that on his salary alone." Her face fell. "He won't let me work. Says the kids need me at home. In some ways, he's right. By the time we pay for daycare, it doesn't really make much sense for me to work a minimum wage job."

Gianna nodded. She agreed with her, but she still had her concerns. "Mrs. Haas, does Derek…is he…"

"Violent? He has a temper."

Gianna forced a swallow. She'd feared as much. But before she could ask anything further, Nancy's doctor walked in. Gianna said her goodbyes, told her that the kids were fine and staying with their aunt, as Nancy had eventually requested, and to call her if she needed her. Nancy teared up again and thanked her. Gianna ducked out and headed down the brightly lit hallway.

Her cell phone rang from her pocket. She recognized the ring tone and answered right away.

"Kiera, hi." She hopped into an open elevator and pushed the button for the lobby. She was surprised to hear from her, especially after their last encounter. Gianna had been afraid she'd said too much and scared her away.

"Hi." She sounded subdued. Perturbed. Something was bothering her. Gianna could hear the wind whistling through the phone. Kiera was talking to her outside, which wasn't a good sign. Whatever she had to say, she didn't want it said in front of Abigail.

For a moment, a split second, Gianna's heart fluttered, thinking that maybe she was going to refer to their kiss. But her hopes were dashed when she heard Kiera exhale, long and hard.

"Something happened this morning."

"What?"

"Abigail started a fire."

Gianna stepped off the elevator and pulled the phone away from her ear. "She what?"

"She lit the stove to put the kettle on, forgot to put it on, and left an oven mitt too close to the burner. It caught fire."

"Oh, my God. Is she okay? Are you okay? Thank God you were there."

"I almost wasn't," Kiera said. "I had stepped out for a few moments to take a dip in the sea and when I came back, there were flames on the stovetop."

"Wait. You went *swimming*?"

"I wasn't gone long and she was still sleeping when I left."

"I'm not accusing you of anything. I just—those currents can be dangerous, Kiera. You shouldn't do that alone."

"I did it all the time back home. As a kid and—" She stopped suddenly.

Gianna walked out the hospital doors and into the overcast sky. "Where is home, Kiera?" she asked softly. But Kiera moved on.

"Anyway, I was calling because I wondered if there was any way we could find someone to come sit with Abigail while I run a few errands from time to time."

Gianna wanted to push the matter and ask her question again, but she let it go. Kiera was obviously unwilling to discuss it and she'd been through quite a bit already that day.

"I'm sure we could work something out," Gianna said.

"I'd ask Henry, but he already does so much for us and you do as well."

"I wouldn't mind sitting with her from time to time."

"I can't ask you to do that after you work all day. You've got to be tired."

"It would be worth it if I got to see you." She paused next to her SUV, feeling more than a little vulnerable at having just shared that. She waited for a response.

She heard Kiera inhale. "I—Gianna. Really?"

"Yes, of course. I wouldn't say it if I didn't mean it."

Silence.

"I don't know what to say. You always seem to leave me speechless."

Gianna laughed and climbed into her vehicle. "Is that a good thing?"

"It's not bad."

"Okay, well, that's something then."

"The truth is…you make me feel things I've never felt before. And I don't know what to do with that."

Gianna started the SUV and sat with the engine idling. "Just do what you feel is right. Follow your heart."

The wind whistled some more into the phone. “Follow my heart,” she whispered, as if to herself.

“Yes.”

There was a brief silence before Kiera spoke again. “I had better get back inside to Abigail.”

“Of course, I’ll let you go. But say, I can stop by this evening if you need to run an errand. You can even take my car.”

“You sure? That would be great.”

“Not a problem. I’ll see you later then?”

“See you.”

“Okay then. Goodbye.”

Gianna ended the call and sat staring through the windshield. Dots of rain flecked the windshield and the wind shook the car briefly. She thought about Kiera swimming all alone in the bustling sea, and chills went up her spine. She didn’t like the idea and she wondered where she’d done it before, where it was that she considered home? It was somewhere along the coast. It had to be.

She put the car in reverse and drove away from the hospital. She couldn’t wait to get back to work to continue her search for answers online. She now had a new plan of action. If she couldn’t find information on Kiera, then she’d try for Abigail. Surely there was something on her. The two had to be tied together somehow.

She was dying to find out just how.

A few hours later, Gianna was pulling up at Abigail’s with excitement thrumming throughout her chest. She’d spent the rest of the afternoon back at the office, grilling Lizzie about Abigail and her past but getting very little in the way of answers. It seemed that Abigail was just as big a mystery as Kiera and the town just seemed to accept that, asking very few questions about the matter.

Abigail was just Abigail. Older, reclusive, private, and cranky. The townsfolk respected her and for the most part, left her in peace.

She'd just always been there, down on Rhydian Hill, living her life quiet and alone. No one was curious as to why.

Until me.

Gianna hopped up the steps with a box of Glenda's donuts in her hands. Kiera opened the door before she even had a chance to knock.

"You brought donuts," she said, eyes wide. "Abigail is going to be so happy."

"I thought she might be." Gianna stepped inside and gave Kiera a wink. "That's why I brought them. Brownie points."

"Ah. Very wise." Kiera shrugged into her coat and hat. She seemed to be in a hurry to get going. "Abigail, look who's here to see you. It's Dr. Walford."

"Gianna, please," Gianna said. She walked over to where Abigail was sitting in her chair. "I brought you something," she said, extending the box of donuts.

Abigail shifted her gaze over to Gianna and focused on the box. Her face lit up. "Are those Glenda's?"

"They sure are. I thought we could sit and chat and eat some donuts."

"Well, make yourself comfortable," Abigail said.

Gianna laughed and set the box on the coffee table as she slid out of her coat and hat to hang on the hall tree. She gave Kiera the keys to her vehicle.

"You have a license, right?" she asked, half teasing.

"Yes," Kiera appeared serious. Almost hurt.

"Just checking." She winked again, resisting the urge to ask to see it, knowing she'd at least see her home address. "Drive careful."

Kiera clutched the keys and nodded. Then she was out the door, leaving Gianna alone with Abigail. Gianna offered Abigail her choice of donuts and she chose right away, plucking a pink frosted one from the box.

Gianna settled onto the couch and munched on a bear claw. Outside, the rain grew stronger and Kiera had already disappeared with the SUV. All that remained was a heavy mist and the sound of the churning sea.

"Henry brings these to me every once in a while," Abigail said. "Brings a whole box of the pink ones, just like I like."

"Next time I'll be sure and do the same," Gianna said with a smile.

"I don't like farting around with the other kind. I know what I like and that's it." She took another bite and Gianna checked the box. There was one more pink frosted donut. Just enough to remain on her good side for a while.

"Do they not have Glenda's Donuts where you're from?" Gianna asked.

Abigail looked at her as if her antenna had gone up. "Where I'm from?"

"I just assumed you aren't from Cliffside."

"What makes you say that?"

"Rumors, I suppose. And I detect the hint of a southern accent."

"Rumors?" She scoffed. "People don't know their head from their asses most days so they got no business discussing me."

"Are you from the south?" Gianna tried, doing her best to sound lighthearted.

Abigail lowered her half-eaten donut. "I've been here fifty years, that's a long time. This here is my home."

"Have I told you that I'm from Arizona originally? Flagstaff. And more recently, I lived in Chicago."

"You told me about Chicago."

Gianna was impressed. Abigail was sharp today, her memory working fine.

"Do you ever miss your home?" Gianna asked.

"I told you, this is my home."

Gianna didn't respond. She knew she was treading lightly. After a long moment Abigail spoke.

"I suppose I miss some things," she said softly. "But not enough to cry over."

"What sort of things do you miss?"

She stared down at her donut. "I miss someone, not some thing."

"Who?"

"Ruby."

Gianna straightened her spine. "Ruby?" Could it be the same Ruby she'd found online? The woman who looked so much like Kiera?

"We were close," Abigail said. "They'll never be anyone quite like her. Though that Kiera comes close."

It was her. It had to be. "Who is she?" Gianna asked. "A friend, a family member?"

"She was a friend. My very best friend. But she's passed on now. Dead and gone. And I'm left here remembering her."

Gianna turned to face Abigail better, needing to see more of her face. "Was Ruby related to Kiera?"

Abigail bored a look right into her. "They were kin."

Gianna's heart leapt. "So that's how you know Kiera. Through Ruby."

"You ask an awful lot of questions. You and Kiera both. About to tire me out with all of them."

"I'm sorry, Abigail, I'm just curious."

"I figured as much. The way you carry on around Kiera and all."

Gianna shook her head. "Pardon?"

"I knew you were curious about her, but me, you ain't got no need to know about me now."

"I'm—" She started to deny her curiosity about Kiera but stopped short. Something told her that Abigail wouldn't buy it. That she'd see right through her.

"I don't know why you're tiptoeing around what it is you really want," Abigail said. "Thought you were braver than that."

"I'm not following," Gianna said.

"You're a dunce too? Now that I didn't see coming."

"A dunce? Abigail, what are you talking about?"

But Abigail sat in silence, quietly eating the rest of her pink donut. Gianna sat dumbfounded, trying to decipher the meaning of her words. She kept coming back to the same conclusion. Abigail knew how she felt about Kiera and she was calling her on it.

How could that be? Was she that obvious? So obvious that a woman in her nineties could pick up on it?

Gianna plucked at her bear claw, not really wanting it. She placed it back in the box and wiped the sticky crumbs from her hands on a paper napkin with the name Glenda's Donuts written in cursive across the front. Then she rose to fix them something to drink. When she came to the kitchen, she could smell the remnants of smoke and see the char mark on the stovetop where the oven mitt had burned. It reminded her of Kiera's request for help. And though Gianna could help every now and then, she knew it wouldn't be enough. Kiera needed someone else in the equation, and thankfully, Gianna had someone in mind.

Her name was Brandi, and she was a college student who had recently conceived. The pregnancy was a surprise, and she didn't have good insurance. So Gianna was treating her in trade. And sitting with Abigail a few days a week seemed like a fair deal. Brandi could sit with Abigail and give Kiera some time to herself, and in exchange, Brandi got the prenatal healthcare that she needed.

It was a win-win.

Gianna brought Abigail some juice, set her own glass on the coffee table, and pulled out her phone. She texted Brandi and proposed the deal. It took a few moments before she replied, but she readily agreed.

"Great," Gianna said.

Now if Abigail would just behave herself and not scare Brandi away.

CHAPTER THIRTY-SIX

The local library was small, with only three available computers and two rooms full of books. The computers were being used when Jenny first arrived so she spent time perusing, taking her time to read the jackets on some of the memoirs. It had been a while since she'd read one and she wished she could check a couple out, but then she'd have to show her real driver's license in order to get a library card, and she couldn't risk that. Cliffside was too small a town and no doubt the librarian would share her real identity with someone, even if just in passing.

She slid the book she was interested in back into its place and hurried over to an open computer. She quickly checked behind her to make sure no one was watching and did a search for news in North Carolina. She prayed her face wouldn't be splayed across the headlines as the police tried to track her down for murder. She was so nervous about it she even clenched her eyes briefly, afraid to look at the screen. But when she opened them, she was surprised to see that there was nothing in regard to her, at least not in the breaking news. Relieved, she went to click on the next page and froze just before she did so. There, at the bottom of the screen, was a photo of a man she recognized. She blinked, convinced she was imagining the likeness. She wasn't. She clicked on the link and a full-page spread came up with Floyd's picture on it.

Jenny gasped, causing the woman next to her to glance over at her. Jenny shrank the page and smiled nervously. The woman refocused on her own computer and Jenny enlarged the page again. She scanned the article quickly, learning that Floyd and his wife, Melonie, had been the victims of a home invasion. Floyd had been stabbed and was still being treated for his injuries. The perpetrator—

"Excuse me," a voice said from behind. Jenny turned, alarmed.

The librarian was standing there with her hands clasped in front of her. "Do you have a library card?"

Jenny stammered. "No—I—no."

"You need a card to use the computers."

"I do?"

The librarian pointed at the sign taped to the desk. It was right there, as plain as day.

Jenny scrambled, wrote down the name of the hospital where Floyd was, and exited out of the article to gather her things. She stood quickly and knocked over her chair. "Sorry," she said, righting it. She started to walk away, needing to escape.

"Don't you want to get a card? All you need is a valid ID."

"No, no thanks. Not today." She tapped her watch. "No time." She forced a smile and pushed out the door. The librarian stood looking confused.

Jenny hurried back to the SUV and crawled inside. Her heart was racing and she felt sick to her stomach. Floyd had been hurt. Someone had attacked him. Was it because of her? Could it be Gary?

She sat and stewed, working over the possibilities in her mind. What were the odds that Gary had found Floyd? Almost zero. It was downright impossible. No, it had to be a random act of violence.

Still, she couldn't shake the notion. Couldn't get past that one-percent probability. She needed to talk to him. To hear it directly from Floyd. And she needed to make sure he was okay.

She pulled away from the library and drove all over town looking for a pay phone. She found a lone one at a gas station near the outskirts. After getting some change from the attendant inside, she dialed the number for the hospital in Asheville. She asked for

Floyd's room, but she was informed that he was unavailable to take calls. She asked why but the operator told her she couldn't divulge any more information.

Jenny hung up and cried. Was Floyd alright? Had he died?

Again, she couldn't help but think it was because of her.

She just had to know. She turned back to the phone and deposited more money. She called Floyd's cell phone, the number she kept tucked away in her purse. It went straight to voice mail. She hung up and went back to the SUV.

She drove home then, back to Rhydian Hill. Her thoughts remained on Floyd, praying that he was okay but still convinced of the worst. When she entered the house, Gianna greeted her with a big smile, one she couldn't bring herself to return.

"What's wrong?" Gianna asked.

Jenny sank onto the couch, not even bothering to remove her coat. "I got some bad news."

Gianna sat next to her. "What?"

"I—a friend. He got hurt. I'm not sure how bad or if he's even okay."

"That's awful," Gianna said, taking her hand. Jenny softened at her warm touch, and tears ran from her eyes. Gianna gently wiped them away. "Can I do anything to help?"

"I don't think so."

"You're trembling. Are you cold?"

"Just upset."

Gianna stood as a car pulled up the drive. "I know just what you need."

Jenny followed her line of sight. "Who is that?"

"That is Brandi. She's going to be helping out with Abigail for a while. She's come to sit with her this evening while you and I go out."

"Oh, no, Gianna, I couldn't possibly." She raised a shaking hand to sweep off her hat. "I'm too upset."

"Which is why you need to get away for a bit." Gianna pulled her to a stand. "We can go to my place. Have dinner. Relax."

"But—"

"No buts. You're going. Put your hat back on and get ready while I introduce Brandi to Abigail and show her around."

Jenny didn't argue. She didn't have the strength. Her mind was still too preoccupied to do much of anything except think about Floyd. She walked over to Abigail and knelt in front of her.

"I'm going to go out with Dr. Walford for a while. You okay with that?"

Abigail peered at her with her dark, mysterious gaze. "It's about time you did if you ask me."

"What's that?"

"Nothing. You go on now. I'll be fine. Even if you are leaving me here with a stranger."

"I'm sure she's very nice," Jenny said.

"I don't need no one to sit with me. I'm not a child."

"No, but you do need help from time to time, Abigail. So let her help."

She waved Jenny off and stared back out at the sea. Jenny kissed her forehead before leaving her to her musings. She met Brandi in the kitchen and helped to explain where everything was. Jenny was relieved to learn that Brandi was a college student, studying nursing, and that she'd helped to care for her grandfather in the recent past.

Gianna also helped by reassuring Jenny that everything would be fine and that she would have her back home before it got too late.

Jenny left with her, giving one last wave to Abigail as they walked out the door.

"I don't like leaving her," Jenny said as they drove away.

"It's good for you, though. Good for both of you. Gives you room to breathe."

They rode the rest of the way in silence with Gianna reaching out to hold her hand. It felt nice, warm, comforting. And it brought more tears to Jenny's eyes. When they reached Gianna's, Gianna led her inside and told her to make herself comfortable while she poured them both some wine. She put on some piano jazz on the sound system and returned to her, offering her a glass of merlot.

"You like wine, I hope?"

"Mm. It's been a while, but thanks."

"It'll help you relax." Gianna rounded the kitchen counter, sipping from her own glass.

Her home was nice, shabby chic and cozy. Lots of whites, creams, and yellows. It soothed Jenny and she made herself comfortable on an impossibly soft sofa.

"How about some dinner?" Gianna asked.

"I don't know."

"You really should eat. At least a little something."

"What did you have in mind?"

"I know a place that has great roasted veggie lavash wraps."

"I don't think I've ever had that." She nodded. "Sure, I'll give it a try."

"Excellent."

Gianna put the order in and sat next to her on the couch. Jenny twisted her glass in her hands, her insides awakening at Gianna's close proximity.

Gianna seemed to sense her disquiet and she carefully took the glass and placed it on the coffee table. "It's okay," she said softly. "Everything is okay."

"I wish I could believe you."

"You can. Just close your eyes and be in the present. Right here, right now, in this moment." She touched her face, stroked her cheek. "Go on, close your eyes."

Jenny's eyes fell closed and she sighed, enjoying the feel of Gianna's gentle touch. It was so light, so tender, it almost felt like a feather. "That feels nice," she said. "I like it when you touch me."

"Then I shall do it a whole lot more."

Jenny smiled and opened her eyes. Gianna was staring into her with a look of powerful longing. "I want to kiss you," Gianna said.

"I want you to, too."

"Then by all means," Gianna said, leaning in to take Kiera's lips with hers.

Jenny fell into her, melting, melding. Gianna felt so incredible, so right. So hot and soft and inviting. Jenny wanted to get lost in her forever. The kiss deepened and Gianna tugged her closer. Jenny moaned in sheer delight and Gianna drew away.

"You okay?"

"Yeah," she breathed. "Really okay."

"Really okay?"

Jenny touched her tingling lips. "Yeah."

Gianna chuckled.

"You've left me speechless, what can I say," Jenny said.

"Speechless in a good way, I assume?"

"Oh, yes."

Gianna pulled her back in. "Good." She leaned in to kiss her again, but the doorbell rang with their food.

"Hold that thought," Gianna said, answering the door. She brought the food into the kitchen and served it on her own plates.

"Should I sit at the table?" Jenny asked.

"If you like."

Jenny settled at the table and Gianna carried over the food. She watched quietly as Jenny bit into her lavash.

"Good?"

Jenny nodded, truly impressed. The flavors were bursting in her mouth. "There's no meat in this?"

"None."

"Wow. It's really good."

"I'm glad you like it."

"And I'm glad you suggested this. You know, us doing this. Here. It feels nice. Right. I just hope Abigail's okay."

Gianna laughed. "I'm more worried about Brandi. But here, let me text and check in with her." She pulled out her phone and did just that. Brandi answered her right away. "There. All is well. They are chatting over tea and cookies."

Jenny breathed a sigh of relief.

"So, you see? Everything really is okay," Gianna said.

Jenny smiled. "Thanks. I guess it is."

"And your friend, I'm sure he's okay too."

"I'm not so sure." She felt her brow furrow. "But there's nothing I can do about it either way."

Gianna rose and took her by the hand. "Come here," she said, pulling her up next to her. "Just relax into me and sway with the music."

"I can't dance."

"Yes, you can. Just follow me. Relax and move with me. Because it's all okay."

They swayed slowly to the music and Jenny rested her cheek on her shoulder, almost convinced that everything was indeed okay. But then she saw a figure at the door and a knock sounded.

Gianna paused. "Who could that be?" She looked at Jenny in confusion. "Just a moment."

She left her to open the door, and her face fell as the woman on the stoop took a step inside.

"What's the matter, babe, aren't you glad to see me?" the woman said.

Jenny searched Gianna's shocked expression. "Gianna, who is this?" Jenny asked.

But Gianna seemed speechless. She stood in silence, blinking rapidly.

The woman came forward with a broad grin. She extended her hand to Jenny. "I'm Tiffany. Gianna's girlfriend. And you are?"

Jenny's heart fell to the floor. She swayed with dizziness but finally managed to speak.

"No one," she said. "I'm no one."

Chapter Thirty-seven

Gary had to be careful. Had to get a new vehicle. The Honda was too hot, he'd had to abandon it at a gas station just outside of Asheville. He'd managed to wash up there though, in the gas station restroom. He'd locked the door and cleaned all the blood off his hands and jeans. He'd had to walk around with damp thighs for a while, but it didn't matter. The blood couldn't be seen. At most, it looked like faded dirt. So he'd walked the roads, trying for a ride. He'd had success twice and reached Tennessee.

Now he could breathe a little easier. He was out of North Carolina. Finally. He hoped the search for him would be less intense. After all, the cops didn't know it was him who'd stabbed Floyd. Or did they? He honestly wasn't sure. He hadn't had access to a TV or newspaper in days. Regardless, he knew he needed to be careful. Very careful.

"Thanks again," he said to the man who drove him across the Tennessee border. Gary climbed from the idle car and gave a wave. The man returned it and drove away. Gary walked the short distance to another gas station. The vehicles parked there were few and far between and only one of them was older. Unfortunately, the driver was already behind the wheel and appeared to be scratching off a lotto ticket. Gary approached carefully, not wanting to startle him. He knocked on the window and smiled.

The man inside eased down the window. "Yes?"

"Hey, how you doing? I was wondering if you could possibly give me a ride? I'd be willing to pay for some gas in exchange."

The man searched his face as if trying to suss him out. "I don't know, I don't usually do that sort of thing."

"I'm not headed far. Just up the road a ways. It would really help me out. Plus you'd get some fuel out of it."

The man hesitated and looked at his lotto ticket. It must not've been a winner because he tossed it onto the dash. "Sure, why not?"

Gary bounced on his feet. "I really appreciate it." He rounded the car and opened the door to climb inside. The man shook his hand, said his name was Dane.

"Glenn," Gary said. "Pleasure." He dug in his jacket pocket and pulled out some folded cash. He counted out sixty dollars and gave it to Dane.

"Thanks," Dane said, sliding it into the pocket of his dash. "Every little bit helps."

"You falling on hard times?"

Dane reversed the car and drove them away from the gas station. They hit the road and accelerated, and Gary allowed the cool wind to whip his face as he rested his elbow out the window.

"Lost my job a few weeks back," Dane said.

"Oh, man. That sucks."

"Tell me about it. I keep praying for a miracle, but so far it ain't happening."

"It will, just hang in there. Good things'll come."

"I hope so."

Gary smiled. Good things were indeed coming, just not for Dane. Unless one considered him being put out of his misery a good thing.

They rode in silence for several miles down the road before Gary put his plan into motion. He clutched his stomach and moaned in agony.

"What's wrong?" Dane asked.

"My stomach is cramping. I feel sick. Can you pull over?"

"Where?"

"Just up there, off to the side near the woods."

Dane slowed the car and pulled off to the side. He put the car in park and watched as Gary crept into the wood line, all hunched over, holding his mid-section. Once he was secure and hidden amongst the trees, he dropped to the ground and lurched, crying out in pain.

When Dane did nothing but call out, he cried some more and rolled onto his side and hugged his knees to his chest. He heard Dane's door open, and he groaned some more and writhed on the ground until Dane was at his side, asking after him.

"It hurts," Gary moaned. "So bad."

"What is it? What hurts? Should I call someone?"

Gary reached into his waistband and retrieved his knife. And as Dane leaned in closer, Gary attacked, thrusting upward, plunging the knife deep into his chest. Dane gasped and his face contorted in horrible shock and pain. Gary thrust the knife in farther and twisted it, ensuring the ultimate damage.

Dane clung to him, his eyes wide with fright, until slowly his grip began to weaken and slide from Gary's shoulder. He fell over and lay helpless on the ground with blood trickling from his mouth.

Gary yanked the knife from his ribs and wiped the smeared blood from the blade on Dane's shirt. Then he tucked the blade back into his waistband and grabbed Dane's arms to drag him farther into the woods. He left him in a heap on some pine needles and made his way back to the car.

He climbed inside and adjusted the seat. After tucking the sixty dollars back into his pocket, he put the car in drive and sped away with the windows down. He smiled as the wind blew against his face, heading westward bound.

Heading to Oregon.

CHAPTER THIRTY-EIGHT

Kiera, you have to believe me," Gianna said again as she pulled into the drive at Rhydian Hill. "She's not my girlfriend."

"Then why did she say she was?"

"I don't know. To fuck with us?" It was a question she'd been asking herself since Tiffany's impromptu arrival.

Kiera reached for the door handle as soon as Gianna stopped. "Kiera, wait. Please. Don't leave like this. Let's talk."

Kiera wouldn't look at her, wouldn't even turn her head in her direction. "I don't think it's me you need to talk to you."

"Yes, it is."

"No," she laughed. "It's not. And you'd better hurry back, you don't want to keep her waiting."

"She can wait all night for all I care. She's not who's important to me."

"Maybe not, but she's the one in your home at the moment, claiming to be your girlfriend. Whereas, I'm sitting here, about to go back inside on my own, wondering what the hell this has been all about."

"Kiera, don't. Don't say that. You know what this is. This… it's wonderful. And I don't want it to end."

Kiera's shoulders slumped as she continued to look out the window. "It's probably for the best, Gianna. I'm not…really in a position to start anything with you."

"Why do you say that?"

"I'm just not, okay? My life…it's very complicated and you deserve better."

"Kiera," She reached for her hand, but Kiera opened the door and exited the vehicle. She turned to finally lock eyes with Gianna. "Trust me on that, Gianna. It's the one thing you can believe." She closed the door and limped over to the porch steps. Gianna watched her go, feeling completely helpless. She had no idea what she'd meant by her last words, but they tore at her heart regardless and she feared that she'd just lost her forever.

"Damn it." She wanted to chase after her, to reason with her, make her see just how much she did care about her, but she couldn't do that at the moment. Abigail and Brandi were inside and she didn't want to have that conversation in front of them. She'd have to find another time, a moment where she could get Kiera alone again. But she had no idea when that would possibly be, especially now that Kiera had just called things off.

Gianna cursed again and put the SUV in reverse. She spun out of the drive and raced back home, fuming over Tiffany. How dare she just show up out of nowhere. What the hell was she thinking?

Gianna's knuckles were white from her death grip on the steering wheel by the time she arrived home. She stormed into the house to find Tiffany lounging on the couch in her stocking feet, drinking her good wine.

"Love what you've done with the place," Tiffany said. "It's very cozy. Very warm."

"Get out," Gianna hissed, removing the half-empty wine bottle from the coffee table. "Now."

"Ouch. Is that any way to treat me after I've come all this way to see you?"

"I mean it, Tiffany. I want you gone."

"Babe, calm down."

"Don't call me babe and it's too late for talking. You should've thought to do that before you cheated on me."

Tiffany downed the rest of her wine and set her glass on the coffee table. "I know. Believe me, I know. And I'm sorry, G. But that's not who I am anymore. I've changed."

"Yeah, right. You've changed. That's why you show up here uninvited and waltz in and start telling lies."

"Lies?"

"You told Kiera you were my girlfriend."

A coy smile broke out on her face. "Semantics. Besides, she's not your type. She's too mousy and obviously you're not that close or she'd know better than to think we were still together."

"How close we are is none of your concern."

"Isn't it, though? Come on, G. I want you back. I need you."

"Precisely. You *need* me. That's the only reason you're here. Because you can't stand to be alone."

"Oh, please."

"No, it's true. Your lover left you and now you're all alone again. You can't handle it."

"You know," she said as she stood. "You really shouldn't try to psychoanalyze me. It's not exactly your specialty."

"Just as telling the truth isn't for you."

"Ouch again." She palmed her heart. "You're throwing some real dingers at me."

Gianna found Tiffany's shoes and tossed them to her. "Put these on and get out."

"G. Seriously? I've come all this way—"

"Then you wasted your time and that's not my problem."

"You're really going to throw what we have away?"

"You've already done that, Tiffany. And don't you forget it."

She marched to the back door and yanked it open. Tiffany crossed the room slowly, holding her shoes to her chest. When she reached the door, she looked at Gianna with big pouty eyes.

"Please, G. Not like this. Give us a chance."

Gianna edged her out the door. "You blew the only chance we had. Goodbye, Tiffany." She closed the door and locked it. She walked away, refusing to look at her through the pane of glass.

She couldn't stand the sight of her and her big pouty eyes. It was bullshit, the whole look. The whole attempt at victimhood.

God, how could she. The audacity. Had she no shame?

Obviously not.

Gianna killed the interior lights and headed up to bed, just in case Tiffany was still lingering by the door. Maybe she'd get the hint once and for all and leave.

"She'd better stay away," Gianna said, sitting on her bed to slip off her shoes. She checked the bedside clock, saw that it was still early, and thought about calling Kiera at Abigail's to apologize again for Tiffany's intrusion. But she knew Kiera couldn't talk privately and she didn't want to add salt to a fresh wound.

So she stripped down and slid into her pajamas and climbed into bed. Her laptop was on the bedside table, along with her notes on Kiera and Ruby and a man named Floyd. She grabbed them all and sat up in bed and opened her computer to begin searching once again.

What had Kiera meant with those last words? Was she referring to her mysterious past?

And how could she find this Floyd?

She did a search for a truck driver named Floyd, along with Ride Right Trucking and then she entered North Carolina since that's where she'd found Ruby's information. She got a few miscellaneous hits, mostly about Ride Right, and she scrolled through them quickly. But then something stood out at her. A photo and a news article about a home invasion. She clicked on the link and opened the full article. She recognized the man at once as the same one she'd seen with Kiera in Flagstaff.

"Holy shit." She sat up straighter and read the article quickly. The man and his wife had been attacked in their home and he'd been stabbed. It sounded terrifying and she struggled to make sense of it and what it could possibly have to do with Kiera.

"This is obviously the friend she's worried about," Gianna whispered. "So why not just tell me about him? Why all the secrecy? Just who are you, Kiera Davenport?" She searched for more information on Floyd, but there wasn't any. And after spending another hour trying to locate any info she could on Kiera, she finally closed her laptop and shoved it and her notes aside.

She sat staring straight ahead, wondering if perhaps Kiera was in some sort of danger. Wondering if maybe Floyd was into bad things and subsequently Kiera was in harm's way somehow. She knew she needed to ask her, but she also knew that Kiera would probably refuse to talk about it, or try to deflect. And now that Kiera had ended things, it would be doubly hard to get her to talk.

Still, she had to try. She cared about her too much not to.

After rising to wash her face and brush her teeth, she walked to the bedroom window to look out into the backyard. Tiffany was nowhere to be seen. Thankful that she'd hopefully moved on, she climbed into bed and killed the light. She had a big day tomorrow, one full of patients with various ailments and she was suddenly exhausted.

She closed her eyes and tried to clear her mind for sleep. But one person's face remained in the forefront. Kiera's.

❖

Gianna didn't sleep much that night, so she rose just as the sun broke over Cliffside, trying to burn through the thick fog. She dressed and laced up her running shoes, deciding that some exercise would do her good, and she set out for a run up to the cliffs.

Tiffany was but a distant memory now that morning had birthed and as she ran she tried to work out how to speak to Kiera. Or more importantly, how to get Kiera to speak to her. She doubted that Kiera would want to leave with her again, so she considered talking to her on the front porch or maybe even in her bedroom. Either way, Abigail would know something was up and it seemed a little rude to try and hide from her in order to have a discussion. After all, she might think they were talking about her and Gianna didn't want her to think that.

Maybe she could have Brandi come back over to sit with Abigail while she and Kiera went for a short walk along the shore. That would be nice and they'd be afforded the privacy they needed.

She smiled to herself, making a mental note to call Brandi later that morning to see when she'd be available. She had a plan and it made her feel better. She decreased her speed as she topped the end of the trail which led to the edge of the looming cliffs. With her hands on the back of her head to catch her breath, she walked closer to the edge and looked out over the fog-covered sea. The sun was glinting off the water in open patches of fog and the seagulls were singing their morning song as they glided overhead. It was a beautiful day, the air moist and crisp and saturated with salt from the sea. She inhaled deeply and turned to head back down the trail. But as she walked away from the cliff side, she saw something else glinting at her through the dense fog.

Headlights.

The vehicle was dead ahead, parked outside the roped off parking area. The engine was running and the driver, whom she could just make out the basic form of, was sitting behind the wheel, unmoving.

She walked closer, curious, wanting to get a better look, thinking it might be Tiffany. But as she drew closer, the vehicle reversed and sped away before she could even get a glimpse of the license plate.

With her heart in her throat, she picked up her pace and ran back toward her house, keeping an eye out for the mysterious vehicle. If it was Tiffany, why hadn't she just gotten out and confronted her? Tiffany had never been shy about voicing her feelings before. And why follow her up that trail? Why not just talk to her as she stepped outside?

It didn't make sense. But then again, with Tiffany, not much did these days. Her showing up unexpected had really been out of character. Tiffany wasn't known to put that much effort into their relationship matters. At least, she never had previously. It had always been Gianna trying to improve things between them.

She slowed once again as her house came into view. She stopped to grab the mail, having forgotten to check it the day before. And as she headed for the front door, she walked past her SUV which was parked in the gravel drive. She stopped, suddenly alarmed, and the envelopes slipped from her hand.

"What the hell?" She crouched down and touched her flattened tire, running her fingers along the large gash in the rubber. She straightened and walked to the next tire, finding it in the same condition. In fact, as she soon discovered, all four tires had been slashed. "Motherfucker." She slapped her hands against her thighs and looked around, searching for the culprit. And there, at the end of her street, sat a vehicle with its headlights on, engine idling.

She took a step toward it, but it once again reversed and sped away, giving her only a glimpse at the fading red taillights.

Mad as hell, she scooped up her fallen mail and marched into the house. Tiffany was obviously angry at her for kicking her out, for shutting the door in her face. Gianna had never done such things in the past. She'd always caved and accepted her excuses no matter how ridiculous. But now things were different. Gianna was different. And Tiffany didn't like it.

She picked up her phone and dialed Tiffany's number, ready to give her a piece of her mind. But Tiffany didn't answer.

Chapter Thirty-nine

Jenny sat very still on the couch, unable to even sip from her now tepid cup of tea. She was frozen, transfixed, her gaze focused straight ahead out the front window, convinced something menacing was about to occur.

Her body shuddered with chills from the bitter morning air, but she couldn't even bring herself to snuggle beneath the blanket, much less get up and light a fire in the stove.

She'd been like this since ten the night before. Since the strange headlights had shone through her bedroom window. Since the strange knock at the door with no one at the threshold.

Who was it?

What had they wanted?

She shivered again and this time hugged herself. The knife she'd pulled from the block in the kitchen sat on the coffee table, her only sense of security. She'd thought about calling the police, but what would she say? Someone parked in the drive, knocked on the door, and then disappeared?

They'd think she was overreacting. And maybe she was. Maybe it was just someone with the wrong address. Or maybe it was just kids playing a prank.

Whatever it was it seemed to be over. She needed to move on. To, at the very least, move from the couch.

She stood and stretched her cold, stiff body. She shoved firewood in the stove and lit it, hoping to warm the house before

Abigail woke. It was nearing eight and she'd yet to emerge, so Jenny went to peek in on her. Abigail was awake but still lying in her bed. Her gaze slid over to Jenny as Jenny spoke.

"Good morning."

"Is it?" Abigail said.

"It is." She smiled, unwilling to tell her about the headlights and the knock at the door. She didn't want to worry her, nor did she want to be called crazy. "I'll go put some more tea on while you dress."

Jenny put the kettle on and sat, waiting for it to whistle. When it did, she poured them both some tea and set the cups on the table. Abigail still hadn't come out of her bedroom. Jenny returned to her room and knocked on the partially open door.

Abigail was sitting on her bed, holding her shirt with trembling hands. She was having trouble dressing.

Jenny didn't speak, she just walked up to her and quietly helped her into her clothes. Abigail seemed to appreciate the silence and she too, said nothing on the matter. When they finished, Jenny helped her into the kitchen where they sat at the table.

Abigail was becoming more and more frail. It seemed to be worse in the mornings now. When her bones were stiff and her mind was not yet awake. She was struggling and it was hard for Jenny to witness.

"Is your tea hot enough?" Jenny asked, wanting to be sure to take good care of her

"Abigail?"

"Hm?"

"Would you like me to refresh your tea?"

She didn't answer. Jenny stood to pour a little more into her cup, careful not to fill it all the way. "There you are."

Abigail watched her but said nothing. She lifted her mug with trembling hands and took a tiny sip. Some of it dribbled down her chin.

Jenny passed her a napkin, but Abigail didn't seem to know what to do with it.

"You've spilt some tea," Jenny said, pointing at her own chin.

Abigail dabbed at her chin as if surprised to find liquid there. She kept dabbing and Jenny had to assure her that there wasn't any more to dab at.

"You ready to go to your chair?"

"I reckon."

Jenny escorted her to her chair and placed her cup of tea on her side table. She covered her with her light blanket and turned on the TV to the morning news. Abigail didn't seem interested though. She was staring out at the sea, taking in the morning along the shoreline and beyond.

It was what she'd been spending most of her time doing lately. Staring out at the churning sea, almost as if it were speaking to her. Whispering to her with every hiss of a crashing wave. She had little interest in her soaps, in conversation, in anything really. Her mind always seemed to be locked away within itself.

Jenny returned to her seat on the couch after checking the lock on the door once again. She picked up the phone and called Gianna, knowing she owed her an apology for the way she'd been behaving.

It had been close to a week now since the night her ex-girlfriend had shown up and though Gianna had called, wanting to come over to talk, Jenny had turned her down. But the truth was, she missed her. Missed the feel of her warm, soft mouth against hers and the way she looked into her very soul, like Jenny was the most important person in the world. She'd never experienced anything like she had with Gianna and her heart, it seemed, wasn't about to let her give that up. With Ken, things had been good and she'd definitely loved him. But it hadn't been like this. He hadn't believed in her the way Gianna seemed to. Hadn't expressed his feelings for her very often. In fact, she'd often had to pry things from him in regard to his feelings. And when she had, he'd gotten upset, defensive even, and told her she was too concerned with such matters. That she needed to just leave things be. Those were the times she'd rather forget.

The phone rang a few times before Gianna answered. But when she did, she sounded winded and a bit unsettled.

"Gianna? It's Kiera. Am I bothering you?"

"Kiera, hi. No, I—I'm just having a hectic morning."

"I won't keep you then. I was just wondering if you still wanted to come by?"

"Sure. I'd love to."

"Great. I'll see you later, then?"

"Yep. Oh, and I'll call Brandi, see if she can come sit with Abigail."

"Okay. But if she can't, I still want you to come. I…really want to see you."

"I really want to see you too."

Jenny said goodbye and hung up. She looked out the window again and saw nothing and no one but the sea. It calmed her somehow, made her feel safe and secure, just like Gianna did.

Her heart warmed at just the thought of seeing Gianna again, and she rose to make breakfast, forgetting all about the strange headlights and the knock at the door.

With Gianna on her mind and Abigail to tend to, nothing else seemed to matter.

She was okay here on Rhydian Hill.

Chapter Forty

Gianna hummed softly as she drove up the drive at Rhydian Hill. She was excited to see Kiera and anxious to give Abigail the donuts she'd stopped at Glenda's to get for her. She'd also brought her some fresh flowers, hoping they'd brighten her mood.

With both the flowers and donuts in hand, Gianna hopped up the porch steps and knocked on the door. The cold wind toyed with her hair, which she'd worn down from her quick shower after work. It was still damp, but she didn't care. She hadn't wanted to take the time to dry it, too anxious to get to Kiera.

It had been a trying day. One full of patients and confusion and anger over the damage done to her tires. She'd had them replaced and also called someone to install security cameras at the house. They were still there working on mounting them to the frame, which made her feel a bit better. Tiffany wouldn't dare do anything with people around. So the house should be safe for the moment, and when the men were done, the house would be protected with the cameras.

She dared Tiffany to come back then.

Gianna knocked on the door again, surprised Kiera hadn't answered already. She heard voices inside and she called out, announcing her presence.

"Kiera? It's Gianna."

The door opened a crack. Gianna smiled. "Hi." But the person peering out at her wasn't Kiera. Or Abigail. It was…a man. A stranger. He opened the door farther and smiled back at her.

"Hi, I'm Gary. Kiera's husband. She's not in at the moment."

Gianna felt heat rush to her face in alarm. "Husband?"

He just kept smiling.

"Where is she?" Gianna asked, needing to see her. To hear this directly from her. Her stomach clenched as she recalled Kiera mentioning men's names before. Had she been trying to tell her something? Like the fact that she was married? If so, if she was really married, then why had she gotten so upset over the Tiffany incident?

"She went into town," the man calling himself Gary said.

"She doesn't have a car," Gianna countered. Something wasn't right about this guy. His appearance was disheveled, filthy even. And his grinning, it seemed maniacal. Something was definitely off.

He hesitated at her statement.

She caught it.

And he saw her catch it.

He lunged at her with a knife and seized her by the wrist causing her to drop the donuts. "Don't fight me," he said. "Or I'll slice you up."

He forced her inside and locked the door. Gianna gasped as she saw Kiera on the couch, curled up in a ball, looking absolutely terrified. She quickly scanned the room for Abigail and found her in her chair, eyes wide, hands clasped tightly together.

"Don't hurt them," Gianna said.

"Shut up." He shoved her in the back. "Sit down."

Gianna sat next to Kiera, placed the flowers on the corner of the table, and held her face. "Are you okay? Are you hurt?"

Kiera shook her head.

The man, Gary, laughed. "What's this? Who is this woman, Jenny? Your new little puppy?"

Gianna glared at him. "Who's Jenny?"

Gary laughed again.

Tears slipped down Kiera's cheeks. "I'm so sorry," she whispered.

"For what?" Gianna asked.

"Everything."

"Both of you, shut up!" Gary said.

"You stop it, Carl," Abigail called out as she tried to stand. "You go on and get now. Leave us alone."

"Shut up, you old bat."

"Don't speak to her that way," Kiera seethed.

"She's crazy," he said. "Keeps calling me Carl. Whoever the hell that is."

"She knows you aren't supposed to be here," Gianna said. "And she's right."

"I'm not the only one who doesn't belong," he said, sitting right in front of them on the coffee table. "Right, Jenny? These people don't even know who you really are."

"I know who she is," Gianna said.

"Do you now?" Gary asked as if amused.

"Yes. In here." She touched Kiera's heart. "And that's all that matters."

"Aww, isn't that sweet?" he said.

Gianna looked him over carefully and saw just how dirty and grimy he really was. His clothes were filthy and his hair greasy. Sporadic patches of hair grew on his jaw and chin, the hair long and wiry. And he reeked with a foul body odor. It was enough to make her gag.

He caught her unfavorable appraisal of him. "Oh, I'm sorry, am I not presentable enough for you, lady?" He sniffed his arm pits. "Woo, I guess not. Oh, well. No time for a shower. Not yet anyway. We've got too much fun to be had first." He stuck the knife in Kiera's face. "We got business to attend to, don't we Jenny? You and me." He tugged on her arm, but she fought him. "Get up!" he shouted, yanking her harder.

"Don't touch her!" Gianna sprang and shoved him backwards over the coffee table. He fell with a crash and cried out as he writhed on the floor, holding his back. The knife was by his side, free from his grip. Gianna rushed for it, but she didn't make it in time before he clutched it again. She fell on him and wrestled him for the blade. He was scrawny but strong, stronger than she'd anticipated.

Kiera screamed and Abigail began yelling at him again, calling him Carl. Gianna rolled on the floor with him, trying first to grab the knife, then trying to protect herself from it.

Gary got the upper hand and positioned himself atop her, attempting to bring the knife down into her chest. She held his wrist, locked her elbow, and strained to hold him back. With her free hand she hit him square in the jaw. It only made him angrier, and spittle flew from his mouth as he bore down harder with the blade.

She grunted with one last rush of adrenaline before her body weakened and the knife inched closer to her chest.

She heard Kiera scream again and suddenly the front door was kicked in with a loud bang. Gary froze to look and Gianna hit him again, this time knocking him from her body. She scrambled away from him and saw a man standing in the doorway. It was Derek Haas.

"Mr. Haas," she managed.

He said nothing, coming straight for Gary. Gary stood and held out his knife, his wicked grin gone. Derek Haas was a formidable opponent, one he obviously didn't want to contend with.

"Who are you?" he asked. "Another boyfriend? Jenny's got a house full of admirers it seems."

"Put down the knife," Derek said. "Before you get yourself hurt."

Gary didn't move. He just swayed on the balls of his feet. "Try it, man."

Derek rushed him and tackled him to the floor. They rolled twice, and though Derek was bigger and stronger, he was no opponent for Gary's knife, which he plunged into Derek's side. Derek groaned and blood trickled from his mouth as Gary mounted him and tried to bring the knife down to stab him once again.

Gianna knew that feeling of helplessness and she knew Derek couldn't hold him off much longer. So she quickly grabbed the heavy crystal vase full of flowers and stood to smash it against Gary's head.

He fell off of Derek at once and Derek rolled atop him and punched him hard in the face, causing a sick cracking sound.

Gary went completely limp, his head lolling to the side. Derek crawled off him and peeled Gary's fingers open to retrieve the knife. Derek straightened and looked at Gianna.

"You alright?"

She swallowed and nodded. Kiera ran to her and flung her arms around her. Gianna held her tightly, whispering in her ear.

"It's okay," she said.

Kiera drew back, her eyes full of tears. "For the first time ever, I actually believe that."

"Serves him right," Abigail said, coming to stand over Gary. "He never was a good man and he'll never hurt Ruby again." She turned and walked back to her chair. Gianna and Kiera looked at each other in confusion.

Derek stood looking down at Gary.

"Is he…dead?" Kiera asked.

"Knocked out cold," Derek said. "He'll come around eventually. Jaw might be broke though." He flexed his hand. "Don't know my own strength sometimes." He tossed the knife down onto the coffee table and held his bleeding side. "Keep an eye on him. He shouldn't wake before the police get here." He looked at Gianna. "Sorry about your tires. I was pissed about you treating my wife again without permission. But I'd say we're square now." With that, he turned and walked out the open door.

CHAPTER FORTY-ONE

Two Months Later

Jenny knocked on Gianna's front door and turned to wave at Henry who sat idling in his truck. Henry waved in return and drove away as the door opened. Gianna's face lit up.

"Well, hello."

"Hi."

"I didn't expect you to drop by today."

"I know, it's kind of impromptu. I hope it's okay?"

"Absolutely, come on in." She moved aside to allow Jenny to enter. But as Jenny walked past her, Gianna gripped her hand and turned her into her for a searing, hot kiss.

"Mm," Jenny moaned, falling into her. "That was nice."

"It was." Gianna closed the door. "I'd like to do it a whole lot more."

Jenny smiled, though she could tell her nerves were showing. So much had happened, so many things were up in the air. She didn't know up from down and she certainly had no idea what the future might bring.

"I know, I would too. It's just with Abigail's failing health and me trying to get all her affairs in order, and having to go back to North Carolina to settle the whole mess with the police and Gary, I'm afraid I've been neglecting you. And you, more than anyone, deserve answers."

"Hey," Gianna said, holding her arms. "You told me the truth. And though I wish you'd done it a lot sooner, I completely understand. You were frightened. Scared for your life. It's hard telling what I would do in the same situation."

"I don't know, Gianna. I think you would've handled it a whole lot better."

Gianna kissed her forehead. "Don't beat yourself up too badly. You survived. And you helped Abigail in the process. How's she doing today?"

"She's quiet. Just sitting in her chair. Brandi tries to converse with her, as do I, but all she can talk about is Ruby and Carl."

"She's still stuck on that, is she?"

Jenny sighed and sat on the couch. Gianna joined her, draping her arm across the back so Jenny could snuggle closer to her.

"Who knew that Carl had been my great-aunt Ruby's husband at one time and that he'd been violent and abusive?"

"No one ever talked about it in your family?"

"No. And I think it's because his death was a big mystery. That and because Ruby and Abigail were rumored to be lovers. Which was very taboo back in those days."

"Yes, it was. They probably weren't permitted to be themselves or to come out as a couple."

"It's so sad." She shook her head. "I look at that photo of them and I just cry. They look so young, so happy, so in love. And to think that no one accepted that."

"Especially Carl."

Jenny closed her eyes. "I think…according to the limited information I've managed to get out of Abigail, that she may have done something to him to protect Ruby."

"You think so?"

"I do. I just don't know what."

"He was found floating in a river, wasn't he?"

"They said he drowned, but they couldn't explain why. They assumed he was drunk and fell in. But I don't know."

"You know Abigail. She wouldn't have killed him."

"Not even to protect Ruby? Whatever happened, it caused her to up and move across the country to Cliffside. She took her life savings and built that house."

"Ruby didn't come with her?"

"She spent some time here, according to Abigail. But mostly she remained back in North Carolina with her two children."

"Oh, right."

"What I still don't understand is, what the favor was that Ruby said Abigail owed her."

"Why don't you ask Abigail?"

"I should. But I'm afraid of the answer. That maybe Aunt Ruby had kept the secret about what Abigail had done to Carl or something. Plus, I feel like I've been bombarding her with questions lately."

"If she minded, she'd tell you. You know, Abigail. She's not exactly shy."

"No. But she's not herself a whole lot anymore."

Gianna held her hand. "I know. But you shouldn't be afraid to talk to her. I'd do it now before it's too late."

Jenny wiped at a tear. "That day is coming, isn't it? Sooner rather than later."

She snuggled into Gianna and held her close.

They sat in silence for a moment before Gianna spoke. "How's your friend doing?"

"Floyd? He's going to be okay, thank God. He's home and getting around pretty good."

"Were you able to see him?"

"Yes. And it was so nice. I gave him the biggest, yet gentlest hug ever."

Gianna laughed softly. "I bet you did."

Jenny frowned as she thought of his injury and the person who caused it. "Gary's pleaded guilty. He's not going to trial."

"He did?" Gianna pulled back to look at her. "Wow."

"The evidence against him was just too great. With Floyd and Melonie as witnesses and his DNA found on the man he killed on the side of the road, not to mention my witnessing him kill Ken. He just didn't stand a chance and I think he knew it."

"Smartest thing he's done yet," Gianna said.

"I'm just glad he's gone away for good."

"You no longer have to worry about him."

"Nope." She cocked her head. "And everything's still okay between you and Derek?"

Gianna stroked Jenny's face. "It is. He's doing fine and we've buried the hatchet."

"I'm glad."

"And I'm so happy for you, Jenny," she said.

Jenny blinked. "Jenny?"

"Isn't that what you want to be called now that I know it's your real name?"

"No. I don't. I want you to call me, Kiera. That's who I am. Jenny, she's the past."

"Okay, Kiera it is." She smiled. "Now, can I kiss you, Kiera?"

"By all means."

Gianna leaned in and kissed her and Jenny closed her eyes and melted into the cushions. It seemed every time Gianna touched her she heated from head to toe and her body thrummed with desire.

"I've missed you," Jenny said, whispering against her lips. "So very much."

"Mm, me too," Gianna said. "I don't ever want to let you go again. In fact, you can't go. Not again. Not ever. You must stay."

Jenny laughed. "I'm not going anywhere."

They leaned in to kiss again, but a knock at the door made them pause.

"Who's that?" Jenny asked.

"I don't know. I'm not expecting anyone."

"It's not another ex-girlfriend, is it?" Jenny said, the nerves evident in her voice.

"Very funny." Gianna rose to answer the door. She shrieked as she pulled it open and the woman on the stoop threw herself into her arms.

Jenny stood, convinced she was witnessing another ex-girlfriend all over again. Only this one seemed to be in Gianna's good graces.

"Holy shit, what are you doing here?" Gianna asked, swinging the woman around.

"Surprise!"

"It absolutely is a surprise. Oh, my God. I can't believe you're really here."

Jenny moved to gather her purse. She felt like an intruder and had the urge to leave. Immediately.

Gianna caught sight of her. "Kiera, wait, what are you doing?"

"You have a visitor. I should go."

"No, no, no. This is my best friend, Lauren. My very best friend. She came to visit from Flagstaff."

Jenny felt her body go limp with relief. "Oh." She smiled. "Okay. I thought for a second…"

Gianna came to her and enveloped her in a hug. "No, love. She's my friend. And you're going to love her."

"Yes, you're going to love me." She joined them in the hug.

"Wait," Gianna said, pulling away to speak to Lauren. "Why are you so dang happy all of a sudden?"

She held up her ring finger. It was bare. "I've finally done it. I've filed for divorce."

"But you…you're…" She touched her belly.

"Still pregnant? Yep. But that doesn't matter. The kids and I, we're going to make it on our own. Well, not exactly alone…"

Gianna raised her brow. "Don't tell me…Jake?"

Lauren nodded.

"Oh, my God," Gianna said. "Just, oh, my God. I'm so happy for you."

The three hugged again, and Jenny once again felt wanted, needed, loved. But most importantly, she felt safe.

Right there, in Cliffside, right there, with Gianna.

Right there with Abigail down on Rhydian Hill.

THE END

About the Author

Ronica Black lives in the greater Phoenix area with her rescue dog, Frankie. When she's not writing, she's creating in other ways, enjoying the great state of Arizona, and spending time with family and friends.

Books Available from Bold Strokes Books

Chasing Her Scent by MJ Williamz. When Sheridan Rousseau walks into Lisette Mouton's charming little bookstore in Quebec City, she unknowingly holds the key to a mysterious box hidden in a secret room. (978-1-63679-900-1)

Heart's Run by D. Jackson Leigh. Hoping to recover an escaped racing mare, stock transporter Tobie Mason locks horns with local wild horse advocate Maggie Wilkes. (978-1-63679-825-7)

Scandalous by Kris Bryant. When a Hollywood actress trades places with her twin sister, everyone's in an uproar about getting duped, but Lindsay's more concerned about finding out which twin she made out with. (978-1-63679-874-5)

The Art of Love by Ali Vali. When Mimi and Bianca both set their sights on Jolly, sparks fly, loyalties are tested, and hearts collide as they navigate the unpredictable nature of their hearts (978-1-63679-719-9)

The Other Side of Forever by Kel McCord. Will Kenzie and Rachel be able to make love work when Rachel's cozy suburban dream feels like Kenzie's worst nightmare? (978-1-63679-812-7)

The Secrets of Rhydian Hill by Ronica Black. A doctor in need of a new start. A woman running from a killer. A love story that could end in tragedy. (978-1-63679-880-6)

Feeling Lucky by Krystina Rivers. What happens when, despite suddenly having enough money to buy almost anything, Lucy and Tanner start to discover that maybe all they need is each other? (978-1-63679-876-9)

Iceberg by Gun Brooke. When Lady Arabella hires Zandra, she never expects to find love, especially not as a disaster looms on the horizon. (978-1-63679-908-7)

It Happened One Semester by Aurora Rey. After a Pride night hookup, can eager new Assistant Professor Hudson Greene and Dean of Advising Callie Shaw overcome the odds and ace falling in love? (978-1-63679-814-1)

It's Kind of a Bad Idea by Sarah G. Levine. What happens when an emotionally unavailable serial dater meets the one woman she can't help but fall for—who happens to be the one woman who told her not to? (978-1-63679-920-9)

Thankful for You by Tagan Shepard. Everyone deserves to find their person, maybe Karen has finally found hers? (978-1-63679-884-4)

What Happens on Location by Nan Campbell. How can Helen produce a successful movie when its director is the woman responsible for the demise of her marriage? (978-1-63679-904-9)

When Love Comes Around by Radclyffe and Ronica Black. Can Maya Sanchez and Nolan Wright trust each other enough to build something real, or will the past tear them apart? (978-1-63679-930-8)

Anywhere with You by Margo Glynn. On a road trip through the Great American Southwest, two friends discover nature, hope, and each other. (978-1-63679-907-0)

Burning Bridges by Lesley Davis. Can Clancy and Jude crack the case of eight missing women—and the secrets of their own hearts? (978-1-63679-872-1)

Dreams Entangled by Sophia Kell Hagin. Amid self-doubt, secrets, a pandemic, fear of attack and attempted murder, Pirin and Gracie's attraction turns to love and their lives will never be the same. (978-1-63679-892-9)

Echoes of Love by Catherine Lane. As Hazel's and Jo's paths intertwine, they're swept up in a whirlwind of long-buried secrets, sizzling chemistry, and memories that won't be denied. (978-1-63679-835-6)

Moonlight Obsession by Sheri Lewis Wohl. All it takes to stop a clever killer is moonlight, love, and a silver bullet. (978-1-63679-831-8)

My Boyfriend's Wife by Joy Argento. Amid betrayal and heartbreak, can two women discover a love that could heal their pasts and rewrite their futures? (978-1-63679-866-0)

Tapout by Nicole Disney. A struggling MMA fighter finds her edge in an underground ring, but as she falls for the magnetic and ambitious promoter behind the matches, their dangerous world threatens to destroy everything they've fought to rebuild. (978-1-63679-924-7)

The Fame Game by Ronica Black. Wild child Hollywood actress Luna Kirkman begins dating Hollywood's leading man, only to fall for his straitlaced sister instead. (978-1-63679-858-5)

An Extraordinary Passion by Kit Meredith. An autistic podcaster must decide whether to take a chance on her polyamorous guest and indulge their shared passion, despite her history. (978-1-63679-679-6)

That's Amore! by Georgia Beers. The romantic city of Rome should inspire Lily's passion for writing, if she can look away from Marina Troiani, her witty, smart, and unassumingly beautiful Italian tour guide. (978-1-63679-841-7)

The Unexpected Heiress by Cassidy Crane. When a cynical opportunist meets a shy but spirited heiress, the last thing she plans is for her heart to get involved. (978-1-63679-833-2)

Through Sky and Stars by Tessa Croft. Can Val and Nicole's love cross space and time to change the fate of humanity? (978-1-63679-862-2)

Uncomplicate It by Kel McCord. When an office attraction threatens her career, Hollis Reed's carefully laid plans demand revision. (978-1-63679-864-6)

Vanguard by Gun Brooke. Beth Wild, Subterranean freedom fighter, is in the crosshairs when she fights for her people and risks her heart for loving the exacting Celestial dissident leader, LaSierra Delmonte. (978-1-63679-818-9)

Wild Night Rising by Barbara Ann Wright. Riding Harleys instead of horses, the Wild Hunt of myth is once again unleashed upon the world. Their ousted leader and a fey cop must join forces to rein in the ride of terror. (978-1-63679-749-6)